Healing Hearts and

C000091328

Healing Hearts
and
Apple Tarts
(and a totally demented Dalmatian)

by
Annie Beaumont

YouCaxton Publications

Oxford & Shrewsbury

ISBN 978-1-913425-00-5
Published by YouCaxton Publications 2019
YCBN: 01

YouCaxton Publications
enquiries@youcaxton.co.uk

For Alexander and Oliver, two fine young men,
with all my love.

Acknowledgments:

My grateful thanks are due to:

Kay Burke, for invaluable help with banking and fraud issues and Irish vernacular!

'Dr Doon', Thai cocktail waiter extraordinaire, for Tequila Sunrise inspiration!

Ray Hoogendijk, for helpful reading of an early draft of 'Nathan'.

Rudi Jennings, for inspirational discussions of his experiences of running a short-holding, particularly lambing!

Matthew Morter, for advice on the law and court proceedings.

Jess Jennings, for sheep story inspiration.

Tess Stebbings, for careful reading of manuscript.

I offer thanks and my deepest appreciation to my writer friends, for your continued encouragement: Jac Harmon; Lorraine Rogerson; Gill Allard; Sabine Meier; Claudie Whitaker; Joanie Phillip.

Thanks also to: Christopher, Dorit, Linda and Patrick, of the *Hua Hin Literary Group* in Thailand, for hearing excerpts from a very early draft of this novel.

Finally, a big thank you to all my lovely readers, who have emailed me such positive feedback and posted on Amazon great reviews of my first novel, *Daughters of Hamilton Hall*. I do hope you will enjoy *Healing Hearts and Apple Tarts (and a totally demented Dalmatian)!*

Important note:
Healing Hearts and Apple Tarts is a novel set in the Norfolk town of Wymondham. While the author has used the actual names of some businesses that do exist in Wymondham, all characters are entirely fictitious and are in no way based on real people, who might happen to work in such establishments.

1

Hetti

Summer 2018

'Daniel, let me in! What's going on?'
Silence.

'Daniel! What's up? Come on, open the door.'

Nothing.

'Daniel! Where were you today? Why didn't you turn up? What happened? Daniel, please, open the door.'

A click.

A shuffle.

A short cough.

'Erm, Hetti?'

I swung around to see my neighbour, Clifford, standing in the doorway of his flat. Sixty years of age. Vest. Joggers. Belly. Hair, what was left of it, standing up in tufts.

'Oh, Clifford... have you...?'

'That's the second time this afternoon that I've been woken up by someone wanting to get into your flat. Can't a bloke get some sleep? I'm on nights!'

'Sorry — who?'

'Some bods came and changed the locks, girl.'

'Changed the locks? But why?'

'How the bloody hell should I know? You paid your rent?' He eyed me up and down, suspicion written all over his face.

'It's Daniel's flat. I don't...'

He held me in his stare. His words measured.

'Well, Miss, I reckon your Daniel's done a runner.'

Deep down, I must have known that his not turning up was more than one of Daniel's memory lapses. His timekeeping was always rubbish. There was Real Time, and then there was Daniel Time. The two were very different.

'What?'

'He was moving stuff out of the flat and into his car when I got in from work.' His voice softened. His brow furrowed.

My world started spinning around the wrong way. The move was barely palpable, but I'd felt it all the same. Realisation slowly started to dawn. Daniel's left. Left me.

I gasped for air. 'But Clifford, he... we... he can't have just moved out, without telling me.'

'True as I'm stood here, my girl, he was moving out when I got in from my shift this morning.' Clifford made an X with his index finger across his chest. 'Cross me heart, Hetti. Cross me heart. I asked him how long he was going to be making a din – carrying things out to his car, banging doors, rolling bloody big suitcases along the corridor. He said he wouldn't be long. And he told me he was moving out and I wouldn't be disturbed no longer.'

No!

My heart raced and my knees trembled. What about...? We'd had plans. We were going to spend our first Christmas together this year, in our new home. Last year I'd invited him to come with me to my aunt in north Norfolk. Well, alright, perhaps not the most exciting of places, but Christmas is about families and loved ones being together, isn't it? And I'd wanted him with me. But he'd had some cast iron reason why he could not come. I couldn't remember what. Now I was beginning to realise. He'd been making excuses. My breath was coming in short, sharp gasps.

Daniel had never wanted to meet any of my friends and, come to think of it, I didn't know any of his friends, either. A very sick feeling swept over me. Why didn't I suspect something before? What a fool I am. And what about our holiday? We were supposed to be going on holiday to the Canaries next week. I'd given him my part of the money – cash - when he'd booked it. Supposedly booked it.

And... and ... no. No! I could not bear to think about...

My mind was darting this way and that. I looked at Clifford, pointing to the door of our — Daniel's — flat.

'My stuff...'

'You'd best get hold of the letting agent, girl. You're not going to get into that flat with that key there in your hand, now are yer?'

I glanced down at the key, still gripped between my thumb and index finger, ready to push into the keyhole.

'But... but... I've nowhere to go.'

2

Nathan

Summer, 2018

'Come and fetch him immediately!'

Mandy spat the words out as a red-faced infant wailed in her arms. I could see my five-year-old son, Ben, in the corner of the screen, his eyes — the carbon-copy of mine — I couldn't deny that he was my son — filled with tears, his lower lip quivered. My heart turned over.

Mandy rarely called me for a voice or video conversation. Her usual mode of communication was restricted to curt text messages, invariably asking — demanding, rather — more money, whenever the mood took her.

'Okay, okay, if that's what you want, I'll come and fetch Ben back to Norfolk. But you do realise, don't you, Mandy, there'll be no going back? If I bring him to me here, I'll be going for full custody.'

'Yes! Fetch him! Fetch him today. I can't —.' She was in tears herself now.

'Mandy,' I softened my voice, 'I can't just drop everything and drive all the way to Carlisle. It needs planning.'

'What is there to plan?' She'd recovered her equilibrium and returned to her usual, obstinate, obstreperous self. There was no reasoning with her. 'You're a single bloke. Get up here, like, yesterday!'

The baby turned up the volume with his lungs-filled-to-capacity-with-oxygen screams.

I had to get Ben out of there. His mother was about to blow a fuse and when that happened, my son would become collateral damage in the fall out.

'Let me speak to Ben, Mandy.' My heart ached to see Ben's sorrowful little face in the background of the Skype screen.

'Nathan, stop wasting time and get yourself up here!'

With that, and before I could utter a word of reply, the call came to an abrupt end.

I'd met Mandy about six years earlier at a New Year's Eve party at a friend's house somewhere between Carlisle and the Scottish border. I was in the area after Christmas as a guest of my best mate, Matthew and his family. Matthew and I met during Freshers' week at uni, were best pals for the whole four years and had remained good friends ever since.

After one night of passion with Mandy at the New Year's Eve party, Ben was the result. At the time of conception, I didn't even know the name of the woman who was to become the mother of my son, and the one who would hold me to emotional ransom at every possible opportunity. Since the day Ben was born, she'd used him as an excuse to extort out of me as much money as she could. I was happy – more than happy – to pay for my son's upbringing – and did so with regular monthly payments, despite the fact that he and I were virtual strangers. It's an odd concept, isn't it? I mean, I loved a virtual stranger. But he was my son, and I did. The situation was not my choice. I'd longed, over the years, to play a more significant role in his life — other than that of a cash cow for his mother — but after years of trying to keep in regular contact and arrange actual, physical visits, in real life and real time — not via a bloody computer — I'd reluctantly and resignedly accepted that I was wasting my time.

God knows how many 'Daddies' my son had been introduced to in his short life. In the meantime, I was reduced to being an image on a smartphone or laptop screen, who popped up now and then and managed to get a few words in before the boy's mother asked for more money and promptly switched me off. I wondered if, in the event I should actually meet my son face-to-face he would expect me to switch off and disappear before his eyes, like I did on Skype? I'm serious! Don't laugh!

3

Hetti

Summer 2018

'Hetti, darling!'

Oscar's smile was as wide as his bright red front door
— momentarily, that is — until he registered my expression.

'Darling! What is it?'

I crumbled into his ample arms, sobbing uncontrollably,
my face wet with tears, my eyes swollen.

'Whatever's happened, darling?'

'Daniel —'

He pulled me across the threshold and kicked the door
shut behind him. Drawing me back into a bear hug, he
soothed: 'There, there, Hetti darling. It can't be that bad.
Had a little tiff with him, have you?'

He handed me a tissue from the hall table.

'There now, blow your nose and dry your tears and tell
Uncle Oscar all about it.' He ushered me through the hall,
towards the sitting room.

Oscar Miller was perhaps not the most outlandish 'queen'
in town, but he was certainly one of them. Mid-fifties, larger
than life and slightly limp of wrist, Oscar had a huge heart,
made of solid gold and was the best friend a girl could have.
Especially in a crisis.

He led me into the front room and deposited me on a soft,
white, squishy sofa, moving several purple and lilac cushions
out of the way.

'If Daniel has broken your heart, I shall slap him, darling.
Do tell all.'

He stroked my head and pinched my cheek, as if I were a
chubby baby, then moved across to the opulent bar in the
corner of the room. Christmas fairy lights trailed across the
bar top and dropped down the sides. It was the beginning
of August, for goodness' sake!

'G and T, darling? Or a nice Rioja? What's your tipple?'

I sniffed and blew my nose again on the now very wet
tissue. Oscar picked up a box of paper hankies from the

bar, moved across the room and placed it on the coffee table in front of me.

'Or perhaps you shouldn't drink alcohol when you're sad, darling? Shall I make you a nice hot mug of cocoa instead? I've got a lovely apple tart, just out of the oven. Can I tempt you?'

'Gin and tonic and make it a big one!'

Blinding sun blazed through a crack in the pink floral curtains. It took me a while to realise that I was in Oscar's spare bedroom. I blinked.

Daniel!

The cheerful sun shining in a bright blue sky seemed so incongruous on the day after I had discovered that my boyfriend of twelve months was not the man that I'd taken him for. Daniel had left me. I couldn't get into the flat to retrieve my belongings and I had nowhere to live. The flat was in Daniel's sole name. He'd been renting it for three years and had invited me to move in with him six months ago. I had no rights where the flat was concerned. What was I to do? Yesterday was supposed to be the day that we arranged the mortgage at the bank, soon to be moving into our lovely little house on Golden Lane. Proper grown up stuff! It would be our starter home, but we wouldn't need a huge mortgage because of my hundred-grand depos —

Oh no! No, no, no! My money! The hundred-thousand pounds that my late parents had left in trust for me until my twenty-fifth birthday. I'd paid it into Daniel's bank account last week, in anticipation of our appointment with the bank manager yesterday. A sizeable deposit would help us secure the mortgage. Daniel had his job and I had given notice at work in preparation for starting university in the autumn.

The breeze blew the pink floral curtains and they billowed towards me like colourful parachutes. Through the window I could see purple Buddleia swaying, butterflies dancing around, as they hunted nectar, collected pollen on their tiny legs.

A little tap on the bedroom door and Oscar entered carrying a tray of tea and biscuits.

'Morning, Dear One!' He placed the tray on the bedside table and sat on the side of the bed. 'I trust you slept well,

Hetti? Nothing like a couple of large Gin and Tonics to knock you out for the count.'

He was too cheerful for my mood. Daniel had very likely scarpered with the better part of my life's wealth and here was Oscar, chirpy as a song bird. Of course, he didn't know the full story. Yet.

Tears welled up in my eyes, but with his back to me now, busy with tea pouring and biscuit distribution, he didn't see until he turned and handed me Earl Grey tea in a bone china cup and saucer edged in gold paint.

'Darling girl, what is it? Don't be sad. You'll sort your life out and — you'll see — you're going to be happier than you've ever been. Why, you'll be starting university soon and you'll soon forget about Daniel. I know it doesn't seem like it now, but you'll get over him and you'll probably end up wondering what on earth you ever saw in him in the first place. Trust me darling. You will. Now drink your tea, there's a good girl.'

I took the cup and saucer from him and tried to force a smile. It wasn't working. My facial muscles were having none of it.

Last night I had told Oscar the story: about going to the bank, sitting waiting... waiting... waiting. Waiting for hours, even after they'd told me I'd missed the appointment because Daniel hadn't shown up.

I'd checked my phone countless times, sent him Whatsapps, called, left voicemails, emailed. And there was no response at all. Nothing. I'd even checked local Accident and Emergency departments, worried that he'd been involved in a terrible accident. Nothing. Just silence. An eerie quietness that had swept through my very being. Daniel had disappeared into thin air.

Over and over in my mind I replayed our last hours, days together. Had he been different? No, he was just the same as he'd always been. Warm, confident, positive.

I'd thought he was the love of my life. He just swept me off my feet, from the moment we first met. Treated me like a princess. Always so attentive, warm and loving. And he was my first love. Oh, yes, I'd had crushes on boys at school and dated a few through my teenage years and early twenties, but nothing ever compared this. And anyway, most guys were shorter than me. I've been six feet tall since I was fifteen.

Daniel was shorter than me too, but he made me feel as if I really was the only person in his life that mattered, so that kind of made up for me being two inches taller than him. He was never interested in us spending time with anyone else and the times he didn't like it when I went out with my friends, well, it just seemed sweet, like he was going to miss me for a few hours. He just made me feel so wanted.

My friends told me, whenever I'd have to cut the evening short to get back to Daniel, that he was being controlling. Coercive control, Louise, my best friend called it. But that was ridiculous, I'd said. Daniel isn't at all violent. 'Violence isn't always physical,' Louise had said one evening. 'I reckon he's psychologically violent!' And at the time I thought she was just being a bit over-zealous with her psychology studies. The very idea that Daniel could be violent was just ridiculous.

How wrong can you be?

'Drink up Dear One. Don't let your tea get cold,' Oscar brought me out of my reverie. 'And do have a biscuit. I always find—'

In haste, I returned the tea to the bedside table, whipped the duvet away and shot out of the room to the bathroom. Oscar followed and rubbed my back, holding back my long, unruly tresses of flame red curls, as I spewed into the toilet pan.

'There, there dearest. It's probably all the upset. Better out than in, eh?' He led me back to bed, and I shivered, despite the warm sun beaming into the room.

'Everything okay, Hetti darling?' Oscar was giving me a sideways glance over the breakfast table. I knew immediately to what he was referring: this morning's bilious attack. I'd explained it away as taking too much gin the evening before, but we both knew there was another possible explanation. I was on the pill — I'm not that stupid — but I'd had that tummy bug a few weeks ago — No! I couldn't be! I refused to even give it head space.

'Yes, Oscar, Of course, I'm fine. I take it you're referring to the sickness this morning?' I looked him straight in the eye. 'I'm fine,' I said, 'really, I am. Just not used to such strong G and Ts, that's all. You know I'm not much of a drinker.'

'Really? Are you sure?'

'Yes, of course, I'm sure. Don't be silly. Can't be anything else but the drinks.'

That was two things I'd omitted to tell Oscar. The hundred-grand that Daniel had more than likely spirited away, and the tummy bug, which could well have interfered with the effectiveness of the pill.

I slurped my morning coffee, took the final bite of my toast and jam, began collecting the dirty crockery and moved from the breakfast room through to the kitchen, calling over my shoulder, 'I've got to go, Oscar. Things to do, people to see.' In fact, I needed to return to the bank to establish whether my hundred-thousand was still in Daniel's account and get them to pay it back to me. I also needed to see the letting agent about getting my stuff out of the flat. Oscar had provided a toothbrush but I needed more than that.

'Don't feel,' Oscar had followed me into the kitchen and now looked straight at me as he spoke, his hand, warm and soft on mine, 'I mean, don't feel you have to dash off just yet, darling.'

'Oh, Oscar, I have stuff to sort out. I'll be back later.'

'No, no, darling. I mean, well, what I want to say is that you're very welcome to stay with Old Uncle Oscar for a while. Well, as long as you need to, really.'

He had the kindest blue, blue eyes that twinkled, even when he was being serious or intense, just as he was now. He gave my hand a gentle squeeze. Tears pricked my eyes and I bit my lip. Oscar wasn't my real uncle. He was my godfather and a close friend of my parents, who'd died together when I was seven. So, he had always been in my life; I could not remember a time when he was not there and I was the nearest thing to a niece that he was likely to get.

Now I hugged him. 'You're such a love. Thank you, dearest Oscar. But I won't overstay my welcome. It's just until I sort myself out.'

'Oh, not a bit of it. Now, off you go and do your stuff, and I'll make dinner and an apple tart for tonight.'

4

Nathan

Looking back... to 2011

And the thing — the really stupid thing — about my oh-so-easy-to-forget drunken sexual encounter with Mandy — was that I already had a girlfriend — Erin — at the time, but she was away home to Ireland for Christmas. And anyway, we weren't sexually involved at the time. Not for want of trying on my part, I should add.

I was in a bar near our student pad with Matthew the first time I saw Erin. 'What can I get you?' she'd asked, with the widest of smiles and the merest hint of an Irish accent.

Laid, I thought, I'd like to get laid — then metaphorically kicked myself up the backside for being so crass — even though it was just an unspoken thought. But you get the picture — the very sight of her working behind the bar had left me with a weakening of the knees and a stirring in the groin.

Erin. Tawny hair, huge green eyes. There was the faintest sprinkling of freckles that dusted the bridge of her nose, and spread just a little way across her cheeks. But it was more than that. It was in the way she moved, the way she'd sort of glide across the room, as she collected glasses from tables, the way she'd push her hair away from her face, the cut of her blouse that hinted at the curve of her breast. The way that she'd touch her lips, lingering with one finger as she was making note of the drinks being ordered. And let's not forget that to-die-for little arse that I'd longed to get my hands on.

She wa sn't easy to persuade. I'd asked her out so many times I'd lost track and although Matt could totally see the attraction, he couldn't understand why, when Erin was clearly not interested, I didn't just move on to the next available girl. After all, there were at least five thousand of them on campus that I could choose from. Easy. But we men don't want it easy, do we? No. We enjoy the challenge. And I'm no exception. I want to have what I can't have. Anyone can have it easy, like I did with Mandy. But a challenge — well, a challenge achieved — results in greater satisfaction.

So, as sexually alluring that many of the girls on campus were, I didn't want any of them. I had my heart set on Erin and for months I kept on trying to get her attention, but to no avail. Despite my best efforts, Erin was having none of it. She served me politely and with a smile every time I went into the bar — and my visits were getting so frequent that I was in danger of becoming either an alcoholic or a bankrupt; whichever came first.

But times changed. Erin's cat, who used to hang around the bar while she was at work, got attacked by an escaped greyhound. As luck would have it, I was close to the scene (being a regular, as I explained, at the bar where Erin worked) at the time of the incident and I frightened the dog away. I picked up Tiddles — that's what she'd named her cat because, as a kitten, Tiddles was in the habit of frequently tiddling on the carpet — and examined her. After applying first aid —well, I *was* studying veterinary medicine! — I took Tiddles to the local vet.

The cat was sedated and kept in the animal hospital overnight.

'If anything is going to kill her,' the vet explained, 'it will be the shock.' Straight out of my Level 2 Veterinary text book.

I took great pleasure in comforting Erin as she anxiously awaited news of Tiddles.

The cat recovered. The greyhound was never seen or heard of again and Erin agreed to go out with me. In her eyes, as I tried to explain to Matt, much to his derision — I'd gone from boring nerd to rescuer-of-cat-super-hero in the space of one afternoon.

Tears now prick the back of my eyes at the memory.

5

Hetti

Summer 2018

'What do you mean, you can't tell me? That money, as you well know, because you served us when we came in together to pay it in, was my hundred-grand. And Daniel Jones has run off with it!'

'I am sorry, Miss Lewis, but once a deposit is paid into an individual's bank account, I'm afraid it belongs to that account holder. I'm sorry.'

'But I paid it in myself, you know I did. Daniel was with me and you served us. We told you it was to be our deposit on the house. And now Daniel Jones has made off with it without so much as a courteous goodbye!'

'I'm sorry, Miss —'

'Stop saying you're sorry! You're not sorry at all! Can't you even tell me if the money is still in his account? He promised me it would be safe in his account until next week when we were going to use it as a down payment on the house. You know he did. He said so in front of you. You know he did. He bloody well promised!'

'I'm afraid that promises are rather like butterflies, Miss Lewis —'

'Butterflies? Butterflies? Daniel Jones has just absconded with my life's wealth and you go all poetic on me? You're bloody useless!' My voice rose as I stood up, pushed the chair out of the way and stormed out of the room, slamming the door behind me.

In the corridor, a young woman in bank uniform stood in front of me and we did that thing when you both step to the side, to let the other by — she to her left, me to my right — and we repeated it three times. Then she stood with her back against the wall so that I could pass and I flounced off, muttering 'Butterflies! Bloody butterflies!' at her, leaving her looking totally bemused.

Outside in the street, tears filled my eyes, my knees trembled and I sniffed in an effort to stem the flow of salty liquid down my face.

'Miss Lewis? Miss Lewis? Hetti?'

I turned to see the bank manager standing there.

'What?' I sniffed and wiped the end of my nose with my fingers.

'Come inside. Please. I have some advice for you.'

He led me back into the bank, into his office and sat me down.

'Please don't think that we don't believe you or that we don't want to help you, Hetti. This is a very serious situation. I will take you now to meet with our group fraud officer. They will investigate the matter from your account. We need all of your details, so that we can investigate internally. What you must do — and I mean immediately — you must report this matter to the police.'

'What will they do? You've already said that because the money is in Daniel's account it's his. You just said that earlier.' I could feel myself getting wound up again.

'Don't upset yourself my dear. You have to give the police all the information and they will investigate too. But we cannot, under any circumstances, disclose to you the details of another customer's account.'

'Yes, so you keep saying, repeatedly. I'm sunk, aren't I? Admit it. You'll never get my money back for me and neither will the police. Otherwise you would just pay the money back into my account, wouldn't you? You know it's mine.' I started to cry.

'Not in the eyes of the law, Hetti,' he said, softly. 'You willingly paid it into Daniel's account and we cannot simply return it to you.'

I got up to leave, feeling every bit as despondent as before. But I did gather myself sufficiently to make my way to the police station to report a crime.

6

Nathan

2011

Even after we started going out, there was nothing going on in the bedroom department. It wasn't easy, but I was holding back for as long as I could. Didn't want to scare her away with my testosterone-fuelled urges. She wasn't just any girl. Erin Byrne was special. She stood out from the crowd. She was a virgin, for Chrissake! A gorgeous one at that. But not only was she stunningly attractive; and not only did she have an air of finesse about her that fired my fantasies night after night, but she also had a wicked sense of humour. I was smitten.

The months went by and I was patiently letting Erin take things at her own pace. I didn't want to rush her. I can't pretend that I wasn't frustrated though. But Erin was a good Catholic girl from Ireland and insisted that she was saving herself for her wedding day.

Personally, I'd rather have stuck red hot needles in my eyes than put a ring on a girl's finger and walk her up the aisle, but I have to admit, I'd have done anything for Erin, even if it meant trading in my confirmed bachelorhood. Yup. I had it bad for Erin.

Matt was totally flummoxed by the whole thing. He just couldn't get his head around my enforced celibacy.

'Come on, mate. Give it up as a bad job. I've never known you go more than a week without —'

'Okay, hold it right there, Matt. I'm a changed man. I'm not interested in putting it about any longer,' I'd said. 'I'm waiting for Erin. She's, well, she's special.'

'Oh, god! Listen to you Nate! What's got into you?'

I just had to shut the conversation down so I got up, picked up my rucksack and headed for the door.

'See you later, Matt. I'm off to the library,' I said, leaving my best mate sitting there shaking his head.

On the way to campus I called in on Erin, who was getting ready for her shift at the bar.

'Hi. Just thought I'd pop by to see how the patient is,' I said, knowing full well that Tiddles was absolutely fine and had fully recovered after her unfortunate encounter with the escaped greyhound. The attack had been weeks ago.

Erin regarded me with those Irish eyes of hers. 'Tiddles is well, thank you,' she said, with the slightest hint of a lopsided smile.

Gently does it, Nathan, I reminded myself.

'What time do you get off work today?'

'Split shift, I'm afraid.' She glanced at the wall clock in her kitchen, just as Tiddles squeezed herself through the cat flap and purred as she wrapped herself around Erin's ankles.

'Hello, my love!' She bent down and stroked the cat. Oh, how I'd wished she'd talk to me like that! She picked up the cat and stroked her fondly. I imagined her stroking me in the same way, but not on my back. I felt myself flush at the thought. The cat meowed.

'Okay, let's feed you and then I'm off to work.'

'I'll make myself scarce, then,' I said, somewhat reluctantly.

There was never a time when I didn't want to be with Erin. She stirred in me a feeling that was something totally new to my experience. And I don't just mean sexual arousal, either. This was something much deeper. More visceral. Every time I saw her, I felt a gut-deep physical response to her very presence. My neurotransmitters were working overtime. My emotions were in a whirl. I was an undergrad, for god's sake, with thousands of nubile female students to choose from, and there I was, as Matt was so fond of pointing out, 'rhapsodising' over just one.

He was right. And I had absolutely no idea what I was going to do about it.

7

Hetti

Summer 2018

So, I stayed with Oscar. I had nowhere else to go. I'd deferred my place at university — too upset to deal with it — all the studying, trying to navigate a new social landscape, a new environment. The prospect just felt too overwhelming.

The letting agent had grudgingly allowed me back into the flat to collect my things. There'd been no time to get sad or sentimental, as I said goodbye to the place that had been my home for the past six months. The letting agent, an officious looking middle-aged man with thinning, grey hair and the hint of a paunch, had stood behind me as I picked things up and stuffed them into my one suitcase and a rucksack. There was one plastic carrier bag filled with my toiletries from the bathroom. Within twenty minutes, all trace of both Daniel and myself had disappeared from our former home. The agent didn't even offer to help me get my stuff — my worldly goods — into the lift. Instead, without so much as a wave of a hand, and as if he was working on getting rid of that paunch, took the stairs — or possibly slid down the bannister — because he'd already reached the bottom and was disappearing out into the street by the time that I'd arrived on the ground floor of the building. I swung the rucksack onto my back, hooked the plastic bag of toiletries over the long handle of the suitcase and made off down the road, taking the first taxi that came along back to Oscar's.

'Welcome home, Dear One!' Oscar greeted me at the door, G and T in hand, kissed both my cheeks, took my suitcase and stood aside for me to enter the house. In his own way, he made me feel as 'at home' and welcome as he possibly could. He shopped, fed me, did my ironing. You'd have thought he was my mother, the way he carried out his caring duties. And, so it went on.

Although I'd missed my opportunity to start my degree course that year, the university had held my place, making it clear that a one-year deferral was all I could expect before losing my place altogether. At least it gave me a chance to get myself organised with a job and settled somewhere.

Leading me into the kitchen, Oscar took an apple tart out of the oven, filling the room with the aroma of spicy baked apples and crusty pastry. He made me a cup of tea and I walked through to the sitting room to find Toby, a love interest of Oscar's, ensconced on the sofa. Thirty years his junior, and, to my mind, too pretentious by far, Toby was like a boomerang the way he came in and out of Oscar's life. He had eyes that were too close together, an aquiline nose and a huge smile. A toothy grin, actually, a rather smarmy one too. Yes, his grin was very toothy, but then so is that of a shark. I wasn't sure that I trusted Toby, but who was I to judge? I'd thought I could trust Daniel, and look how that ended!

'Well, hello there, Hetti!' Toby's grin seemed even broader and even more toothy than ever. There he sat, naked apart from a bath towel around his waist and a half-empty glass of wine in his hand. It had occurred to me — fleetingly — that he might whip the towel off any minute, just for the shock effect. But he didn't, thankfully; instead he placed his now empty wine glass on the coffee table, his little finger crooked, got up, strolled across the room like a catwalk model and up the stairs.

'Hetti darling, have you finished your tea?' Oscar came bustling into the room. 'Do come and take your jacket off and let's get you unpacked and settled into your room. I'm so looking forward to having you to stay.'

And that just did it.

I mean, Oscar was always so loving and caring, but after the bank had told me where to get off and the stony-faced letting agent had perfunctorily opening the door to let me into the flat to get my stuff — well — all it took was that little warm gesture from Oscar to set me off. What could I do? I'll tell you what I did. I crumbled, not for the first time, into Oscar's enveloping arms and let it all out.

As usual, his kind platitudes and gentle pats on the back and to-die-for hugs meant that in no time at all I was sniffing and getting back my emotional equilibrium and smiling through my tears.

'Darling child,' Oscar soothed, 'all will be well, I assure you. Come!' And with that, he was picking up my rucksack and plastic carrier bag, as I took hold of my suitcase on wheels and we proceeded to 'my' bedroom.

Once inside, he closed the door firmly behind him, heaved the suitcase and rucksack onto the bed and took me into his arms once again.

'It will all be fine, darling,' he said, as he tried to comb through my unruly curly locks with his chubby fingers, pushing my hair back from my face. He regarded me, then glanced down.

'Hetti, my dear, Toby is going to stay for dinner. That okay with you?'

I nodded and shrugged my shoulders. What could I say?

'I've got a lovely duck braising in the oven and some creamy, herbed mashed potatoes and some wonderful mixed root vegetables and orange sauce. And apple tart for afters. How does that sound?'

Delicious. Amazing. That's how it sounded and I felt an appetite coming on. I wrapped my arms around his neck and kissed both his slightly rosy cheeks. After the couple of days that I'd just had, Oscar's culinary delights were just what I needed. He left me alone, closing the bedroom door behind him.

I unpacked my belongings, such as they were, hung my few clothes in the wardrobe, hooked my toiletries carrier bag over the back of a chair and plugged in my laptop to charge the now very low battery. A few short moments later, Oscar called me from the bottom of the stairs and I skipped down the stairs, feeling rather better than I had for some time. Well, since Daniel had left me waiting in the bank like a jilted bride at the altar. I'd still not heard a word from him — no surprise there — but the bank fraud people were on it and the police had been informed, so although I held out little hope of ever seeing my money again, at least there was a report on file in the event that the thieving reptile ever tried to swindle some poor unsuspecting woman again.

8

Nathan

2012

It took a long time to win her over, but Erin was worth waiting for. She was perfect. Warm, funny, intelligent, kind and — yes — very, very sexy. It pleased me no end that she'd 'saved' herself — and that it was me that she was doing it for. Saving herself, I mean.

The sex was phenomenal. It was my first time with a virgin. And it was mind-blowing. I like to think that I taught her, but that would be doing Erin an injustice. For her, love-making came naturally and I literally drowned in her, our bodies melting into one.

While our nights were exquisite journeys into ecstasy, our days were low key. We walked around the campus lake, fed the ducks, spent hours over coffee in street cafés in Norwich, played with the cat and cooked Sunday lunch together. Slowly, slowly, we got to know each other. It was bliss. Simple, sheer, undiluted bliss.

We walked on a Norfolk beach early one morning after a night of sweet passion and watched the sunrise. We talked about Mick Jagger and Tequila Sunrise, even though it was long before our time that the Rolling Stones had popularised the cocktail drink and The Eagles had immortalised it, with their song of the same name.

We talked about the three children we would have and their names and hair and eye colour and academic achievements and then laughed as we were getting ahead of ourselves. Although a devout Catholic, Erin had gone to the women's clinic and acquired the contraceptive pill. She'd struggled with the conflict, saying that her parents would be very disapproving, should they ever find out, but common sense ruled over parents' views, religious affiliation, belief and faith.

Another Christmas came and Erin went home to Ireland to see her family. I suppressed the urge to beg her to stay, spend Christmas with me in Norwich or come with me to my folks. But I knew how important her family was to her.

She had a twin sister, she told me, called Áine (pronounced 'Awn-ye', she explained). I couldn't imagine another like Erin. 'That's a very fine name,' I'd commented and she told me its English equivalent was something ordinary like 'Anne' or 'Anna'. I'd thought the Irish version was preferable.

Christmas passed, Erin returned to Norwich and we settled into January. Snow fell heavily on campus and we built a silly snowman by the lake. Ducks waddled across the frozen water and dog walkers' breath made white clouds as it was exhaled into the cold air. When snowdrops peeked hopefully through the twinkling, frozen ground we anticipated spring and bluebells carpeting the woods.

Matt had thought that my preoccupation with Erin would negatively affect my degree work, but if anything, I was more productive. The anticipation of seeing Erin spurred me on to get my head down and work all the harder.

'Have to admit, mate,' he said, over a pint one evening when Erin was on shift, 'being in love suits you. Never thought I'd see the day.' His grin was wide and his eyes glimmered.

'Yeah. It feels just right, Matt.' And it did.

Summer approached and end of year exams loomed. I set up a revision programme that included time with Erin on her days or nights off. Those times with her felt like a reward to myself for focusing on my exams and working hard. Being with her seemed to rejuvenate me so that I was more energised to study. She was laid back and easy-going and oh, so supportive. We talked about the possibility of her embarking on a physiotherapy degree the next academic year and it all seemed so real, and entirely possible and absolutely the right thing to do. And not only that, but it would be a natural step forward for her and for both of us, because, wouldn't we be together? She'd encouraged me throughout my studies and I would do the same for her.

I passed my end-of-year exams with flying colours and we celebrated by drinking wine and making love all night long.

Dad's old school friend, Jed Bailey, offered me a summer job on his smallholding on the outskirts of Wymondham, a little market town near Norwich. I jumped at the chance to earn some money, gain more experience of working with animals and — crucially — stay close to Erin. It was a long, hot summer and the outdoors work gave me toned muscles and a 'tan-to-die-for', according to Erin.

September arrived and my final year at uni beckoned. Although I'd been getting great grades, I knew how much my final results could make or break my career as a vet. Erin encouraged me in that quiet, reassuring way of hers and again I setup a timetable to fit in study time and Erin time. Everything was going to go well. I was in my final year of uni and Erin was still with me.

And then the phone call came.

9

Hetti

Summer, 2018

Toby stayed not only for dinner, but for breakfast, lunch and dinner again. It wasn't that I objected to his presence (how could I? I was living rent-free in Oscar's house, after all), but there was something about Toby's presence that made me feel uncomfortable. Oh, he was charming alright. Never discourteous or impolite, but yet, even though I was there at Oscar's invitation and I was his goddaughter, so we were sort of family, I felt like the interloper.

Toby stayed another night. And another. There was nothing I could put my finger on. It was just that, well, I worried that he might be taking advantage of Oscar's good nature. It wasn't as though Toby didn't have a home of his own. Apparently, he enjoyed a rather opulent penthouse somewhere in the more upmarket end of the city. And coming for dinner and staying several days just didn't sit well with me. After Daniel, well, I just found it rather difficult to trust a man — any man — apart from Oscar, of course. But then, I'd known Oscar for all of my life. He was the nearest to family I had left, apart from my Aunt Pat up in north Norfolk.

So, there I was, playing the gooseberry to the full extent until one morning — well — that's what did it, really. I'd woken up early, and feeling nauseous, had dashed to the bathroom, only to find that Toby was locked in there, singing away to himself in the shower. Y-M-C-A by The Village People, if you don't mind, and I bet he was doing all the arm movements while he sang his heart out.

Despite my frantic banging on the door, he just carried on enjoying himself in there. I didn't know if he was deaf from an ear full of shampoo suds or just being bloody difficult and ignoring me. Oscar appeared on the scene, just in time to witness me throwing up all over the landing carpet. Fussing over me like a clucking hen, he banged on the bathroom door with the full might of his fist and shouted at Toby to get the hell out of there. He led me back to my bed and went off in search of warm, wet flannels and drinking water. His 'there-theres' came into full force as he patted me gently on the back and rubbed it softly.

'Oh yuk! Who's thrown up?' Toby's voice shrieked from the landing. 'How positively revolting!'

Oscar was out of the bedroom like a shot. 'It wouldn't have happened had you not hogged the bathroom so unnecessarily, Toby. Poor little Hetti is not feeling well.'

'Evidently,' I heard Toby's contemptuous tone as I tried to sip the water that Oscar had brought for me.

Oscar popped his head around the bedroom door. 'Alright sweetie? Feeling better?' I nodded pathetically.

'I'm just going to clean up the landing darling and then I think we need to have a little chat.'

This was it, I thought. He's going to kick me out. It was obvious that he and Toby were on the verge of a full-blown relationship. Perhaps Toby had promised to become Oscar's One-And-Only after all the to-ing and fro-ing of recent months.

I refused to believe that I could be pregnant. I mean, that would be very unlucky, wouldn't it? Pregnant after one little incident of a thrown up contraceptive pill during a food-poisoning incident? Surely not. Even more unlucky would be getting pregnant and then abandoned by rat-face Daniel. The same rat-face Daniel who had evidently stolen my parents' trust money from me. How could he? What an absolute rat! My stomach churned every time I thought about it, my palms growing sweaty and clammy. No wonder I was nauseous. Who wouldn't be? I convinced myself that the cause of the sickness was the trauma of not only being left in the lurch by Daniel but having my hundred-grand stolen to boot. I'd heard nothing from the police and the bank people were still remaining tight-lipped about the whole sorry affair. I really was well and truly stuffed. And I simply could not be pregnant! No way. Nevertheless, I resolved to find out once and for all and take myself off to the pharmacy for one of those very expensive pregnancy test kits.

Returning from the trip to the chemist's later that day, I walked in to hear Oscar and Toby having a humdinger of a row. And it seemed to be about me.

'Toby, dear boy, Hetti will be staying here with me for the foreseeable future. That is how it is.'

'But Oscar, darling,' I heard Toby say, 'you and I — well — we need our space, don't we?'

'Toby, Hetti stays and that's that.'

'But why? Can't the girl fend for herself?'

'It's not about that. She's my niece — well — alright — my adopted niece, but also my goddaughter, I'll have you know.'

'So! This means, does it, that you put her before me? Before our chance of happiness?'

'Toby!' Oscar voice was raised now. His blood pressure would be sky high at this rate. Then his voice was quieter, though not softer. 'I thought better of you!'

'I'm sorry —'

'Patience dear boy. Patience.' Oscar's tone now sounded placatory. 'And be a little kind. This is not all about you.'

'Well, no, Oscar. I actually thought it was about us. You and me.'

'Toby, my dear –'

'And what's all the throwing up about? I mean, it is disgusting, darling. She's probably up the duff! Have you thought about that? Are we to expect a screaming brat disturbing our lives any time soon?'

I shuffled uncomfortably and tried to head, unnoticed, up the stairs. I would pack. Leave as soon as possible.

'Hetti, my dear! I'm so sorry. You weren't meant to hear that.' Oscar appeared at the foot of the stairs.

'Evidently, Oscar. I'll just pack my stuff and leave you both in peace.' I turned, nearly toppling down the three stairs I'd just climbed.

'No need for that my lovely. Just a little domestic — nothing serious.'

Oscar stood there, looking more than a little embarrassed — no — mortified was more the description. Yes, mortified. That was the word.

'It's okay, Oscar. I should go and give you and Toby some space,' I said, gripping the bannister in an effort to try and regain my balance, both physically and emotionally.

10

Nathan

Autumn, 2012

'I have to go to Ireland.' She said it very matter-of-fact. Just like that: I have to go to Ireland. She lifted her rucksack from the wardrobe.

'What's up?'

'It's Áine.'

'What about her?'

She carried on putting clothes into the rucksack. She was calm. Quiet. Business-like. She opened a wardrobe drawer and took out her passport.

'She has a problem with her kidneys.'

Was that it? Some kind of kidney infection?

'Kidneys?'

She folded a sweater meticulously, methodically.

'Yes.'

I took hold of her arm and tried to twist her around to face me.

'Erin?'

She gently but firmly removed my hand from her arm and moved towards the wardrobe again without even looking at me.

'Erin? Speak to me.'

She took a bra and some knickers and socks from the same wardrobe drawer and stuffed them into the rucksack.

She was scaring me now. Her silence cut through me.

'Erin? Speak to me, for Chrissake!'

'No need to blaspheme, Nat'an,' she said, in that Irish lilt, quietly but with conviction.

'Well, speak to me, will you?'

'I told you. Áine has a problem with her kidneys and I need to go home.'

'What's wrong with her? I mean, alright, it's her kidneys, but why do you have to go home? Surely some anti-biotics will —'

She stopped dead. Turned to face me. Her countenance was one I'd never before seen. Not on Erin, I'd not. It was as though we were strangers.

'Nat'an. No amount of anti-biotics is going to fix Áine. She has kidney disease. She could die.' And, in that cool, calm and practical way of hers, she carried on folding clothes and putting them into her rucksack as though the conversation had not taken place.

'Oh. I'm, er, really sorry. I had no idea.'

'Why would you, Nat'an? I've never mentioned it before.' She didn't even look up as she said it.

'Well, no, you haven't. And I'm just wondering why. I mean, I thought —'

'What, Nat'an? What did you think?'

Now I really was alarmed. Everything that I thought we had seemed to be crumbling before my very eyes. Where was my lovely Erin?

'Well,' I took a deep breath. 'Well, I thought that we were close. I mean, we were – are – close, aren't we? I'd have expected you to tell me about something like your twin sister having a potentially fatal illness.'

Now she stopped and looked at me. It was a look that I found very unsettling. Where was the lovely, fun-loving, soft, gentle, warm Erin? She squinted at me as if the sun was shining in her eyes. It wasn't that though. There was no sun in her eyes. It was more like as if she was scrutinising me for the first time.

'I don't have to tell you everything, Nat'an.' Her words fell, icy-cold, on my ears.

11

Hetti

Summer, 2018

I sat cross-legged on my bed, tapping away on my laptop. 'Have you not heard of Airbnb?' Toby had snorted at me. This, from the man with the posh-end-of-town penthouse that stood idle and empty while he helped himself to Oscar's generosity, hospitality and good nature. Priceless.

Airbnb? I'd searched and explored every possible style of accommodation, but anything suitable was way beyond my means and what I could afford involved a pokey little room, with a single bed, no WiFi and a shared bathroom. No, thanks very much! But I'd had enough of waiting — green around the gills — for Toby to vacate the bathroom whilst I was in the middle of a queasy attack. I needed my own space. At least the nausea had settled down. I'd done the pregnancy test and it had showed well and truly negative, but I'd heard that there can sometimes be a false negative, so I knew that I would need to repeat it.

Now, there was a gentle tap on the bedroom door and Oscar's head popped in. Just his head, with a placatory smile across his face.

'Hetti darling, can I get you anything? A nice cup of tea? Hot chocolate?'

I had to smile, despite myself. 'Thank you, Oscar. Hot chocolate would be lovely. But hey, let me make it. I moved to climb off the bed and the rest of Oscar entered the room.

'No, no, Sweet One. Let me do it. I'll be back in a mo,' he said as he reached for me and planted a kiss on my forehead.

I leaned back onto the bed. 'Okay, thank you.'

He left the door ajar and I carried on with what was clearly becoming a fruitless search for accommodation. Had I taken up my place at university, I could soon have been moving into halls of residence and I was really wishing I'd taken up my place, but my mind was all over the place after the shock of what Daniel had done. Studying would have been difficult to focus on in my current state of mind. But, anyway, no point in having regrets, except, of course, the inescapable regret of being stupid enough to pay my money into the bank account of a man I should never have trusted.

I scrolled down the pages of 'homes' available for impossible amounts of money. Oscar had said multiple times that he wanted me to stay, but despite my reluctance to trust Toby's motives, I did want Oscar to at least give the relationship a go. He wasn't getting any younger and I worried that he might not get many more chances. And anyway, Toby might be a good guy for all I knew.

I looked up to see Oscar coming in with a tray containing two mugs of hot chocolate and a cheese sandwich. It was the tail end of summer, so hot chocolate seemed somewhat incongruent with the season and the weather, but as Oscar has always known, it's my go-to-comfort drink.

'There we are my lovely. This will do you good,' he soothed, as he placed the tray on the bedside table and handed me a mug of hot, comforting liquid and the sandwich. I let out a little sigh, took a bite of the sandwich and a sip of the drink.

'Be careful not to burn your tongue, now, although I did put cold milk in too.'

'It's perfect, Oscar,' I said and smiled.

'That's my girl,' he said, tweaking my nose, like he used to when I was a small child. 'Any luck?' He nodded in the direction of my laptop, now discarded on the bed, lid down.

'No. Airbnb might be okay for a holiday but not for long term. I'll need a place for a year to take me up to starting Uni, when I'll be able to live in Halls for the first semester. I haven't the money for a deposit on a flat and with no job now —'

'You do know, don't you, that you don't have to go, darling?'

'Oscar, we've been through this. I know I'll always be welcome by you, but if you and Toby are going to get it together...'

'Don't think about that now, Hetti. Who knows what will happen?'

'Well, nothing will happen for you while I'm squatting here like the proverbial gooseberry!'

'Don't ever feel like that, Dear One! You will always come before anyone else in my life. Even Toby.'

I finished the sandwich and my drink and reached for my laptop.

'If you really must leave and if you won't let me help you out financially, at least let me help you find somewhere.'

He took the computer from me and started tapping away, his chubby little fingers flying across the keyboard.

'Ah! Bingo! Here we are,' he beamed as he handed the laptop back to me.

'Housesitting?'

'Yes, darling, why not? Some people make a career out of it, and dog and cat sitting too. Free accommodation, all in, apart from your food. And some of these places are really rather plush. Why not give it a go?'

12

Nathan

Autumn, 2012

I took her to the bus station in Norwich and hugged her tight as she made to step onto the bus. Her eyes glistened with tears as she tried to smile. It was the first time I'd seen any emotional response to the situation and the reason she was going back to Ireland.

'Take good care of yourself, Erin.' I touched her cheek.

'To be sure it's Áine that needs the taking care of,' she said, and sniffed — just a little — and I knew that it wasn't a cold that she was getting but more likely that she was trying to hold back the tears.

'Let me know when you get to the airport — I wish you'd let me come with you to Heathrow.'

'What for? I'm perfectly capable of getting myself to the airport on a bus, Nat'an. I've done it many times.' And she smiled, just a little.

'Okay. But I need to know you're safe. So, let me know, won't you? And I wish all the best to your sister. I hope she recovers soon. Please keep me updated.'

She smiled. It was a thin smile. Not an Erin smile at all. Then she turned again and got on the bus. I watched, desolate, as the bus took Erin out of the station and onto the road to London.

But she didn't.

She didn't let me know that she'd got to the airport or that she'd arrived safely in Dublin or how her sister was. Nothing. Just an eerie phone silence that I found so disquieting that I could barely function. I sent so many texts to her that I started to worry that I'd become a stalker. I struggled to come to terms with the fact that Erin, the one woman I'd ever loved and who I'd been so sure loved me too, had just got on a bus and disappeared out of my life. Just like that. Gone. No communication at all.

Thinking about it, I realised that we'd never had a voice call whenever she was in Ireland. It had been a plethora of text messages but never a voice or video call in real time. Was she telling the truth? Was her sister really ill, or was there something else that she didn't want me to know about? The anguish consumed me. Misery devoured me in great gulps. Matt tried to get me out to the pub, but pints of beer, once a source of pleasure and relaxation, now held no appeal. It was the same with food. I didn't want to eat, let alone go out to buy ingredients and cook for myself. Matt invited me round to his place and tried to coax me to eat, but I had absolutely no appetite.

'Come on, mate. You can't go on like this. No woman is worth it.' He held my arm as he spoke, shaking it a little as if to emphasise his point. I'd let him persuade me to go for a drink that I didn't really want. Eerily, as we sat down with our pints, Erin's cat sauntered into the bar and came over to me, rubbing herself against my legs. Tiddles had taken to spending more and more time at the bar and eventually stayed there, full time. True to a cat's nature, she went where the food was.

'I just can't understand why she wouldn't keep in contact. She's getting all my messages, I can see that she's read them, but she's just not responding.'

Her boss at the bar hadn't heard from her either. I'd asked him several times, until he'd said, exasperated, 'for the umpteenth time, mate, I'll let you know if she makes contact.'

'Bit cruel, if you ask me, Nate,' said Matt. I knew he was only trying to support me but I felt angry at the suggestion that Erin could ever be cruel. Not my Erin. Never. But never before, either, had I seen that cold look in her eyes the day that she got the phone call and started to pack her rucksack.

Somehow, I managed to bury myself in my work and tried not to think — or overthink — Erin's disappearance. In some ways, work was therapeutic, but there remained the feeling of a heavy stone in the pit of my stomach and, despite it being a reasonably pleasant autumn, I felt cold, day and night.

I'd grown used to nights spent spooning with Erin and waking up next to her soft body. Now, she was my waking thought and the one thing on my mind as I tried to sleep at night.

Every morning, I checked my phone in the hope that she'd sent me a message, but the silence was chilling. I tried to resist the overwhelming urge to text her but all of my willpower was spent. Sometimes I'd hear myself calling her name out loud as I cycled to or back from campus. There seemed to be a great hollow where my heart used to be. Eventually, I managed to get my daily text messages down to two per day.

1. *Good morning, Erin. I love you.*
2. *Good night, Erin. Sweet dreams. I still love you.*

I became accustomed to being ignored, but was determined not to give up, unless and until she told me categorically to stop all communication.

Days turned into weeks and September became mid-October. I was beginning to believe that I'd never see or hear from Erin again, when, one Sunday morning, as I sat on the sofa in my boxer shorts and hoodie, reading up on veterinary principles and practices, there she stood. Slowly, I got to my feet. She dropped her rucksack in the corner of the sitting room floor and flew into my open arms.

No words.

No words, at all.

She pulled me to the bedroom and kissed me so hard that I could hardly breathe. She slipped out of her shoes and her knickers but left on her long flowing skirt. I was so turned on I lost my speech. I was on my back with her on top of me and inside her before I could blink. She didn't even stop to take off her tee shirt or bra.

Much later, she lay in my arms, her skirt discarded but her long top and bra still in place. I tried to speak. My voice came out as a croak.

'What happened, Erin?'

'Shush.' She placed her hand over my mouth. 'Shush.'

She held the gold crucifix that she always wore on a chain around her neck, rubbing it between her thumb and forefinger.

I stroked her arms, ran my fingers through her hair, kissed her cheeks, held her close.

She looked up at me, with raised eyebrows. 'Your hair's getting long and you look like you haven't shaved in weeks.'

I cleared my throat.

'Yeah, well, I've been a bit — hey!' I was half sitting up by now. 'Hang on a minute. Never mind criticising my unkemptness — where have you been all these weeks, Erin? And why did you not keep in touch? I've been —'

'Not now. Come on, I want you again. Now!'

And what Erin wanted, Erin got. For hours.

At one point, I went to remove her tee-shirt — she must have been very hot in that top what with all our strenuous activity — and anyway I was desperate to get at her gorgeous, pert breasts.

But she stopped me. Taking my hand away.

'What's up?' I was genuinely puzzled and not a little perplexed.

'Shush.'

13

Hetti

Late summer, 2018

And that's how I came to be at Wisteria Cottage. "You'll find the keys underneath the plant pot to the left of the back door", the emailed instructions for check in had stated. She's either a very trusting soul or completely bonkers, I thought. "There is a small cactus plant on top, so do take care." Oh, well that'll keep burglars out, then!

I'd almost expected to find that the keys were missing and that some other house sitter or even squatters had moved in before I'd got there. But, no. There, as described, underneath an upturned plant pot by the back door stood a glass jar containing a bunch of keys. And each one of them clearly labelled: 'back door'; 'front door'; 'garden shed'; 'living room writing bureau'. Talk about make it easy for the burglars! It flew in the face of sanity to advertise for a house sitter — presumably for security reasons — and then leave a bunch of neatly labelled keys in the first and most obvious place that any self-respecting burglar would look.

I let myself in the back door and found myself stepping straight into the kitchen. Red and white gingham cotton curtains hung at the tiny window and a small wooden table with two mismatched wooden chairs stood in the middle of the room. I heard the whirring sound of the fridge as I scanned the space, taking in a kettle on the stove, a butler sink, with wooden draining board and flowering potted plants lining the kitchen window sill. Assorted saucepans and an oddment of cups and mugs dropped down from hooks that hung beneath wall cupboards and from crowded shelves. Dried lavender and rosemary, tied up in bundles hung from the curtain track. A wine bottle containing a burnt red candle with solidified multi-coloured wax that had dripped down it sat in the middle of the table.

And that's when I saw it: the note propped against the bottle on the table. I picked it up. Broad, confident strokes in bright green ink, obviously from an authentic fountain pen with a proper nib, spread across the page.

"Hello there, Miss Hetti," I read. 'Thanks a million for looking after the old place for me. There are two bedrooms; you can take the second bedroom that looks out front. You are not to enter my bedroom under any circumstances. I hope that's clear. Just as a precaution, I've padlocked it. I'm sure you are trustworthy, and I know you passed security by housesitters-r-us.com, but one simply cannot take any chances."

Not take any chances? She'd left the bloody keys under a plant pot by the back door, for heaven's sake!

"Everywhere else in the house you have free reign. Do make yourself at home. The WiFi is fibre optic and superfast. The user name is Wisteria and the password is Lollypopsarered."

Ye gods! She's even advertising her username and password for anyone to see!

"Couldn't get little Tosca into kennels so I've left him with a neighbour. Be a love and offer to take him walkies – he only needs out a couple of times a day – but the old girl isn't up to that."

A dog? Nobody said anything about a bloody dog. I've never owned one. How was I meant to know what to do with a dog? It wasn't that I didn't like dogs, it was just — well — I wasn't used to them. Only contact was petting the dog of a friend I might be visiting and that was only to say hello. I was happy to leave it at that. As for taking a hound for a walk, well, don't they have to be disciplined by owners? I had no idea what to do to make a dog behave.

"There's milk and bread, fruit and yogurt in the fridge for your breakfast — after that you're responsible for feeding yourself. There's plenty of tea and coffee — you'll find it all in the cupboard."

I took a glance inside the fridge and opened cupboard doors to peek inside.

"Be careful with the washing machine..." Oh, where was that? I looked around and spotted it tucked underneath the draining board...

"... it was making a bit of a rattling noise last time I used it, but I didn't have time to get it fixed. If you have a problem, though, be a love and call Jack on 07799424244. He'll sort it for you."

Hmm, I thought. I'm sure he will — for a price! I wasn't expecting to have to fork out for other people's maintenance issues, but, hey, I had a roof over my head and I was warm and dry. And no rent to pay. I resolved to not worry about little problems but to enjoy my sojourn to Wisteria Cottage in Wymondham in the heart of the countryside, south of Norwich. The owner was to be gone for a year – on some around-the-world trip to make up for missing out on a gap year in her youth, so my housing problem was sorted for the foreseeable future.

"Jack is quite handy for all manner of things house-related, so do get hold of him if you need anything at all.

All best wishes, Olivia Hargreaves-Brown."

Sure, Olivia, I will do that. You enjoy your trip while I get work done on your house for you. No problem.

"P.S. Finally, if you're a driver, you can make use of the land rover. It's parked by the garden shed. Keys are in the ignition." Well, of course they are. Where else would they be?

I wandered out of the kitchen, through an archway and into a tiny sitting room. By the open fireplace, in a recess, was a white wooden rocking chair, covered with a throw and a big, plump, multi-coloured cushion. In the recess on the other side of the fireplace stood the writing bureau to which I had been trusted with a key.

On another wall stood floor-to-ceiling bookshelves and a CD player, next to which was a large collected of CDs. I took a little look. Hmm. She liked her opera, that much was evident, as I flicked through her collection. Puccini, Wagner, Mozart, Verdi, Rossini, Wagner. The woman had taste. Although I wouldn't admit to most of my contemporaries, I do love a bit of opera. In fact, come to think of it, I might have known that Daniel was never going to be soulmate material when I found out he hated opera and was more interested in 1980s pop and — seriously — rap! A rap fan with a penchant for stealing thousands of pounds from his girlfriend. Stop thinking about it, Hetti!

I took a deep breath and looked around the room. A small, two-seater sofa with a throw matching that on the rocking chair, and three matching cushions sat snuggly against another wall, sandwiched between two pine bookcases stuffed to capacity. The small window, facing out front, was dressed in identical red and white gingham curtains as those in the kitchen.

A second archway led me through to the tiny hallway with stairs, bare and dusty. Climbing up to the tiny landing I discovered that they were rather rickety and had a loose bannister that felt like it might easily rip from the wall if held too tightly.

This cottage might just turn out to be a veritable death trap!

14

Nathan

Autumn, 2012

So, I shushed. It was just so good to be with her again, feel her, smell her, to be totally sucked into her, that I didn't want to argue. However, although she was still, in many ways, my wonderful, familiar Erin, somehow, something — I wasn't sure what — had changed. I didn't care, I told myself. I was just so glad to have her back and so I went along with anything she wanted to do.

Dusk fell and I'd eaten nothing all day. I was fed to the brim on Erin's love. I'd earnestly wondered if I was dreaming, but this was real. I mean, very real. Very, very real.

'Is there any food in the flat?' I'm sure she knew that there wasn't a crumb. When Tiddles had eaten all the cat food, she had taken up permanent residence at the bar. I was surprised that Erin had not noticed the cat's absence.

'Come on. Let's pop down to Tombland and get a pizza and a bottle of red.'

The cobbled streets of Tombland, a historic and much-loved area of Norwich, was the go-to place for students who wanted a good meal for a decent price and there would be at least one place that would offer a buy-one-get-one-free on a Sunday evening, when things were pretty quiet after the weekend. And with a student card discount of twenty-percent, there was always a good deal to be had on any day of the week.

I suddenly felt ravenous — for food, I mean, not for Erin — though I always had an appetite for her.

She hopped off the bed and skipped along to the bathroom. I followed. We'd often taken a shower together, but this time she slammed the bathroom door and locked me out.

'Erin? Erin? Why d'you do that?'

No reply.

The sound of the shower water cascading onto her body rendered any protests of mine unheard.

'Go. Shave. Shower. I'm hungry,' she said as she emerged from the bathroom five minutes later, wearing nothing but a towel. At the sight of her I wanted her all over again but she batted away my advances and I retreated into the bathroom.

Hand-in-hand, we walked the streets of Norwich after stuffing our faces with pizza and drinking glasses of wine. Despite my happiness at having Erin back, I had a niggling feeling that she was keeping something from me. I'd asked her about Áine, several times, but all Erin would say was that her sister was now fine. Things just didn't add up. There was something that she was not telling me. I was reluctant to pry, not wanting to push her away and risk losing her. The weeks without her had been sheer torture. And, I could not forget, I'd seen that scary look in her eyes the day she'd left for Ireland; a look I'd never seen before and one that I had no desire to see again. So utterly consumed with joy at having Erin back was I that there was no way I was going to jeopardise anything. Those weeks without her had been like a living hell.

When I'd asked her why she'd ignored my messages and not kept me updated about her sister's health, she'd just said what did it matter, now? She was back, she'd said, and, more importantly, her sister was fine now.

The morning after her return, Erin made a phone call to her boss at the bar, then locked herself in the bathroom again while she took a shower. I grabbed a bit of breakfast, gathered together my textbooks and laptop and was just packing my rucksack for uni when Erin started searching through her unpacked rucksack that still lay where she'd left it yesterday in the corner of the sitting room.

'Oh, feck it. What have I done with that?' She muttered the words but I could hear her perfectly.

'What you looking for?' I went and stood at the bedroom door.

'My hairclip. I'm sure I packed it,' she said, as I walked into to the sitting room. She was tossing the contents of her rucksack, one item at a time, onto the floor.

'You've got loads of hairclips, Erin, there must be one around here somewhere,' I said, turning around to go back into the bedroom. I opened the drawer of the cabinet on

Erin's side of the bed. Sure enough, I found a large black clip that she often took out of her hair and threw into that drawer last thing at night.

'Here! There's one here, Erin.'

'Oh, great!'

I lifted the clip from the drawer.

And that's when I saw it.

And I knew.

Straight away, I knew.

A state of anxiety, as cold as a winter chill swept over me as I lifted the packet and looked at the last day that one of the tiny pills had been taken. It was a Saturday. But which Saturday? It couldn't have been the Saturday this past weekend. She wasn't here. And she hadn't unpacked a thing since she arrived back yesterday.

'What are you doing?' Erin stood behind me, as I stared at the packet.

'Erin?' I could hardly get the words out. 'Erin, did you, er, did you forget to take these with you to Ireland?'

'Give those to me.' She made to grab the packet of pills but I held them away from her.

'Erin. I'm waiting. Did you forget to take these to Ireland with you?' I already knew the answer.

'Yes. No big deal.'

'Erin, what do you mean, "no big deal"? We've had sex and you weren't protected.'

'I said give them to me, Nat'an!' Her eyes blazed.

I stood there with the hairclip in one hand and the packet of contraceptive pills in the other and a heavy feeling in the pit of my stomach.

My phone pinged with a text message and I glanced down at the lit-up screen of my phone as it lay on the bed. I dropped the pills packet and the hairclip on the bed and picked up the phone.

Hi stranger. You're a hard man to find. Took me a while to extract your number from my friend's boyfriend. Just to let you know I gave birth to our son a week ago. How about you send me some money? Mandy.

15

Hetti

Late summer, 2018

Incessant banging on the cottage door, accompanied by scratching sounds and barking dragged me from my slumbers. I squinted as the morning sun peeped through the crack in the bedroom curtains. More rapping on the door. I staggered downstairs and opened the front door. A blur of white and black whizzed by as I held onto the doorframe to prevent me getting knocked over.

Looking down at the wizened old woman who stood before me, I thought she was the size of a sparrow; or so it seemed. She had piercing grey eyes that twinkled, yet threatened simultaneously. Her face lined and pinched, lips pursed, like a cat's backside. She held a walking stick in her right hand and I wondered, for a moment, if she was going to hit me with it.

Inside I could hear destruction on an industrial scale going on in the kitchen, along with whimpering and frantic barking. I looked behind me then back at the old bird, my mouth agape. I was barefoot and still in my pyjamas and didn't know which way to turn.

A loud crash sent me running into the kitchen where the fruit bowl was no longer on the table, but smashed to smithereens on the floor and apples rolling around like balls that had just been hit by a billiards cue. I saved, in the nick of time, the candle-waxed wine bottle from tumbling from the table. Two enormous paws landed on my shoulders and a large, pink, very wet tongue proceeded to lick my face. The huge creature whimpered, barked, then licked some more. I was getting very wet. Standing on its hind legs, the thing was almost the same height as me. I grabbed its collar and pushed it down.

'Sit!' I shouted, trying and failing to sound authoritarian and not scared (which I was; scared, I mean, not authoritarian).

It took not a blind bit of notice of me but licked some more then bounced around the kitchen, knocking over more things as it went. I managed to catch last night's wine glass before it fell off the draining board.

The demented creature was a ginormous spotty dog, presumably a Dalmatian, going by the white background and black marks scattered across its body. What was it doing here and who was that sparrow I'd left standing at the door? I tried to grab the lead in an attempt to get the dog out before it totally destroyed Wisteria Cottage, but he wasn't having any of it. He was just too quick for me. I chased him around the kitchen until eventually, after what seemed like an hour (it was probably only a couple of minutes) I managed to tread on the lead. I then wrapped the lead around my arm and held onto the dog's collar as well before proceeding to get him out of the house. I got him to the front door just in time to see Sparrow Woman disappearing through the garden gate.

'Hey! Hey! Lady! What's with the demented dog?'

She turned and held me in her gaze as I walked towards her, dragging the dog behind me. The dog pulled on the lead, nearly upending me in the process.

'Take your dog, Madam. You can't just dump him on a stranger.' My navy-blue pyjamas were covered in white dog hairs. My feet were bare and cold on the morning dew that sparkled on the grass beneath me.

Closer now, I could see Sparrow Woman's mutinous expression. The dog pulled on the lead, dragging me to the ground. I now had not only dog-hair-covered pyjamas with wet trouser bottoms and cold, wet feet but also a cold, wet bum to match. Sparrow Woman started to walk away as I got up, still holding tight onto the lead.

'It's not my dog. It belongs to that cottage you're staying in.' She pointed a crooked finger towards the house.

The owner's elegantly written note left on the kitchen table sprang to mind.

"*Little Tosca*", she'd written. Would I kindly take little Tosca for a walk twice a day?

Either the dog had suddenly grown to its gargantuan proportions since she wrote that note or she was a blatant liar.

'You keep the dog. It belongs at the cottage. You look after him. I was only minding him while you got here. You're fit and strong. Much easier for you to have him than me. And you're bloody welcome to him. My house is wrecked and so am I, might I add!'

Just as I suspected. 'Is this Tosca?' I called to the back of her head and she carried on walking away from me and the dratted animal, who continued to tug left, right and centre. He'd throttle himself at this rate, and quite honestly, the way I felt at that moment, it wouldn't be such a bad thing.

'Tosca. Yes.'

'Hey! What about food? What does he eat?'

'Hah! What doesn't he eat?'

Waving a thin hand in the air, Sparrow Woman disappeared into the distance, marching purposefully and determinedly, walking stick and all. I stood there, watching her go while Tosca leapt up and licked my face with much enthusiasm and intensity.

'Down boy!' I commanded, only to be ignored. I pulled on the lead, which had become somewhat disentangled from around my arm, and wrapped it around my wrist to shorten it.

'I said down!' Had no one tried to train this animal?

Dew from the grass, relentlessly, continued to soak my feet and seeped further up my pyjama pants, the seat of which was soaking wet and my bottom numb with cold. Summer was beginning to fade, all too soon. My face was still wet from Tosca's saliva and my dry mouth screamed out for a big mug of coffee. Clearly, I needed to sort myself out — as a matter of priority — but what to do with the dog in the meantime? I couldn't leave him on the loose; he had the capacity to destroy the whole house and the garden too. And goodness knows what else he could get up to. At this rate it wouldn't be long before he started chewing his way through the tyres of the land rover.

I looked around for a suitable post to secure him to. The garden gate posts were already starting to show signs of rot, so a slight tug from Tosca would doubtless rip one into splinters. Looking around, I noticed the remains of a rusty gazebo that led from the front garden to the side and then to the back of the house. I inspected it, gave it a bit of a shake. Well, it was neglected, but sturdy enough, or so it seemed. I wrapped the lead around it several times and attempted a tight knot. I say 'attempted' because Tosca was in no mood to cooperate and bounced around so forcefully that I feared he'd pull my arm out of its socket.

'Sit!' I yelled at the top of my voice, tugging on the lead.

A whimper. A pitiful look on his face. I wasn't having any. I looked him straight in the eyes.

'Sit, Tosca!' I pressed down with my fist on his rump.

'Sit!'

He sat. He actually sat.

I tied the lead to the gazebo and admonished Tosca to 'stay!'

Another little whimper and that look of doleful forlornness on his face again.

I took a deep breath and exhaled fully, turned around and walked into the house, my shoulders pulled back and down and arms swinging at my sides.

Once inside, I washed my hands at the kitchen sink, put the kettle on for coffee and rummaged through the recycling bin for the ready meal container from last night's dinner. I gave it a cursory rinse under the tap then filled it with water and took it out to the dog. Tosca was now lying on the grass, napping. Well, it's alright for some! I quietly placed the water next to him, tiptoed into the cottage and started clearing up the mess he'd made.

Three cups of coffee later, breakfasted, showered and dressed in clean, dry clothes, I ventured out to check on the Tosca situation. He was still asleep. Obviously, wrecking kitchens and ripping arms out of sockets is exhausting work for such a creature. He stirred, lifting a single eyelid, which then drooped to a close.

It's okay, Tosca, you slumber while I try to figure out how on earth I'm going to cope with a crazy spotty dog.

16

Nathan

Autumn, 2012

I fled the room, ran out of the house.

My first lecture was at nine o'clock and then I had back-to-back lectures and seminars for the rest of the day. My hair flew behind me as I cycled towards campus, weaving in and out of the city traffic, which was always at gridlock point at that time of the morning.

A son. I have a son. I have a son.

Spots of rain hit my face.

I'm a father.

The wind grew stronger and the rain came in earnest now.

I have a child.

Hailstones threw themselves down, hitting the ground like machine gun fire and assaulting my face like bullets on a pillow.

A son.

On campus, I abandoned my bike against a tree and headed for the lake. I couldn't face lectures. Couldn't face the carefree demeanour of my fellow students and I certainly was not in any mood to hear a grey old fossil of a professor going on about some aspect of veterinary surgery. Not this morning.

The hailstones had stopped and the sun cheerfully tried to shine through clouds that now dispersed like fluffy, grey cotton wool, to reveal a blue, blue sky.

I'm a father.

I'm a father.

I'm a father.

Oh god. I was a father.

But wait. How did I know for sure? Mandy was an easy lay, so if she'd do that with me, she'd do it with any dude, wouldn't she? Why pick on me? I made a quick calculation in my head and realised that the dates added up exactly. There was every chance that I was the father, but I'd need proof. Seems that all Mandy was interested in right now was getting money out of me.

I rummaged in my rucksack for my mobile. Several more texts pinged through, all from Mandy, each one becoming more and more abusive.

I needed to think. I started to walk around the lake and the ducks quacked in unison, like they were laughing at me, for being such a fool. For Chrissake! Nobody these days does this. Gets a girl pregnant on a drunken night out. Why did I not...? Well, no point in worrying about that now. I knew that I hadn't used a condom. I didn't have any with me because I'd had no intentions of getting laid.

'You bloody fool!' I yelled across the still waters of the lake. 'You stupid, fucking fool!'

Ducks took flight and left the water, flapping their wings feverishly, as I disturbed their quiet morning.

I'm a father.

I have a son.

My phone rang out into the stillness of the waters.

Erin.

I couldn't resist.

I had to answer.

'Nat'an. Don't be angry. You don't understand.'

'Too bloody right, I don't understand, Erin. What were you thinking of?'

'I couldn't take my pills back to Ireland. If my parents found them — oh, you just don't understand.'

'Erin, we should have used condoms. It is sheer madness to risk a pregnancy,' *said the idiot who had done just that last New Year's Eve.*

How was I going to tell Erin? Not only had I been unfaithful to her — well, alright, technically, I wasn't unfaithful, because we hadn't started having sex yet — but that was irrelevant now — the point was that I was now a father. How was I to tell her that? It would be curtains for our relationship. I'd lose her forever.

'I know, Nat'an. I know. But I'll pray to God and the Holy Virgin Mary that my period comes next month.'

The sheer innocence (or blind stupidity?) of her comment left me with no words.

'Nat'an? Are you there?'

Her voice was soft and sweet and conveyed her contrition at the risk she had taken without my knowledge.

'Yes, babe. I'm here.'

'Nat'an, there is a lot you don't understand.'

'Yeah, right. And you don't do much to help me understand, do you, Erin?'

'It's so difficult to make you understand. You don't understand the Cat'olic faith or the Irish culture. My parents —'

'Your fucking Catholic faith? Irish culture? Your fucking parents? Erin, you're a grown woman, for fuck's sake!'

'Nat'an! Don't speak to me like that! It is so disrespectful.'

'Disrespectful? Disrespectful, is it? Well, Erin, you're a fine one to lecture me on lack of respect. You totally disrespected me when you let me slide inside of you without a bloody condom!'

Silence.

'Did you pray to the Holy-fucking-Virgin-Mary while we were shagging each other's brains out, Erin? Huh? Did you?'

Silence.

'In the misguided hope that my sperm wouldn't mingle at a party with your fucking eggs?'

Silence.

'Did you, Erin?'

Silence.

'Erin?'

I looked at the phone.

She'd gone. Hung up.

17

Hetti

Late summer, 2018

'A Dalmatian? You have a Dalmatian? Darling! How perfectly splendid!' I could almost hear the beaming smile on Oscar's face as we talked on the phone.

'Oscar, I don't know the first thing about Dalmatians and this one is totally bonkers. It's so badly behaved and it's wrecking the joint. The owner could have at least trained the bloody thing before leaving it to unsuspecting house-sitters while she swans off to trot the globe.'

'But Hetti, my love, it will be a good companion for you. Stop you feeling lonely out there in the sticks.'

Oscar had made one of his daily calls to me, just to check that I was still breathing and safe. Part of me felt he was fussing too much — after all, I was a twenty-five-year-old woman, perfectly capable of looking after myself — but another part of me felt warm and fuzzy and extremely grateful to have a kindly 'uncle' looking out for me. His call had come through as I was letting Tosca out into the garden to perform the necessaries. Now I sat on a rickety garden chair while trying to keep an eye on the dog.

'Hetti, darling, have you seen or heard anything from Daniel? Or the police?'

My heart flipped over and I felt the never-far-away tears at the back of my eyes. It was still so raw. The betrayal. The deceit. The theft of my trust money.

'Nothing, Oscar,' I managed to say. 'I think Daniel and my money are gone forever.'

'Don't give up hope, my dear. The police have the report and he's only got to put one foot wrong and they'll be onto him.'

'I don't hold out much hope at all, Oscar. Both the bank and the police told me that the money belongs to the person whose account it was paid into. It's not as if I paid it in by mistake. And the man in the bank knows that. He was there when I went in and paid it into Daniel's account. Oh! I have been such a fool!' The tears flowed freely now, unchecked.

'Hetti, darling. Don't upset yourself. Oh! I'm so sorry. I am an insensitive ass at times! Didn't mean to make you cry. There, there, now.'

I could almost feel him there in the garden with me, holding me in his big bear hug arms and patting my back.

I sniffed and took a tissue from my pocket, blowing my nose rigorously.

'It's okay, Oscar. It's nothing you've done. Just me being silly.' I tried to smile, as if to reassure myself that all would be well, as Oscar always said it would.

'Not silly at all, my dear. Not at all.'

'I'm so lucky to have you for an uncle, Oscar. Thank you for being there for me.'

'Oh, none of it, my precious! None of it!'

I took a deep breath and slowly exhaled, trying to rid myself of the tears.

'Tell you what: how about I come over tomorrow. I could bring a home-made apple tart and a lovely hot roasted chicken from Sainsbury's, and we can bake some herbed potatoes and —'

'Oh, yes please!' I squealed, not giving him a chance to finish his sentence, 'oh, yes, Oscar. Oh, but what about Toby? Will he come too?'

'No, Dear One. Toby is away for a few days. It will just be me and you — and of course, the demented dog.' He chuckled as he said it.

'Okay. Erm, is everything all right with you and Toby? I mean, I thought once I moved out —'

'Oh yes, my Love. All good. He's just had to pop off for a few days. No drama. No probs. All good.'

Why didn't I believe him? I really wasn't sure that 'all' was 'good', but didn't say so. I was so excited at the prospect of seeing dear old Uncle again that this took priority over any Toby-type concerns.

The dog. Where was the dog? An ominous quiet hung in the air. What was he up to?

'Gotta go, Oscar. See you tomor —'

The sound of breaking glass.

I ran back into the cottage to find a flower vase smashed on the kitchen floor, the flowers — picked yesterday from the garden — strewn everywhere. Water flowed along the kitchen table and trickled onto the floor. The bacon and sausages that I'd taken from the fridge for breakfast that morning, were missing from the table. All that remained were shreds of grease proof paper. Tosca licked his lips.

'You bad dog!'

Tosca cowered, hung his head. At least he was beginning to develop a conscience.

'You've eaten my breakfast raw and the wrapping paper too!'

I took hold of his collar and heaved him out of the house, picking up the lead from the hook by the back door as I went. I tied him firmly to the gazebo and went back into the cottage to clear up the mess.

What was I to do with this unruly creature? At this rate, there'd be nothing left of the house by the time the owner got back. Part of me thought that it would serve her right, however, I did want a half decent house to live in for the coming months. Summer was showing signs of turning into autumn and I stopped to think about the prospect of having to take Tosca out for long walks in freezing cold weather. And, not only that, but he was eating me out of house and home.

The dog whimpered and let out a single bark, as if to apologise for smashing the vase and was asking my forgiveness. I went outside and patted his head.

'Okay, Tosca. You and me, well we are going to have to set some ground rules. You cannot continue to smash things. At this rate, there will be nothing left. And eating my breakfast, or any of my food, for that matter, is definitely a no-no. Got that?'

Tosca put his head to one side, and whimpered again, in a but *I'm only a puppy and I didn't mean to break anything and your bacon and sausages were delicious and I love you really* kind of way.

That evening, glass of wine at the ready, I searched the internet for information on how to train a Dalmatian.

'A good Dalmatian,' I read on one website, 'can be trained to be a dependable, dignified and gentlemanly companion.'

Hah! Dignified? Gentlemanly? You've got to be kidding! I took a slurp of wine and continued reading.

'A young Dalmatian can be high-spirited and playful.'

High-spirited? The dog was a thug. Isn't 'high-spirited' the posh term for downright hooliganism? I yelled at my laptop screen. There was no one else to yell at. The dog was asleep. Obviously worn out by his day of meaningful destructiveness.

'Unfortunately, there are many poorly-bred Dalmatians,' I know! I've got one! *'which, if not trained properly can have devastating effects.'* Yes, I've noticed that. Well, trust me to end up taking custody of one of those!

'You have to show him who's boss!' Well, I keep telling him I'm the boss, but he's not listening!

'Your Dalmatian needs companionship, a loving home and plenty of exercise. A confined Dalmatian, who suffers from insufficient mental stimulation, is perfectly capable of destroying your home.'

Yup. He's more than capable of wrecking Wisteria Cottage in the space of five minutes.

On reading further, it said that a Dalmatian is a very athletic dog (as if I didn't know that already!) and that I should be taking him out jogging with me, or even on a hike or a rigorous bike ride. At least once a day. *'You need to get out and exercise your young Dalmatian to keep him stimulated and out of mischief.'* Huh! Which one of us needs to burn off excess energy, me or the dog?

'If you cannot give your Dalmatian sufficient exercise, then it needs to be left to romp around in a safe, enclosed and good-sized area. An obstacle course is preferable to give the dog both the exercise and the mental stimulation that he needs to thrive and grow into a responsible, gentleman.' I had to laugh at the way they kept referring to the dog as a "gentleman". Tosca was many things, but a gentleman he was not. *'The average sized back garden is not really big enough for a young Dalmatian dog to get the amount of exercise he needs. A dog lover should only keep a Dalmatian if they have plenty of space for it.'*

So, that was it. He needed a lot more exercise, some serious obedience training and much more space. According to this website, a Dalmatian will shed its coat all year round, so it seems I'll be clogging up the vacuum cleaner on a regular basis. I looked down at my black jeans, covered in white dog hairs that clung on obstinately. Thanks Olivia! What was Olivia Hargreaves-Brown thinking of? Who gets themselves a Dalmatian pup and then leaves it with strangers? Not that Tosca has ever treated me like a stranger. How could I forget our first encounter when he licked the face off me?

18

Nathan

Autumn, 2012

I slung my mobile into my rucksack and took off at a sprint around the lake. The leaves from the surrounding trees were starting to turn into gold and yellow and brown. Some had taken the lead and were floating down to the ground, making the beginnings of an autumn carpet for me to tread on as I ran and ran around the water's edge. The fringe of the lake was an estimated one-kilometre circumference and when I reached the spot where I'd started to run, coming full-circle, I carried on, doing more and more laps. My breath came in sharp gasps and I began to slow down. Despite the autumnal weather, sweat dripped from my forehead, down my temples and onto my chin.

I picked up speed again and started to chant as I ran: *You fucking stupid dick. Stupid dick. Stupid fucking dick!* How could I have got myself into this mess? A son in the north of England born to a woman I knew nothing about except that she had enormous knockers and a strange accent and a propensity to shag at first sight. Then there was the strong possibility of a second kid on the way, here in Norfolk.

I was due to graduate in the summer and then I'd have a job to find. And a son to keep. And possibly another child too, if Erin's period didn't arrive next month.

You fucking stupid dick. Stupid dick. Stupid fucking dick! I chanted the words, as I jogged around the water's edge. I stumbled and sat down on the grass. It was a bit damp, but what did I care? A pair of wet jeans was nothing compared to the monumental problem that I faced. A dog ran up to me and started sniffing. Its owner followed and admonished the mutt to leave me alone.

'Sorry about that,' he said, with a smile and I realised he was one of the lecturers.

'Oh hi, Professor. No problem at all,' and I patted the dog before it ran ahead.

The professor walked on and I sat there, looking across the lake at the unique shape of the campus buildings. A large expanse of grass with huge, imposing trees spread across it gave the campus a stunningly natural beauty. Virginia creeper clung to grey buildings like an autumnal coloured cloak. Thin, young saplings lined the walkway from the lake to the lecture rooms. There was a dried-up old tree trunk, that people used as a bench, lying on its side at the edge of the water. Rumour had it that the tree had been a casualty of the October storms in 1987. To think, it had been lying there like that since before I was born. As I stared at the campus buildings, I recalled my first year, living in Halls, and the amazing sexual opportunities that it brought. God, I'd been like a kid in a sweetie shop. But I was more sensible in my younger days than I had been as a supposed adult! I never took a girl's word for it, if she told me she was on the pill; I used a condom anyway. Better to be safe than sorry.

So, what had got into me last New Year's Eve? Jumping into bed with a woman I'd met only a few minutes earlier and not taking precautions? Alcohol. That's what. There was a lot of booze at that party and the northerners and the Scots sure knew how to knock it back. I couldn't keep up.

No. There's no point in trying to push responsibility onto anyone else. No-one had held a gun to my head and made me drink myself senseless at that party. I did it of my own volition and now I had to face the consequences.

I gazed across the water and contemplated my time at the university. It had been, by and large, fantastic. I had been loving my course, working hard, playing hard and building great friendships. Now, had I thrown away my chances of the career I'd worked towards since I was doing A-Levels as a seventeen-year-old? What a total idiot.

I sat there with my head on my knees, my arms wrapped around my shins. Oh, god. What was I to do?

19

Hetti

Early Autumn, 2018

You know when you get the feeling that someone is watching you, and you look around and there's absolutely no one there? Or like when you suddenly shudder and say, Someone's just walked over my grave! Well, I know, it is impossible, isn't it, for someone to walk over your grave, when you can't possibly be in it, because you're not dead. You're still alive and living and breathing. And you wouldn't be able to say it, would you? I mean, you'd be dead wouldn't you, if you really were lying there in your grave? But you know what I mean — it's that sense of something a bit strange or other worldly, isn't it? And we just describe the feeling as though someone has just walked over the grave.

Well, anyway, there I was, getting busy with the weeds in an effort to thwart their attempts at strangulating the wisteria that hugged the side of the cottage like a thick lilac coloured blanket when, all of a sudden, it seemed to me that I was being watched.

But if there really was someone lurking around in the background, somewhere in this little cottage garden, well, it would be a bit of a surprise because apart from me and the mad spotty dog, there weren't many people for miles around. Unless, of course, it was Sparrow Woman.

Well, actually, there was the other house sort of next door, but not that close to the one I was staying in (and not Sparrow Woman's house, because she had wandered off in the opposite direction when she'd dumped the dog on me), but there didn't seem to be anyone living there. No smoke coming from the chimney, for example — well, okay, so it was still only late summer, but this was rural England and it got pretty chilly in the evenings.

Perhaps the occupier, if there was one, came from one of those Scandinavian countries or somewhere like that, in which case, they would be unlikely to feel chilly on an English summer's evening, wouldn't you think?

I shrugged, and carried on with trying to extricate the weeds from the poor wisteria, which, despite the best efforts of the weeds, seemed to thrive anyhow.

A crack of the undergrowth, now. A rustle of leaves and I shot round to see — to see nothing. A movement of the breeze, surely?

I carried on with my task of separating the good from the evil, the wisteria from the weeds. With every weed that I pulled from the ground I imagined that I was ripping an appendage off Daniel's body. It felt good. And there were plenty of weeds for me to pull, so I had great opportunities to try and get the scheming, cheating bastard out of my system.

You'd have thought the owner would have sorted the garden before globe-trotting off to Thailand, wouldn't you? Or Cambodia or Vietnam or whatever Southeast Asian location she'd headed off to.

And the bloody dog! Huge great, totally crazy canine that loved to slaver all over my face in the morning. I wasn't expecting a dog at all, any kind of dog, come to that. The ad had specified 'house-sitter wanted', not sitter for a demented spotty dog!

20

Nathan

Autumn, 2012

The October light was fading and I'd been sitting there at the water's edge all day. I'd missed all my lectures, received copious messages from lecturers and admin staff asking as to my whereabouts, and ignored them all. I'd eaten no food since breakfast. I'd had a bottle of water in my rucksack but that was empty now.

I was furious with Erin, but even more furious with myself and with Mandy. Yes, bloody Mandy. She had to take responsibility for her part in this. Why did she take that chance? Alright, I took a chance too, but why was I only finding out about the pregnancy now? Why not when she first found out? I was beginning to wonder if the child really was mine. I needed to speak to her, but I had not the strength of mind nor the inclination, to be honest, not right now. Her text messages tailed off eventually, but there were at least thirty of them that I'd left unread.

Matt tried to call me but I declined the call. I just couldn't face anyone, not even my best mate. Text messages followed but I only read the text visible in the preview and I could see that he was wondering where I'd got to.

I started to feel cold, as the sun and light faded and I got to my feet, slung my rucksack over my shoulder and headed off the campus. Standing on the side of the road, it suddenly occurred to me that I'd left my bike behind and went back for it. God, I was so distracted. There it was, still leaning against the tree, where I'd left it that morning. I marvelled at the honesty of people.

Walking the bike off the campus I jumped on the saddle and instead of heading home, took off down the cycle track towards the little village that skirted the university area. There were a couple of gastro pubs, a bank, some small shops and a hairdresser's salon on the corner. I turned right and cycled out of the village. I rode for miles, along narrow, winding country lanes. It started to rain. I came to a bus shelter on the outskirts of another small village. Alighting from the bike, I sat on the bench inside the shelter and caught my breath.

A voice startled me. I hadn't seen her. An old woman in a green woolly hat, a long grey coat that looked as if she'd been wearing it since the 1960s and a pair of black Wellington boots.

'What? Sorry, what did you say?'

'I says, it's a grim old evening to be out, and thass a fact.' She spoke with a broad Norfolk drawl and had a front tooth missing.

'Um, yes. I suppose it is.'

'You alright, little old boy?'

'Pardon?'

"I says, are you alright? I mean, you look a bit glum, to me, that's all.'

'Um, yes. Yes, thanks. I'm okay.'

'Huh. Don't look like it to me, boy. What's troubling you?'

I regarded the woman from a sideways glance. Her skin was like a crumpled up brown paper bag and her fingers had nodules on the knuckles. She had a turned-up nose and her eyes glistened in the evening lamplight.

'Come on, boy. Ain't nothin' can be that bad. Trouble shared is a trouble halved, as my old mum used to say.'

I puffed out my cheeks and exhaled through my mouth. Who was this woman, anyway? I'd probably never see her again. What was to stop me from unloading my double-whammy day onto her and then walking away?

'Well?' She had a lovely smile, despite her missing tooth and her wrinkly face. From the pattern of the lines on her skin I could see that this was a woman who had smiled a lot over the years.

'I, er —'

'Yes?'

'Oh, it's a long story. I wouldn't want to burden you.'

'Do I look like I might be burdened by your problems? I've lived a lotta years, boy, and I've seen a lotta grief. Telling me what's on your mind ain't gonna burden me none and thass a fact.' She reached out and squeezed my lower arm. She had a gentle, yet firm grip.

'I, er, well, I found out this morning that I've got a baby son.'

'A baby son? Why, thass a blessin' boy, not somethin' to be grievin' about.' She clapped her hands as if in celebration.

'Well, you see, it's this girl up north. I only met her once, at a party at New Year, and — well — you know — I went all the way with her and — well — I never saw her again, but now she's telling me —'

'She's tellin' you that you's the father of her little un, is she?'

I nodded, gazing out across the country road and into the far distance.

'And you? What do you think?'

'What do you mean?'

'Well, do you think you're the father of this baby, or not?'

'Well, no, I don't know for sure, but the dates add up, yes. I could well be the father.'

'Right, now. Well, you'd best make sure this little 'un is yours and then if he is — then what?'

'I don't know. I mean, I don't understand why she didn't have an abortion. I mean, we didn't even know each other. I feel such a fool —'

'You and half the young men in the country what's been caught out like this, my man.'

I thought about that for a moment. She was right. How many dudes had been 'caught out' as she put it, by an unwanted pregnancy and then events had taken an unexpected turn that affected them for the rest of their lives?

'Have you spoken to the mother? How did you find out about the baby?'

'She sent me a text this morning. Said she's given birth to our son and that I needed to send her some money.'

'Oh, I see.' She looked away, as if considering this information for a moment.

'Well, I reckon it's the best thing if you ask for one o' them there DNA tests and make sure you know what you're paying for. There's plenty men around what's paying for children what isn't really theirs. And they probably have no clue, either.'

I pondered this for a while. Of course, I already knew that a DNA test was the way to go and I was aware that asking for it was going to probably upset Mandy no end, but the old lady was right. If I was going to be financially supporting a child, I needed to know that it actually was mine.

I took a deep breath and exhaled fully.

'Thanks,' I said to the old lady sitting next to me. 'Thanks. I will ask for a DNA test and then take it from there.'

'No need for thanks, boy. That ain't rocket science, is it? Thass just common sense.'

'And I have a girlfriend. Here, in Norwich. We had a bit of a falling out this morning.'

'Well, I expect that she wasn't too pleased to hear that you're the father of another girl's baby, was she?' Her tone went up and down in her Norfolk drawl.

'She doesn't know, actually. The row was about something else.'

'Oh? Want to tell me about it?'

I didn't know if I could. The possibility of Erin being pregnant was turning me inside out. How could she be so bloody reckless? And her an Irish Catholic, too. Who cares if her parents saw her taking the pill? If she was pregnant, she was not going to be able to hide that from them, was she? And abortion was out of the question. According to Erin's religion, abortion was murder. She'd never reconcile killing her unborn child with her Catholic faith.

'Well? Are you going to tell me?'

I looked at her, looked away, then back at her. 'Well, you see, it isn't just that there's this baby by, there's also a possibility that my girlfriend might be pregnant.'

'Oh, my giddy aunt!' The old woman slapped her forehead with the palm of her hand.

'It wasn't my fault! Really, this one wasn't. She forgot her pills.'

I heard the engine of a bus, signalling its approach. The old lady stood up and took my hand in hers.

'Well, thass my bus now. Nice talking to you. Now remember, everybody makes mistakes. Ain't nobody on earth what's not made a mistake. You made a mistake. Learn from it. Forgive yourself. Get your DNA test done and move on from there.'

The bus pulled in and the old lady stepped aboard.

21

Hetti

Early Autumn, 2018

'He really is rather frisky, isn't he darling?' Oscar was petting the dog and had become exceedingly close to being upended and landing on his back on the kitchen floor. Tosca was the proverbial bull in the china shop. Oscar grabbed hold of the edge of the butler sink, just in time.

'Bad dog!' I admonished Tosca. He whimpered, cocked his head to one side and took on that hang-dog expression of his,

'He needs boot camp training for dogs, my dear,' Oscar suggested, not unhelpfully.

'Well, I was reading on the Internet last night that you have to give Dalmatians — especially young ones — lots and lots of structured exercise — they even mention an assault course!' I was, I must admit, somewhat sceptical. 'Do you suppose they really do have boot camps for dogs? Sounds very X-Factor/Simon Cowell-esque to me.'

'Let's take a look after lunch. Right now, we need to get this meal in the oven.'

'Yes,' I replied, 'and we need to keep that cooked chicken out of the dog's way, otherwise he'll eat the lot!'

'Oh dear, yes,' Oscar popped the chicken he'd brought into the microwave, out of harm's way, but left the machine turned off. 'I defy him to get it out of there!'

I laughed and started to place vegetables in an oiled oven tray. I was looking forward to this dinner, having lived on ready meals for too many days now. If Oscar knew, I'd get a lecture on the importance of taking good care of myself and eating a healthy, balanced diet.

'He shouldn't be eating chicken, anyway, darling. It's got purines in it.'

'Purines?'

'Yes, my love. Purines, I believe, can cause kidney stones in Dalmatians.'

I was confused.

'But what are purines, Oscar? I've never heard of them.'

'Well, I only know about them because of my gout!' He gave a little wince, that turned into a chuckle.

'I have to avoid purines to prevent my gout playing up.'

'Oh, I see,' I said, popping the tray of vegetables into the oven and wondering at the same time why we were having chicken for lunch if Oscar was supposed to be avoiding purines. I kept quiet about it though.

'And last night,' Oscar continued, 'I did a little online research into a healthy diet for the Dalmatian.'

Tosca scratched at the back door and gave a single bark, a signal that he needed to go out.

'Come on, you,' I said, taking the lead from its hook. 'But I'm tying you up once you've done your business, so no barking or creating a ruckus, okay?'

'Tying him up in the garden is no substitute for a jolly good run in the countryside, darling. You really do need to formulate a suitable exercise regime.'

I opened the door and led Tosca out. 'I will,' I said, over my shoulder, 'I will.'

Walking back into the house, I found Oscar sitting at the kitchen table, searching on his smartphone.

'Just looking up the info about Dalmatians and diet, Hetti. It's very important that you feed him correctly. And his excessive exuberance could be due to a bad diet.'

'Well, I'm feeding him dog food from the local shop. Surely dog food is okay?'

'Not for Dalmatians, I'm afraid. Sorry to deflate you!'

Once again, I imagined myself throttling Olivia for leaving me in this situation. I was supposed to be housesitting, for goodness' sake, not taking on full responsibility for feeding, exercising and training her mentally deranged pet! And as if own-brand dog food wasn't already eating into my tight budget, Oscar's special diet for Dalmatians was beginning to sound exceedingly expensive. I could see myself, at this rate, spending more on the dog's food than on my own.

'Oscar, a specialised diet sounds very expensive and I'm not exactly flushed with money at the moment.' I gave all thoughts of Daniel's thieving betrayal a hefty shove to the back of my mind.

'Okay, here's the plan: we'll have luncheon and then do a thoroughly good internet search, so that you're all clued up on how to feed and train your Dalmatian. Perhaps it won't be too expensive.'

He reached for the wine bottle and two glasses.

22

Nathan

Autumn, 2012

There was little doubt. The DNA test results showed that there was a ninety-nine percent chance that I was baby Ben's father. A hundred quid and forty-eight hours to confirm that I had a son and that I'd be financially responsible for him at least until he turned eighteen. I held the paper in shaking hands and read it over and over, as if by rereading it the result would change before my very eyes.

I called Mandy.

'Well? You going to take responsibility for your son now that you have the scientific fucking proof that he's yours?' I recoiled at her coarse manner.

'There was never any question of me not supporting him, Mandy. I just needed to be sure that he is mine.'

'So, you reckon I'm some slut who goes around shagging anything with a dick, do you?' God, how did I ever create a little human being with this monster of a woman? *Everybody makes mistakes...* I recalled the old woman's words as she'd squeezed my hand at the bus stop that evening.

'I never said that, Mandy. It's just that we don't know anything about each other. I had to be sure.'

'Well, now you are sure. No fucking doubt. You got me up the duff and now you've got to pay.'

I swallowed hard in an effort to avoid hitting back with some smart-arse reply.

'I'd like to see the baby, Mandy. May I come up to visit?' I trod carefully.

'Sure. But bring your cheque book. You're not going to get away with this.' She made it sound as if I'd forced her into bed that night, when, in fact, it'd been her who'd taken me by the hand, her other hand fondling my crotch, as she led me to the bedroom.

'It's not about me "getting away with it", Mandy.' God, I could hardly remember what she looked like, and I certainly did not recall her being so common. 'I would like to see my son. Our son.'

'Please yourself.' No pleasantries. Nothing. As she ended the call, I struggled with the incredulous situation I'd landed myself in.

At uni, a 'reading week' was coming up. I decided to get ahead with as much work as possible, so that I could use some of the time that week to travel to Carlisle. I set up a work timetable, printed it and pinned it up on my notice board.

I had no idea how I was going to break the news of my son to Erin. She'd not known that I'd even been to a party in a northern town, let alone slept with another woman. I felt so unclean at the memory. At the time, I told myself that it wasn't really cheating, because Erin and I were not yet lovers — and I hadn't got laid since I'd first set eyes on Erin. I'd wanted no other woman. I knew, though, that I was just making excuses for my behaviour and, now, I was feeling pretty disgusted with myself.

That evening, I met Matt for a drink in a pub near campus. I needed to have a talk with him, tell him everything, but I could not risk Erin or any of her colleagues at the bar overhearing us.

'You're looking a bit peaky, Nate, what's going on? Erin keeping you up all night?' He laughed at his own crude suggestion before realising that I was just sitting there, staring into my pint.

'Christ, man! What's up? You ill, or something?'

I slowly raised my eyes to look my best mate in the eyes.

'I'm in the shit mate. Big time.'

As he sat listening in silence, I explained the whole sorry situation to Matt. Only when I'd finished did he speak.

'Jeezus Christ on a bike, Nate! You're a dad? What, with that little scrubber at the party? You sure it's yours? She's got a right reputation, mate, I can tell you.'

'I'd rather not know about that, Matt,' I said, feeling queasy at the thought of the numbers of sexual partners Mandy had probably had before me.

'The baby is mine Matt. DNA can't lie. I'm going up there in reading week. I need to see him. He's my son, Matt. My little boy.'

'No way out of this one, is there? You're well and truly screwed.'

'Well, thanks for the support, Matt!' I bit back at him. Talk about rub it in. And this was my son he was talking about. I didn't want a 'way out' of it.

'Oh, sorry Nate. I didn't mean — I mean, it's a helluva mess, but what are you going to do?'

'He's my son, Matt. What do you think I'm going to do? I want to be in his life. He needs a dad.'

'You sound like an old bloke, mate.'

'Thanks. For Christ's sake, Matthew, I thought you'd be a little bit more supportive than this. We've been best mates all this time. Now I've got myself into this mess, and all you can do is laugh and make stupid, tactless jokes.' I slammed my half empty glass down on the table and made to stand up. He grabbed my arm.

'Oh mate! Sorry! I didn't mean it — come on, sit down and I'll get you another pint.'

'I thought better of you, Matt. I really did.'

I walked home in the rain. It was that autumn rain that made clear, with the merest hint of a chill, that winter was not far around the corner.

I don't know if it was the beer or my situation that brought it on, but I found myself weeping as I made my way through the streets of Norwich towards the flat that I shared with Erin. A homeless man asked me if I could spare him some change for a coffee and when he clocked my tears he grunted, 'Cheer up mate, it may never happen.' I wanted to punch his fucking lights out.

At home, I showered and got straight into bed. Often, when she was working an evening shift, I'd meet Erin at the bar to walk her home, but on that particular evening, I had not the inclination nor the energy.

I turned out the light and, much later, I awoke to the sound of Erin quietly opening the bedroom door and felt her slip into bed beside me. With her arm around my waist, she spooned me. And, yet again, she kept her tee-shirt on.

I pretended to be asleep.

Like some cosmic joke, one week after the DNA test result had arrived in the post, confirming my status as a father, Erin's period failed to arrive.

23

Hetti

Early Autumn, 2018

I was beginning to get cabin fever, out in the sticks in this solitary cottage, so I decided on a trip into town. I just fancied a wander around the little independent shops in Wymondham, stop for a coffee somewhere, walk along the Tiffey riverside, maybe check out the thousand-year-old Abbey — anything for a change of scene.

It was a week since Oscar had visited and the dog was the only living creature I'd spoken to. The only human voices I'd heard were on the television or on Olivia's CDs.

Last night, as I stretched out on the sofa with a glass of wine in hand, dog at my feet, I listened to an opera singer invoking images of Wagner's 'Tristan' dying and his heart-broken 'Isolde' having some ecstatically mystical experience that left me wondering if she'd died too or was just so grief-stricken that she'd lost it altogether. I think they ended up together in some version of heaven. I do like a happy ending. And the singer had me gripped with her vocal acrobatics.

But I digress. That was last night. Right now, I needed some human interaction and a decent cup of coffee at a nice coffee shop and a walk along the Tiffey riverside. I looked forward to enjoying the early autumn fresh air.

But, what to do with the dog? Tosca wasn't just any dog. Tosca was the most disorderly hound tearing around the planet; of that I was sure. According to the Wymondham community website, it was permitted to take a dog along the riverside, so long as it was on a lead. That was all well and good, but I really wanted to have a bit of time to myself. As I sat on the sofa, the dog asleep at my feet, I toyed with the idea of asking Sparrow Woman to take Tosca for a short while, but quickly dismissed that mad idea. For one thing, I didn't know where she lived and I hadn't set eyes on her since the day she dropped him off at Wisteria Cottage and if her (then) demeanour was anything to go by, she was not going to greet me with any enthusiasm if I went to ask her to dog sit for a couple of hours.

Tosca gave a little whimper in his sleep, as if he'd heard my thoughts and they'd made him cry. His legs started to twitch. I leaned forward, placed my tea cup on the occasional table and patted his back.

He awoke, jumped up, placed his paws on my shoulders and gave my face a jolly good lick.

'Oh, do stop slobbering, Tosca. Get down!'

I pushed him to the floor and got up from the sofa.

'Come on. Out to the garden. Run off some of that excess energy.'

Grabbing the lead from its hook, I opened the back door and Tosca made a run for it. Before I knew it, he'd leapt over the fence and was on his way to freedom. The white and black blur disappeared across the fields.

'Tosca! Get back here immediately!'

Futile command.

He was well out of ear shot, even if he'd been the sort of dog to obey.

I ran around to the side of the cottage and jumped into the land rover. The keys were, indeed, where Olivia had said she'd left them — in the ignition. I threw the dog's lead onto the floor of the passenger's side and turned the key in the ignition. The engine whirred a little, stuttered and stammered and choked a bit before coughing and jerking into action.

Reversing out of the gravel driveway, I changed into first gear then stopped to look for Tosca. The land rover was like one of those driven by Vera in that TV police drama set in the North East of England. I was mortified with embarrassment and hoped that no one I knew would see me driving this monster of a car.

Now early September, the start of autumn began to reveal a selection of gold, red and brown colours as flowers and trees began to change. The vivid colours spread out before me like a magical carpet of nature. In the distance, I could see what looked like sheep, grazing. Sounds of faint bleating filled the air. Last night's rain had left puddles lying on the sides of the road and the sun in the now clear blue sky left golden rays across the surrounding wheat fields.

Where was Tosca? I squinted in the sunlight and shaded my eyes with my hand.

More bleating. Not gentle now, but a louder, alarmed sound that increased in volume. Peering over towards the sheep field I spotted a blotch of white and black charging around.

Oh no! Was that Tosca, worrying the sheep? Please, no!

I pressed down my right foot and accelerated down the lane. Puddles from last night's rain edged the sides of the road and splashed the ancient land rover as I sped along.

Drawing closer now, I could see Tosca rounding up terrified sheep that crowded into a corner of the field. I parked close to the ditch and jumped out of the land rover, grabbing the lead from the foot well. A small bridge over the ditch led me into the field. Evidence of last night's rain lay in the bottom of the ditch.

Tosca was thoroughly enjoying his exercise and the sheep were definitely not happy. Bleating and barking filled the air, the frantic sounds carried along by the summer breeze.

'Tosca! Stop that! Stop it now! Heel, boy. Heel!'

No response.

Sheep bleated.

Tosca barked and ran in circles.

I sprinted towards the dog but he ran, much faster, in the opposite direction.

'Tosca! Come here right now!' My throat burned and my voice grew hoarse.

The dog ran and ran in circles, jumping over any sheep that got in his way, like a racing horse leaping over Becher's Brook in the Grand National at Aintree. A group of sheep swerved to avoid him and I stood, transfixed, while they ran past, rendering me surrounded by the woolly beasts. I don't think I'd been in such close proximity to sheep in my life and I was, all at once, quite frightened, yet fascinated. And that is when I realised: these sheep were very young, not yet fully grown, barely weaned from their mothers and here they were, already out in the fields to graze. And that pesky dog was worrying the life out of the poor creatures.

'Tosca! Get over here right now!' I yelled, but he was having far too much fun to notice or to care.

A solitary sheep tore past, knocking me to the ground, which was still wet from the rain. Now my hands and knees were covered in mud and I found myself slipping and sliding as I tried to upright myself.

My hair was blowing in my face, so I twisted it around and around into a 'rope' and tucked it into a knot on top of my head. Now I had mud in my hair, as well as on my knees and hands.

There must have been two or three dozen young sheep now, darting in opposite directions, trying to avoid the crazy dog, who continued to bark and run at them.

My initial alarm and concern for the sheep now turned quickly to fury, as I tried to catch Tosca, only to find myself flat on my face in the mud again. This damned animal's days were numbered. If I ever caught hold of him it would be first stop the dog pound. Not for the first time, an image came to mind, of me with hands around her throat, squeezing the life out of Olivia Hargreaves-Bloody-Brown.

And then it would be the dog's turn. And let's not forget Daniel, whose deplorable behaviour had landed me in this situation in the first place.

'Tosca! Come here!' I tried again, as he chased a lone sheep towards the edge of the field. It was perilously close to the ditch.

The sheep ran onto the little bridge, slipped and, unsuccessfully, tried to get up, as I ran towards it and Tosca.

I was torn between trying to prevent the sheep from sliding into the ditch and taking the opportunity to grab hold of Tosca, who was now hurtling towards me, as if he'd only just noticed that I was there. He jumped up on hind legs, paws on my shoulders and proceeded to slaver all over my face.

'Tosca! You bad dog!'

Taking hold of his collar, I fixed the lead and dragged the dog towards the land rover.

'You do not worry sheep like that, Tosca. It's doggie boot camp for you!' I said, for the hundredth time and with all the authority I could muster. It wasn't working. He just licked me again, as if I'd just told him what a good boy he was. 'And you're supposed to be a Dalmatian, for goodness' sake, not a bloody sheep dog!'

I opened the passenger door and shoved him onto the seat, slamming the door on him.

Meanwhile, the lone sheep (all the others were crowded into the far corner of the field, probably totally traumatised) was bleating away in the ditch.

24

Nathan

Autumn, 2012

Erin was pregnant.

She sat on the edge of the bath, sobbing as she held the pregnancy test kit in her hand. Showing me, she said, 'It's positive, Nat'an. Positive. I'm to have a babby. What am I to do? What will I tell my parents? They'll disown me. Oh, I'm so ashamed.'

Ashamed? A whole gamut of emotions swept over me but 'shame' wasn't one of them. I was bricking it. I felt the fleeting feeling of anger at Erin. How could she let this happen?

My mind was in utter turmoil. What was I meant to do? I had a baby son after a one-night-stand that I still hadn't told Erin about and a girlfriend with a baby on the way. No-one could ever accuse me of firing blanks. It would be funny, were it not so absolutely terrifying. My dad always told me never to let my libido get in the way of my intellect. Never let your brain get in the way of your libido, Nathan, more like. I could have kicked myself.

I took her in my arms and held her close and tight. Just couldn't help it, despite my angst. I buried my face in her gorgeous tawny hair and could smell her shampoo. She was doing a really good job of giving her tear ducts a workout and her shoulders moved up and down with every sob.

I let her cry. Kept quiet and just held her while she wept.

Eventually, she stopped, sniffed, reached for the toilet paper and blew her nose.

I took her by the hand and led her to the sitting room. I brought water and coffee and sat beside her on the sofa.

Here goes. No more procrastination. We had to have the conversation.

About why she'd left her contraceptive pills behind when she'd gone to Ireland.

About why she didn't just tell me and let me use condoms, instead of just jumping on me as soon as she walked through the door.

About why the bathroom door was always securely locked behind her.

And about why she would never take off that bloody tee-shirt.

There was no more putting it off.

'Erin. We have to talk about things. Come on, dry your tears,' I handed her a box of tissues. 'Please tell me whatever it was that you should have told me weeks ago.'

'I'm to have a babby, Nat'an. What will I do?'

'That's not what I meant. I already know that the pregnancy test is positive. So, isn't it more a case of what will we do? This is my baby too, isn't it?'

'Well, to be sure it's your babby, too, Nat'an! Who else's babby might it be?' Shock and indignation swept across her face. I thought she might hit me.

'Erin. Listen. I am not saying for one moment that I think the baby is not mine. It's ours. My responsibility as well as yours. Whatever we decide, we must decide together.' Oh god, I was up to my neck in it. How the hell...?

She took my hand. 'Please, Nat'an. Help me.' She looked so miserable and forlorn sitting there that I felt my heart would explode into tiny fragments. While Erin seemed to be inordinately worried about bringing shame and disgrace on her family, I was more concerned about the responsibilities involved in bringing a baby — another baby — into the world. Unlike Erin, I knew for sure that I could rely on the support of my parents, even if Dad would call me a stupid pillock for getting a girl pregnant. Quite right too. But god knows what they'd say when I had to tell them that it wasn't one, but two girls I'd — oh shit. Sheer panic gripped every cell in my body.

Right now, though, I needed to know why Erin had acted so recklessly when she'd got back from Ireland. I braced myself, trying to get up the guts to broach the subject. We'd been skirting around it for weeks.

Deep breath.

'Erin, you left your pills behind. Why?'

'I couldn't risk my parents seeing them. You don't understand what it would be like, if they found out I was no longer a virgin.'

Too right, I didn't understand. This was a twenty-one-year-old woman we were talking about, not a thirteen-year-old kid, for Chrissake.

'Erin, you're an adult. What business of your parents is your — our — sex life?'

'It's alright for you to say that, Nat'an. You don't understand the Cat'olic faith nor the enormity of the social stigma that is attached to an Irish girl who gets pregnant out of wedlock.'

'But Erin!' I jumped up from the sofa, my anger surfacing, and stood facing her. 'You wouldn't be fucking pregnant if you'd taken the fucking pill!'

She shuddered and started to cry again. 'Don't say that, Nat'an,' she managed to say through her sobs.

'It's fucking true, Erin! You stopped taking the pill and didn't tell me and now you're fucking pregnant! How do you think that makes me feel?'

'Feel? Don't talk to me about your feelings! What about my feelings and the feelings of my family and the feelings of our babby and don't keep swearing at me.'

What? I was facing a cataclysmic situation; this bit none of my own making and she was telling me not to swear about it?

I sighed, audibly.

'Don't teach me my manners, Erin, not when you did something so totally disrespectful and inconsiderate as to let me screw you when you knew full well that it could result in an unwanted pregnancy!'

She flinched at my bluntness.

'I didn't do it on purpose! I was just so happy to see you. And I just forgot. What with all the — well — there was a lot going on with Áine. Don't judge me!'

Okay, I know, recriminations were not helpful, but I could feel the blood vessels in my neck begin to protrude and my face to flush and I wanted to scream in frustration. My heartbeat kicked up a pace. I should have been reading for my vet's degree and instead I was talking about an unwanted embryo that I'd unknowingly helped create while struggling to process the news that I was now the father of a baby boy in some distant part of England.

Erin was crying in earnest now. Great big tears rolling from her beautiful green eyes and her whole body shaking.

I softened.

'Erin, look, I'm sorry, okay?' I moved to sit next to her but she shifted to the other end of the sofa.

'Look, we are both het up.' I took a sip of coffee, which was now getting cold, and replaced the mug on the table.

'Het up? I'm not het up, Na'tan. I'm frightened.'

My every instinct was to take her in my arms and hold her and reassure her until she calmed down, but the truth was, I was in need of someone to reassure me. We hadn't even touched on the rest of my problem. What would Erin do when I told her, which I'd inevitably have to, that I was already the father of a new-born? I was terrified. Absolutely bricking it.

'You and me both, Erin.'

And without any warning, it seemed, the sheer magnitude of my dilemma hit me fully and I was crying too. Not one of those silent cries that men tend to do, you know, embarrassed and trying to hide and not let the sobs out, but a high-decibel, full-on primal yell, several times over and above normal human hearing levels. My howls hit out into the room. My mouth wide open, my facial features distorted, I let rip with all my might, the pent-up fear and anxiety I'd been experiencing in the weeks since I found Erin's packet of pills and received Mandy's news.

Erin jumped up, turned around and stared at me. 'Oh Nat'an, Nat'an!'

Then, in a moment, she was beside me, sitting on the arm of the sofa, her arms around me, rocking me like a small, distressed child.

'Hush, now, Nat'an. Hush, my love.'

25

Hetti

Early Autumn, 2018

Looking down from the bridge, it was evident that some of last night's rain was still laying in the bottom of the ditch. The sheep bleated pathetically, as I tried to reassure it.

'Okay, little Bah-Bah, I'll get you out.' Except that it wasn't all that little, as young as it was. I had no idea how many kilos it might weigh, but by the looks of things it might be quite a few.

And I wasn't sure how I was going to get down into the ditch to catch hold of Bah-Bah (no, she wasn't a black sheep, just in case you're wondering), but I couldn't leave it there, could I?

I crouched down and got onto my belly and reached down into the ditch, trying to get a hold of the sheep's front legs. It was just a few inches too far away for me to reach it.

I slithered like a snake so that I was closer to the edge of the ditch and reached down again. Nope. Sheep was too far down.

I was now covered in damp earth and grass and other greenery and I was feeling most uncomfortable. My clothes were preventing me from sliding down any further and anyway, I could end up in the ditch myself and then that would be two of us stuck. The sheep continued to try to tread its way out of the ditch, bleating frantically as it did so.

'Okay, Bah-Bah. Hang on in there. I'll get you out.'

Who was I kidding? The sheep or myself?

Tosca barked and I barked back at him to shut him up. It didn't work. He upped the ante and barked back.

'Shut up! Just shut up!'

He cocked his head to one side, in that way that he did, and lay down on the front seat of the land rover.

Bah-Bah bleated some more. I tried to get closer, lost my footing and joined the woolly creature at the bottom of the ditch.

The muddy water splashed my face, my hair, my eyelids. I attempted to wipe my eyes and made things worse by using a finger covered in dirt.

'Okay, Bah-Bah, work with me on this one.'

I tried to lift the animal but it was even heavier than it looked.

I got behind it and tried to shove it up the side of the ditch. It wasn't even co-operating. Just left me to do all the work.

'Come on, Bah-Bah, help me out here. We both need to get out of this ditch before nightfall, so at least try.'

It bleated.

I grabbed its woolly coat and tried to drag it, but the recalcitrant beast didn't budge.

Tosca barked. I looked up, hoping that he was barking at a person — someone who might help — but, no. He was just attention seeking.

However, getting my attention like that gave me an idea — Tosca's lead!

I tried to climb out of the ditch but every time I took a step up, I slid backwards.

After several attempts, I managed to get hold of a bit of the bridge and with extreme effort hauled myself out.

Grabbing the dog collar as soon as I opened the car door, I unbuckled it as quickly as was humanly possible considering my filthy, muddy hands, and slipped it off. I only hoped the collar would be big enough to fit around the sheep's neck.

The lead was still attached to the collar and I slammed the land rover door tight shut to ensure the horrible hound didn't escape. My sweater and jeans were dragged down by the weight of the mud and silt, now well and truly caked all over me. My red ballet flats were completely ruined. I'd only bought them a few weeks ago and they'd been my favourite go-to footwear. Good for just about any occasion — except for rescuing sheep from ditches!

I climbed down from the bridge and into the ditch, where Bah-Bah was bleating with all her might.

It was obvious straight away that the dog collar was too small to go around her neck so I wrapped the lead around the top of Bah-Bah's body, just behind her front legs.

Taking a deep breath and exhaling a long sigh, I tried to coax the sheep.

'Come on, Bah-Bah. Let's go.'

I tugged on the lead and tried to get myself out of the ditch and onto the bridge under which was beginning to trickle water. My stomach turned over. All manner of catastrophic situations flooded my mind.

The sheep bleated again and that's when I saw it. One of Bah-Bah's hind legs was obviously injured and the poor animal must have been in a lot of pain. No wonder she wasn't co-operating.

I looked around and up and down the road to see if I could muster some help. Not a soul in sight.

What to do? I had a lunatic dog in the land rover, an injured sheep in a ditch, I was covered in muck and had left my mobile phone in the cottage.

I took a deep breath and tried to think.

Clearly, this injured animal needed to be rescued from the ditch and taken to a vet, or at least to the farmer, whoever that was. I peered around the fields and up and down the road again.

I looked back at Bah-Bah. The thing bleated and my heart sank. There was every possibility that this creature could die in my care, and if it did, I'd never forgive myself.

With supreme effort, I heaved at the lead and fell back on my bottom. My clothes were so heavy with rain water and mud that they were impeding my efforts. Taking a huge inhalation of oxygen, I pulled on the lead for all I was worth.

'Come on, Bah-Bah. Come on!'

And that's when I landed on my back in the ditch with an almost fully-grown sheep on top of me. And that's also when Bah-Bah emptied her bladder on me.

26

Nathan

Autumn, 2012

The light had faded when I awoke and I reached for the bedside lamp.

We'd both cried so hard that I thought we'd never stop. Erin cried because of the shame her pregnancy would bring on her family, while I cried because I was petrified of having to take responsibility for two children when I was not much more than a kid myself. I felt like I'd wrecked my life when it had hardly begun. Would I have to leave university, give up my career in veterinary surgery and get some menial job to pay for two kids I'd never planned on having?

We'd moved from the sitting room to the bedroom and now lay on the bed, our bodies entwined. I watched Erin as she lay there, sleeping. Her long tee-shirt had ridden up and that's when I saw it. I reached out and touched her belly, running my fingers along the thin, red line. What the hell had she been doing in Ireland?

She stirred in her sleep and opened her eyes, quickly pulling down her tee-shirt.

'Erin, what is that on your belly? What happened in Ireland?' I pulled her tee-shirt up and she let me, this time.

'It's from the surgery,' she said, quietly.

'Surgery? What surgery?'

She looked at me briefly, then looked away as she spoke.

'Áine needed a kidney transplant. I was her donor.' She touched the scar, as if it were something very delicate. So: that was the mystery of the tee-shirt cover-up solved. She didn't want me to know. But why? And now, I realised, there was another aspect to this.

'Wait a minute, Erin. Are you telling me that you underwent kidney donor surgery a few weeks ago and now... now... now, you're pregnant?' My mouth was dry, my lips stuck to my teeth and my throat felt like sandpaper. I could hardly get the words out. I reached for a bottle of water at the side of the bed and took a swig.

'She would have died. I had to help. Mammy and Daddy said it was my duty, as Áine's sister, to donate one of my kidneys.'

'Wait. Are you saying that you were coerced into doing this?'

'No! I wanted to do it! Áine is my sister. My identical twin. I was the perfect match. It was the most natural thing to do.'

'But, Erin,' I was careful here, not wanting to sound too alarmist, but at the same time, needing to know, 'there must be complications involved in a pregnancy so soon after a surgical operation in the abdominal area. Can't you see that?'

Holy fuck.

27

Hetti

Early Autumn, 2018

Scrambling out of the ditch, I leaned in and took hold of the lead still wrapped around Bah-Bah's torso. With a great heave-ho, I was, once again, on my bottom but the sheep was out of the ditch, bleating feverishly. Picking it up — it was heavier than I'd imagined — and mindful of its injured leg, I staggered to the land rover and dumped the sheep in the back. I bent over, trying to catch my breath, taking in great gasps of air, my hands resting on my shaking knees.

The dog was barking and the sheep was bleating.

'Oh, just shut up, the pair of you!' I managed to say, still gasping for air. I looked down at the state of me and wanted to cry. I was exhausted and just wanted a hot shower and a hot drink, but I had to get this injured animal to either the farmer or the vet. I didn't know where the farm was, so it would have to be the local vet.

I sniffed, and wiped my face with the back of a muddy hand, then kicked off my shoes, stripped off my clothes that stank of sheep's urine and jumped into the driver's seat.

Tosca, delighted to see me, licked my face enthusiastically.

'Oh, get off me, you pesky mutt! Dog Boot Camp for you and that's a promise!'

I gave the dog a shove, much to his chagrin and turned on the ignition.

As I drove down the road, wearing nothing but my bra and knickers, with a totally mad dog and an injured sheep in the car, it really didn't occur to me at that particular moment in time, that I must have presented a rather odd sight to anyone I might encounter.

The vet's was closed. Bah-Bah bleated pathetically and Tosca whimpered as if he knew that he was responsible for the sheep's pain and was trying to say he was sorry. I wasn't feeling any sympathy for him. Indeed, had there been a home for stray dogs within a five-mile radius I'd have dumped the delinquent hound in it forthwith!

Torn between searching for another vet (the likelihood of an alternative practice in the immediate area was, I thought, unlikely) and going home to a long shower, clean clothes and a stiff drink, I turned on the ignition and drove down the lane towards Wisteria Cottage.

Glancing in the rear-view mirror I noticed a group of women of all ages, arms crossed, watching me drive away. Great. They must have seen me, bra, knickers, no shoes, peering into the vet's practice window. Bloody great! My reputation would be in shreds and I imagined being known, for as long as I lived in Wymondham, as the mad woman from Wisteria Cottage who goes around in her underwear, covered in mud and with a lunatic Dalmatian and a sheep in her car. Oh well, could have been worse, I suppose. At least I wasn't wearing a thong. I have always been less of an *Ann Summers* girl and more of a *Reebok*-Sports-Shorts-and-Crop-Top one.

At home, I left the sheep in the back of the land rover and tied Tosca to the gazebo. Indoors, I stripped off and had a hot shower, which took a while because I needed to get mud and silt off every part of my body as well as out of my thick, wild hair.

A loud rat-a-tat-tat on the cottage door and Tosca barking agitatedly startled me as I wrapped a towel around my head and another around my torso.

Rat-a-tat-tat!

Oh, for goodness' sake! Now what?

Whoever it was, had no intention of giving up because they just kept on banging, so I went straight downstairs, still wrapped in towels, and opened the front door to a rangy young man sporting blue jeans, an un-ironed black tee-shirt and a panama hat that looked the worse for wear. I'd never seen him before in my life.

'What are you doing with my sheep in your vehicle?' With one finger, he pushed his hat to the back of his head, to reveal a pair of startling dark eyes, thick, black eyebrows. His black wavy hair almost reached his shoulders, and he had several days of beard growth. He had a scowl on his face and his hands on his hips, making him look confrontational.

Feeling somewhat vulnerable, I held the towel tighter around my chest, worried it might fall, which it might well have done and if it did the consequences would have been more than a little embarrassing.

'It's injured.'

'What have you done to it?'

'Nothing.'

'So,' he regarded me with a sideways glance, 'what is it doing in your land rover?'

'I told you. It's injured. It was in the ditch and —'

'In the ditch.' It wasn't a question, so much as a term of derision.

I had no desire to argue with him while wearing nothing but a towel, so I said, 'I need to get dressed.' And with that I closed the door and skipped up the stairs — the same rickety stairs that would probably come crashing down one of these days and kill me — well, it would be the stairs or Tosca or a sheep landing on me that would end my days — and slammed the bedroom door behind me. Tosca barked. I hoped he was still securely tethered to the gazebo.

I removed the towel from my head and rubbed my hair a bit to get the drops of water off. Drying myself I could see the beginnings of bruising obviously caused by Bah-Bah when she'd landed on me. Pulling on some clean underwear, a pair of leggings and a tee-shirt, I went back downstairs and opened the front door. The man was still standing there as if I'd never left.

'My sheep,' he said. 'I believe you owe me an explanation as to why and how my sheep got into your car.'

'I told you. It was in a ditch. It was obviously distressed and in pain and I got it out and I didn't know who the owner was so I brought it back here.'

'Did you now?'

'Yes, I bloody did! And to great inconvenience to myself, I might add. I nearly got stuck in the ditch myself trying to rescue your animal and I got absolutely filthy and ruined my brand-new red ballet flats in the process. But don't bother thanking me. Just take your bloody sheep and clear off!'

28

Nathan

December 2012

'Having a baby is perfectly fine, but I was ill-advised to become pregnant for at least twelve months after your transplant, Erin.'

We sat in the obstetrician's surgery, holding hands. I listened to the words and wondered what planet I'd landed on.

'Some of your medications after transplant can cause problems to the foetus, you see. Developmental problems, that is. Didn't the kidney transplant team explain this to you, Erin?'

I felt as if a freezing cold wind was blasting right through me.

The doctor regarded her carefully, waiting for an answer.

I looked at Erin and then back at the doctor.

'Well, no, you see,' I started, 'no —'

Erin squeezed my hand, as she spoke. 'It was a rather delicate situation, doctor. As you can tell, I'm Irish. Not only that, but I come from a very devout Cat'olic family background. As a single woman, I am not expected to even be sexually active, let alone get pregnant.' She blushed slightly. 'The doctors didn't even mention pregnancy.'

'I see. But you should have told the transplant team, Erin, that you have a boyfriend. It is a significant factor that needs to be considered.'

'The doctors told me that I'd be in hospital for a few days, which I was, and then it would be perfectly safe for me to go home. They said I'd have a wee bit of discomfort for a couple of weeks, but I didn't. They gave me pain killers and I didn't even need to take them.'

'But you came back to England after a couple of weeks, and resumed your normal life?'

'Yes, I was fine.'

'Maybe you were not in any discomfort, Erin, but you needed between six and eight weeks to heal, so you didn't give yourself sufficient time for the healing process.'

I shifted in my seat. This did not sound good.

'But don't worry. We will closely monitor you and hopefully there won't be any problems.'

Hopefully? Not exactly comforting. I needed cast iron reassurances, which I felt in my gut I was not going to get. This was looking decidedly dodgy. It seemed to be bordering on a medical emergency, just waiting to happen. Erin's family finding out that she was pregnant and the inevitable fall out from that, paled into insignificance with the news that we could end up with...

I gathered myself.

'Doctor, are you saying that the baby could be born disabled in some way?' Well, someone had to say it and it didn't look like Erin was going to.

'Well, there are two issues, here,' the doctor spoke carefully, quietly, yet firmly. 'There is the matter of Erin's health and then the question of the developmental issues that could affect the foetus. As I've explained, her body needed time to heal before getting pregnant.'

This was sounding serious now; very serious indeed. The baby was at risk and so was Erin. He'd just said so. Oh god, could things get any worse?

'What exactly could go wrong, doctor?' I needed to know. We needed to know.

'Let me reassure you that most women who get pregnant after kidney donation have a trouble-free pregnancy. The problem we have with Erin is that the pregnancy came so quickly after she donated her kidney. Her body was not totally healed at the time of conception.'

'Yes, I understand that, but what sort of problems, exactly, can we expect?'

'Well, hopefully none at all, but —'. That word again, hopefully...

'Doctor, no disrespect,' I cut in, 'but "hopefully" isn't good enough. I need to know what we might expect to go wrong, so that we can do whatever we can to try and avoid it.'

'I understand,' he said, with an exaggeratedly patient air about him. 'With any pregnancy involving a recent kidney donor mother, the most common problem is preeclampsia.'

'Preeclampsia?' Erin and I said, in unison. We looked at each other, then turned back to the doctor.

'Yes. It is a kind of high blood pressure, which, if it occurs, needs close monitoring.' He looked first at me, then at Erin, his expression difficult to read. 'It can be a very risky situation for both mother and baby.'

29

Hetti

Early Autumn, 2018

I slammed the door in his face, then watched through the window as he picked up Bah-Bah from the back of the land rover and walked off with the animal tucked under his arm. The sheep seemed a lot lighter to him than it had been for me. He made it look effortless.

Tosca barked. Well, he would, wouldn't he? Any excuse to cause a ruckus. I walked out and untied him from the gazebo.

'You'd better behave yourself from now on, Master Tosca. You've got enough black marks against you to last a year!' I said, trying to sound like I meant it. Well, I did. In fact, I meant every word of admonition that I'd ever spoken to him, but it all went in one ear and out the other, where Tosca was concerned.

He jumped up and dutifully licked my face.

'And just so you know, there's no need to bark when a person is *leaving* the property. It's sufficient to just alert me if there's an intruder.'

Inside, I fed and watered the dog, telling him he really didn't deserve it and warning him yet again that any more bad behaviour and he'd be in big trouble.

He cocked his head to one side, as if I was talking a foreign language.

Gathering together the ingredients for a pot of soup, I began chopping vegetables. Bending down to take a big saucepan from the cupboard, I felt the effects of my encounter with the sheep in the ditch. I'd be well and truly covered in bruises the next day, I just knew it.

I took bread rolls from the freezer, microwaved them before smothering them with butter and garlic then stuck them under the grill.

I opened a bottle of wine and reached for a glass. Tosca snored contentedly on the hearth rug, as I walked through to the sitting room, glass of red in one hand and plate of garlic bread in the other.

My mobile phone lay the coffee table, where it had been all afternoon. Several missed calls from Oscar, umpteen text messages from friends I'd been neglecting for weeks and a missed call from an unknown number.

I'd call Oscar later. For now, I needed sustenance in the beautiful shape of a glass of wine and hot garlic bread.

The soup was ready and I was just ladling some into a bowl when my mobile went off. Torn between feeding my face and taking a call, it didn't take long for the food to win and I didn't even look at the phone.

Another glass of wine and I was nodding off on the sofa when the phone startled me back into consciousness.

Oscar.

'Hetti, darling! Where have you been? I've been trying to get hold of you for hours!' He sounded frantic.

'What's up, Oscar?'

'It's Daniel, darling.'

A cold chill ran down my spine.

'Daniel? What about him?'

'Well, darling, Toby was in Norwich city centre today and he thinks he saw him.'

Daniel was in the city? My heart beat a little faster and I didn't know if it was a longing for my former boyfriend or the anticipation that I might be closer to getting my money back from him.

'I didn't realise that Toby knew Daniel.'

'Well, darling, he doesn't exactly know him, but he did meet him that one time, remember? When we bumped into you both?'

The memory was vague, but I took his word for it.

'And, of course, he's seen photos of you both together.'

So, Daniel had the nerve to show his face in Norwich, even after pilfering my hundred-grand and running off with it. What self-respecting criminal hangs around the scene of the crime, for goodness' sake?

I took the stairs two at a time, ran into the bathroom and threw up.

30

Nathan

Early summer, 2013

The baby died inside her.

Erin laboured day and night to bring into the world a lifeless infant who couldn't make it beyond seven months' gestation. 'Preeclampsia', they said had caused it. A complication of pregnancy that is more likely to occur in a kidney donor mother, especially if she becomes pregnant too soon after donation. Just like the doctor had warned us. After thirty-six hours, my tiny little girl lay still and pale like a plastic doll in the palm of my hand. She was perfect. Simply exquisite. Flawlessly formed and utterly beautiful. I felt helpless and hopelessly inadequate by my inability to help her. My heart bled with grief.

Erin, exhausted after her ordeal, lay sleeping; her hair wet with sweat stuck to her forehead and spread across the pillow. A gentle hand touched my shoulder.

'Nathan, you have to say goodbye now. We need to take care of Baby.' The voice was soft, yet the words felt hard and impossible for me to comprehend. How could I possibly say goodbye to this tiny girl that I'd helped create, yet would never get to raise? I loved her already. Who would take care of her, safeguard her, now that it was impossible for me to do so? A father's role is to protect his child. That privilege had been ripped away from me.

'She's so little. What will you do with her?' My voice was not my own. It sounded weak and small.

'You don't need to worry yourself with that, Nathan. Let me take the little one, now.' The voice was gentle, controlled, calm. Kind.

A blue surgical-gloved hand reached towards my little girl.

'Let me take her, now, Nathan.'

I pushed the gloved hand away, angry suddenly.

'Get off her. She's mine.' The woman stepped back. I touched my baby daughter's head, cradled it. I leaned forward and kissed her cheek.

I placed the baby's face next to sleeping Erin's cheek. Moments later, I handed my daughter to the nurse.

Have you ever heard the sound of a heart breaking?

I have.

My own.

'Holy Mary, Mother of God... pray for us... pray for us sinners now...'

Although Erin's voice was weak and almost inaudible, as she drifted in and out of consciousness, I got it that she was praying to her holy virgin, Mary. I wasn't sure what good it would do. I also got it that she was going to be tormented with guilt about this whole sorry, sad episode for the rest of her life. That, I was sure about. She'd see it as god's punishment for her sins. I stroked the back of her hand and pushed her hair back from her pale face. She looked so small, lying there. Almost like a child herself, yet she had done the most grown-up, courageous thing any woman can do; she'd brought our already perished daughter into the world. I would forever be grateful to Erin for the chance to meet and spend precious moments with the little girl who would never grow up.

Nurses drifted in and out of the room, checking Erin's vital signs, as she lay there sleeping. I sat by her bedside, overwhelmed with grief and anxiety. Grief for our tiny baby daughter and anxiety over Erin's recovery. The Internet is a cool piece of kit for research, but it can also be a source of enhanced fear and angst. I'd been searching on my phone for information and knew that eclampsia was a real possibility for live kidney donors and I was terrified that I'd lose Erin too.

Erin stirred, as the nurse took her blood pressure and made other examinations. My hands felt empty when I had to let go of her while the medical checks were regularly carried out.

At some point in the night, having been awake for over forty-eight hours, I fell asleep in the chair, still holding Erin's hand in mine. Images of my baby girl's doll-like face crowded my dreams. I jerked awake as my head nodded forwards and lolled to one side. Erin slept peacefully. I stroked her hair and squeezed her hand.

Fitfully, I dozed through the night, stirring only when a nurse entered the room. My neck felt like a twisted, iron rod and my lower back ached.

'Nathan? Nathan?' A hand on my shoulder, gently shook me.

I looked up, blinked, to see a nurse standing over me.

'Huh?'

'Nathan, why don't you take a little break? Go to the canteen and get yourself some coffee and breakfast? We're here to look after Erin.'

I looked over at Erin, sleeping, it seemed, so peacefully. Was she oblivious to what had happened?

'I don't want to leave her,' I croaked, with tears pricking my eyes.

'Go, Nathan. Get some food inside you. You'll need your strength and energy to take care of and support Erin when she's well enough to leave hospital.'

Reluctantly, after leaving a lingering kiss on Erin's forehead, I left the room.

The canteen was busy with medical staff and people I assumed were patients' relatives. The queue for drinks and food was long. I sat at a table, waiting for the room to clear a bit. I looked at the pictures of Full English Breakfast displayed on walls around the serving counter. I could smell coffee and tea and bacon and toast. My belly rumbled. I yawned, swiping my hand across four days' worth of beard growth.

Erin's parents knew nothing of what had taken place. They didn't even know that she'd been pregnant, let alone that she'd given birth to a stillborn daughter. I took out a paper serviette from the table and wiped my eyes and the tears that threatened to roll down my face, hoping no one would see. I really was in over my head, but at least I'd been able to confide in my parents and Matt had been a good listening ear, even if he was a little bemused by the whole thing.

This time last year, life had been so carefree and full of hope. I'd won the affections of the girl of my dreams and everything seemed so perfect. Erin was worth waiting it out for. I'd never been so happy. My studies were going well — they still were — up to the point of Erin going into labour. No matter what was going on, my degree studies never suffered. Matt said he thought I was mad and heroic in equal measure.

I looked up to see that the queue at the servery was thinning out. It was only six in the morning and I marvelled at the numbers of people looking for breakfast in a hospital at this ungodly hour.

The hot coffee made me feel more human and the Full English filled my belly.

I made my way back to the ward.

31

Hetti

Early Autumn, 2018

I hadn't dared to buy a second pregnancy test kit before now, but all these bilious attacks were a tad worrying, so I thought I'd better pay a visit to Wymondham pharmacy. I really needed to face up to the fact that I could be pregnant, and if I was not, then I needed to find out what was causing the sickness and missed periods.

And anyway, I felt like having a little outing, after the events of yesterday, so I grabbed my handbag and the dog's lead and locked the cottage door behind me. Tosca was snoozing by his gazebo and jumped to it when I whistled at him. I shoved him into the back of the land rover, securing him with the lead. A nice walk by the River Tiffey, a pot of tea and some cake and a trip to the pharmacy were the order of the day. The mutt had just better behave, that's all.

There was a definite autumnal feel to the air as I parked the land rover and walked through Wymondham. Taking the Tiffey bridge, I looked over to see the soft white foam of the water as it bubbled below. Across the water meadows a dozen, or more, Great White Egrets explored their surroundings, their heads, as they peered around, looked too small for their bodies. Tosca, spotting them, pulled on the lead, heading for the water.

'Oh no, you bloody don't!' I warned him as he pulled me along behind him. For goodness' sake! If it wasn't sheep it was birds. Can't the damned dog just leave the poor animals alone? He picked up a pace and I was in danger of being pulled down and dragged along on my belly.

'Stop! Heel!' I shouted at the top of my voice, but he was having far too much fun to listen to me.

Egrets took flight in a white flurry.

'Don't yell at him, he thinks you're as excited as he is about the birds and that you want to play with them too.' Tosca came to a halt, so that I nearly toppled over him.

I turned to see Sheep Man standing there with a smirk on his still unshaven face.

'You!'

'Yup. Me,' he said with a grimace, 'and you need to train that dog of yours.'

The cheek of it.

'He's not *my* dog and for your information he was already trained when I got him. Trained in inappropriate behaviour, but nonetheless, trained. He's not my responsibility. I'm just — just — looking after him for someone.'

'Oh, yes, and that would be mad old Olivia, would it?'

He knew her?

'I don't know about the 'mad' or the 'old' bit — I haven't met her — but yes, the owner's name is Olivia.'

'And she won't have done any training with this pooch,' he said, stroking the backs of Tosca's ears, 'I can assure you of that.' The dog then proceeded to lick the man's hand rigorously.

'Well, he seems to like you,' I said, a little miffed. 'He's calmed down a bit.'

'Hm. Interesting, because this breed is not the most sociable of dogs.'

Positively unsociable, judging by his behaviour so far!

'But let me offer you a little advice,' he continued, before I could react, 'you see, the thing is, you don't want to bombard him with your commands. Be consistent, but don't keep hassling him. He's a bit like a bloke, like that. Doesn't want to be nagged at.' He grinned. 'He'll find it irksome and, also, just like a bloke, he'll just switch off.'

Who was this guy? Some kind of expert?

'Yes, well, that's all very well for you to say. You're not the one who's had the beast foisted on you. I was supposed to be housesitting, not taking care of a crazy dog.'

'Okay, only trying to help. See yah.' And, whistling for a small, caramel coloured terrier, who, from nowhere, it seemed, came tearing up to him, off he sauntered. Irritating bugger.

Tosca pulled on the lead and made off in hot pursuit of Sheep Man and terrier, dragging me behind him.

With two hands and all my might I yanked on the lead and somehow managed to pull him to heel.

'You just stop that, immediately, pesky dog! No more repeats of the sheep incident, thank you very much.'

Tosca looked at me with that dejected expression of his then jumped up and licked my face.

Hearing a hearty guffaw, I looked ahead to see Sheep Man standing on the Tiffey bridge, laughing his head off.

'Okay, Tosca. Listen very carefully. Stop humiliating me in public, or it's the dog pound for you. And this time I mean it,' I said, pointing my finger in his face, which he promptly licked.

We made our way from the Tiffey and up towards Market Place. I could see Market Cross, the iconic landmark, looming ahead. I reached Market Cross and noticed the *Mad Hatters Tea Shop* on the opposite side of the road. It seemed a fitting place to go, considering I had a mad dog in my charge.

There was just enough warmth in the air to remind me of the lovely summer that was now about to take a farewell bow and make way for autumn.

A couple of old codgers got up from a table on the pavement outside the tea shop and one of them doffed his flat cap at me. They toddled off down the road and I moved to take a seat. The walk had made me warm so I took off my cardigan and wrapped it around the back of the chair. Peering through the window, which was dressed with half-way-up pretty, floral, blue and pink curtains, I could see oddments of bone china tea cups, saucers, mugs and teapots adorning the shelves. Pastel coloured bunting framed the counter, which displayed an assortment of homemade cakes. Customers sat at tables that were crowded with cake stands and an assortment of china cups, saucers and teapots.

A smiley lady, wearing a pinafore with a strawberry pattern and blue frill round the hem came out of the tea shop and took a wary look at Tosca.

'Oh. It's okay,' I said, trying to sound confident and reassuring, 'I'll keep him under control.'

'Oh, don't you worry about that, my woman. People brings their dogs here all the time. What can I get you?' More smiling.

'I'd like a pot of tea and a slice of that delicious looking carrot cake, please.'

'My pleasure. Coming up!' She scribbled on her notepad and disappeared indoors.

I took the lead and secured Tosca to the leg of the table and also to the leg of my chair.

Moments later, Smiley Lady emerged from the tea shop, carrying a tray containing a floral teapot, a bone china cup and saucer and a huge slice of carrot cake on a mismatched plate. She placed my order on the table and with a jolly 'enjoy your tea and cake', went back into the tea shop. I lifted the teapot and started to pour. Without warning, Tosca made a sudden dash for freedom, with table and chair, still secured to him by his lead, rattling along behind him.

A searing pain shot across my bare arm.

Nathan

Same day, early autumn, 2018

I heard a noise and looked up the street to see a blob of white and black hurtling towards me, dragging a table and a chair behind it. Before I knew it, the Dalmatian was on top of my terrier, Toffee, trying for all he was worth to hump her, a table and a chair — I kid you not — attached to him by his lead. At the same time, the cries of someone very obviously in considerable distress caught on the wind and reached my ears.

The thing was — I really didn't want a bloody great animal like that impregnating my young terrier, even though, given the differences in their sizes, it was highly unlikely that the Dalmatian could choreograph it. Pulling them apart, I took the bigger dog by the collar and untied it from the table and chair. A woman with a pushchair containing a sleeping toddler stopped and dutifully up-righted the table and chair on the side of the road, then carried on walking, as if it were the sort of thing that she did every day.

The commotion at the tea shop fifty metres up the road continued and I could see someone lying on the pavement, the woman from the café fussing around her. I took both dogs by their leads and ran up the road to the scene where I found that it was the hot redhead on the ground in some distress.

A broken teapot and other crockery were strewn around the area, and the poor girl was hugging her arm. It didn't take long for me to realise that she had been scalded by hot tea. One of the women from the *Mad Hatters' Tea Shop* was holding a tub of butter, trying to persuade the girl to let her rub some on the burn. A small crowd of villagers formed around the scene, each one offering some old wives' tale remedy for scalded arms. It was, rather appropriately, turning into a version of *Alice in Wonderland's Mad Hatter's Tea Party*. I almost expected a fully-clothed white rabbit and Tweedle-Dum and Tweedle-Dee to turn up at any moment.

'No! Don't put butter on a scald! Worst thing you can do!' I yelled, then scanned the group for a couple of suitably able people to hold one dog each and keep them apart.

'No, butter ain't no good. You wants Vaseline, thass the best thing,' one woman then suggested, rather unhelpfully, because she was as wrong as the butter woman.

'No Vaseline, either,' I said. 'That'll only prevent the heat from escaping. We need to cool her down.' Jeezus! What was the matter with these people? Bloody butter and Vaseline, for fuck's sake!

'We need to get her to a cold water tap immediately, and do you have any cling film?' I asked the woman, who obviously worked in the tea shop because she was wearing an apron and still had the tub of butter in her hand.

Butter Woman nodded, 'come inside, my man,' and walked into the tea shop.

I knelt down to the patient, placed my arm around her shoulders and helped her up. Her hair fell in her face and I moved it back, looking straight into her downcast eyes. She winced in pain.

'Take it easy, now,' I said, trying to be reassuring and manly and not at all sure that I was managing it, 'we need to get that arm under cool, running water for a while and then I'll put some cling film over it to keep it clean and protect it from the air.'

Her hair sprung back into her face. I could smell her shampoo and the faintest hint of her shower gel. The Dalmatian barked and let out a whimper and tried to move towards her. Luckily, I'd put a hefty young dude in charge, who yanked the lead, pulling the dog back. Toffee was in the capable hands of another lad, who looked to be the younger brother of hefty dude man.

We trod our way through the debris of broken china, entered the tea shop and went behind the counter, where Butter Woman turned on the cold-water tap.

'Here, put your arm under the running water. You need to leave it there for a while. About twenty minutes. We need to let the heat inside escape.' I unnecessarily pushed her hair back from her face and tried a little smile. She still winced in pain and I felt, well, pretty helpless, really, despite my best efforts at first aid. It was that feeling — helplessness — that I had felt all those years ago, when —. Well, I never wanted to feel that way again.

Customers were paying their bills and leaving the shop, while another member of staff cleared up the wreckage on the pavement, obviously caused by the Dalmatian. She really needed to get that hound trained.

She hadn't spoken a word, but now with her arm held under the running water, she looked at me and murmured, 'thanks.'

'No problem at all. Happy to help,' I said, then, to try and lighten the mood, I added, 'we really can't keep on meeting like this.'

She gave me a look, then turned her attention back to the water as it poured over her red arm, saying, 'Like what?'

That arm was going to be sore.

Hetti

Same day, early autumn, 2018

It was as if I was having my arm held over a live flame. All I could see were jeans-clad legs and blue and pink pinafores and there was a cacophony of suggestions for dealing with scalded arms. The smiley Mad Hatters lady was trying to get me to let her put butter on my burning arm and even with my rudimentary knowledge of First Aid I knew that butter or grease of any kind was the last thing you should put on scalded skin.

That blasted unruly dog was definitely in trouble now. He really was the limit. As irritating as I found Sheep Man's unasked-for advice on dog training earlier that day, I had to admit that he had a point and what he said — about badly-behaved dogs being like badly-behaved guys — sounded about right. Now he was standing over me — god knows where Tosca had got to with that table and chair — and he was taking over with all the confidence of a fully-trained paramedic. I must say, it felt reassuring to have someone taking control, but there was no way I was going to say so.

He helped me up and we trod through all the broken crockery and went into the tea shop, where he gently put my arm under the cold-water tap. The cool water was immediately soothing to the burning pain that the hot tea had inflicted on me. He asked someone to fetch paracetamol. I'd need it, that was for sure. What with the pain from the hot tea and the bruises from my sheep-rescue gig and then getting knocked to the ground by Tosca this afternoon, I anticipated being in considerable pain for quite a few days. After what seemed like forever, he removed my arm from the running water, patted it dry and wrapped it in cling film.

'Where's my dog?' I asked, as he studiously went about his paramedic duties. I was surprised at how the pain eased considerably with the application of the cling film.

'I put two youths in charge and they've taken the dogs for a walk.'

'I need to go home. Where did they take the dog?'

'Don't know, I'm afraid. I was otherwise engaged on medical duties,' he said with a rakish grin that I wished I could wipe off his face. Who did he think he was, trying to flirt with me? I didn't owe him anything. Okay, so he had fixed my arm, but so what? Hadn't I rescued his blessed sheep? Okay, it was the dog that I was supposed to be looking after that caused the sheep to... oh well, let's not go over that again.

'Who's got him, then? Can you tell me that much?'

Nathan

Same day

She was gazing at her sore arm and biting her lip in pain. She was still standing at the sink and I glanced around for somewhere for her to sit. The shock must have been pretty unpleasant.

Butter Woman handed over a glass of water. 'Do you think she needs to go to the hospital? Or maybe the health centre?'

'No, I think the first aid should be sufficient.' The girl winced in pain again. 'Does anyone have any paracetamol?' I said, looking around for an answer, but no one could help. Wymondham people must be pretty robust if they never needed a painkiller. I took a fiver out of my back pocket and handed it to Butter Woman. 'You couldn't get someone to nip to the chemist for some paracetamol, could you? Would you mind?'

'I'll get my girl to go,' she said, with a smile.

'Thanks. And I think our patient needs to sit down. She'll need to keep her arm under the running water for a while longer.'

'O'course. I'll fetch a stool,' she said, with a smile. 'And I'll make a nice pot o'tea and get some more carrot cake for yer, me dear, alright?' She said, looking at the girl, whose face was very pale. 'Yours is all over the pavement!'

A teenage girl came in and handed me a packet of paracetamol and my change.

'Did you hurt yourself, when you fell?' I asked, handing her two tablets and some water. Butter Woman's suggestion of taking her to hospital had made me think. 'I mean, have you any other injuries apart from this scald?'

'I'll probably have a few more bruises on top of the ones I sustained rescuing your sheep,' she said, without the hint of irony or even a smile as she swallowed the tablets and knocked back the water. Bloody hell. She really was pissed off with me. Well pissed off. But I deserved it, to be honest. I was a bit of a prick that day when I found out that she had one of the sheep in the back of Olivia Hargreaves-Brown's land rover. She'd been driving down the lane, towards Wisteria Cottage, and I'd seen her as I walked Toffee. She looked a right mess and she didn't seem to be wearing much. Jed would be well hacked off with me if I lost one of his sheep, so I had to go after it. I was depressed that day. Even after all these years, it still came over me without warning. A horrible black mood would descend over me and cause unanswered questions to run around in my mind. How old would my little girl be now? It didn't bear to think about. The scenarios played over and over in my brain, like a Netflix movie that wouldn't turn off. The memories would never fade.

No excuse for behaving like a pillock though.

Butter Woman came in and told us that the two guys I'd asked to hold onto the dogs had taken them for another walk. I'd actually forgotten all about them.

Getting back to the conversation with her, I ventured, 'I'm… I'm sorry about — er — you know, when I came to your house. I realise that I was rude. I knew that you couldn't have stolen the sheep or anything like that. I was —'

'What? Having a bad day?' She shot me a look that was also a warning, like, 'don't mess with me,' sort of thing.

I felt suitably chastened. I also felt something akin to anger rising up in me, bubbling up to the surface. I tried to hack it back down again. It bloody hurt though.

'Yes, I was having a bit of a shit day, but no excuse, I know.'

And the thing of it was — the real shit thing — was the feeling that the brick that now hung where my heart used to be, never got any lighter. And I couldn't believe for one moment that it would ever decrease in weight, let alone leave me altogether. And in a really morbid, maudlin sort of way, I had grown used to it and sometimes wondered what life would be like without those feelings of hopelessness and despair. The grief had ripped the guts out of me and torn my life from me, it seemed.

'Yes, well, I'd had a shit day too, trying to rescue your sheep, and I didn't know who it belonged to and getting covered in mud and greenery and having to drive the animal to the vet, only to find the practice was closed for the afternoon.'

'You did? Well… well, thank you. I had no idea that you'd done that.'

'Of course, you didn't. You never asked.'

'That was very bad mannered of me.'

'Yes, it was.'

'I apologise.'

'And I was hanging around outside the vet's in my underwear.' She said it without a hint of humour, irony or self-consciousness, while inside I was pissing myself laughing. Was she actually telling me that she'd been in the middle of Wymondham wearing nothing but her underwear? The image of it started a stir where I didn't need one.

'Your underwear?'

'Yes. My clothes got so muddy that they were weighing me down. And my shoes — my best shoes, that is — were completely ruined. I should send you the dry-cleaning bill and an invoice for replacement ballet flats!' I detected a tiny twinkle in her eye as she said it, but nonetheless, I felt bloody awful about it.

Maybe this was my chance?

'Erm, please allow me to make it up to you. How about —?'

She shot me a look. 'Don't even go there!'

Butter Woman busied herself behind us, served customers as they came in, retold the story of the afternoon's events as she went along, seeming to enjoy the sudden, if temporary celebrity status. She handed me roll of cling film. 'You need this?' She said it with a wink and a smile so warm it could have melted the ice I felt coming from the girl.

'Thanks.' I said, taking it. I collected some of the running water and poured it over the scalded arm. She'd had her arm under the running water for at least fifteen minutes and the redness had faded a bit. I turned the tap off. There was a roll of kitchen paper on the wall above the sink and I took a few squares of it, to pat the girl's arm. She winced as I did so.

'Sorry.' I looked into her eyes.

'It's okay.' She murmured it without even looking up.

I unrolled a sizeable piece of the cling film and took the girl's hand in mine.

'Just keep your arm still for me, while I wrap you up,' I said, trying to sound reassuring yet light-hearted, if not a little suggestive. She just gave me a withering look that put me firmly back in my place.

32

Hetti

Same day

Back at the cottage I phoned Oscar and told him the events of the afternoon.

'Hetti, darling, I'm coming over right now. Have you eaten? No? Then I shall bring sustenance.' He was knocking on the door an hour later, food in hand.

We feasted and sat by the unlit fire, he with his arm around me and me with my head on his shoulder.

'I think you need an early night, Dear One. I'll make up a bed down here with the cushions. Come now, up to bed with you.'

I did as I was told.

I took Tosca for a walk the following morning, then made breakfast. I'd dreamt about Daniel, the night before. In the dreams, Daniel was standing over me, fifty-pound notes in his hands, shuffling them like a deck of cards and laughing in my face, as he threw the notes in the air like confetti. Over breakfast, I told Oscar about the dream.

'I don't think I'll get any peace of mind until I find him and retrieve my money, Oscar.'

'The thing is, Hetti dear, he is bound to slip up sometime and then when the police have some evidence and know where he is, hopefully they'll arrest the bounder. And if they don't, then may he enjoy his karma.' I wished I could share his confidence in both the police and bloody karma.

I still struggled with Daniel's betrayal and I knew that I had little hope that I would ever see my money again. Where could he be?

'I'm going into Norwich, Oscar.' My dear uncle looked up from buttering his toast.

'Really dear? What do you need?'

'I want to look for Daniel.'

'Is that wise, Dear One? How will you know where to look? He's probably miles away by now. He's hardly likely to stay around after swindling you, is he? Anyway, you need to rest your poorly arm.'

'But you said that Toby had seen him.'

'Thought he'd seen him, darling. He could have been mistaken.'

'I have to do something, Oscar. I cannot just wait and hope for the best. If I could see him, speak to him, I could get some answers and hopefully my money back.'

'Hetti, darling, Daniel has no scruples. He will wriggle out of it. Why not just leave it to the bank's fraud people and the police?'

'Because the police are useless! They couldn't care less! And the fraud people at the bank haven't been in touch either. All bloody hopeless, they are.'

I jumped up from the table and started to clear away the breakfast dishes.

'But where will you look for him? I mean, where will you start? Norwich is a big city.'

But I had to try. I just had to. A long shot, I know and Oscar was right — Norwich is a big city — but I needed to find Daniel.

He'd ghosted me since the day he'd failed to show up at the bank and moved out of the flat. What a coward.

'Please, Oscar, take care of the dog for me while I go to the city,' I pleaded.

'But Hetti, my love, think about it. What are you going to do in Norwich? Where will you start? It's not a good plan, darling.'

'I have to try, Oscar,' I said. 'I'll start with all his favourite haunts, hang around, ask around, hope he'll appear.'

'You'll be wasting your time, Hetti. Is he likely to return to his former watering holes? I doubt it. You should let the police and the fraud people do their job.'

'Yes, so you keep saying, but what have they done so far? Nothing! I'll be drawing my old age pension before I see my money again if I leave it to them. They just think I'm a silly girl for trusting Daniel in the first place.'

Oscar and I took our coffee to drink in the garden and sat with blankets over our knees. I gave a little shudder. The cooler weather belied the weak sun and clear blue skies. Tosca slumbered, tied to his gazebo. Oscar patted my knee.

'We don't agree on this my dear, but I do respect your need to find Daniel. I'll stay and look after the dog and I might as well make myself useful and do a bit of tidying up in the garden.'

The wisteria was still thick and a vibrant colour as it clung steadfastly to the cottage walls.

I leaned in and kissed Oscar on the forehead and he gave me a hug. Getting up from my rickety garden chair, I was surprised to see Sheep/First Aid Man — if I'd been told his name, I'd forgotten it — standing by the fence, with what was — I could see from where I was sitting — a thunderous look on his face. I was going to offer him a cup of coffee, but he turned around and walked away before I had the chance to speak to him. Tosca, useless guard dog that he was, snoozed on.

I went and grabbed my jacket and handbag from inside the cottage. 'See you later Oscar,' I called over my shoulder as I made for the land rover. 'Shall I bring something home for dinner?'

'How long will you be?'

'Dunno. Maybe a couple of hours?'

'Okay darling, do bring food and I'll cook for us this evening.'

I blew him a kiss through the car window as I drove away.

33

Nathan

Same day

I got home after the Mad Hatters drama, gave Toffee some water and went to check on the injured sheep. I'd kept her penned separately from the others, while she healed. It wouldn't take long. She just needed a bit of rest and that leg would be in good working order in no time. I shut the pen and went into the house. Time to get some food in my belly.

Later that evening, my thoughts, as they frequently did, went back to the flame-haired goddess. I thought of paying her a call the following day on the pretext of asking after her scalded arm and to thank her properly for rescuing the injured sheep. Any excuse to see her again. I was aroused at the very sight of her. It had been a long, long time since I'd felt like that about a woman. She was hot, I mean, really hot, but in an unassuming sort of way. She just seemed to take herself for granted. Standing there at the door that afternoon with one towel wrapped around her head and another around her body and that Amazonian, lithe frame, she looked so hot. When she'd come back and opened the door again minutes later, with all that wild red hair still damp and hanging around her shoulders and down to her elbows, god, she almost sizzled!

She was feisty too — I loved how she had told me to 'clear off' and the way she looked at me like I was one arrogant bastard, when I tried to teach her how to train that dog down at the Tiffey. It made me positively horny, the way she could stand up for herself without being too belligerent or loud-mouthed. I didn't believe for one moment that she was aware of how sexy she was. And even less aware of what she was awakening in me. It had indeed been a very long time.

After the first time I saw her, I'd found myself fantasising about her and trying to think of ways to cross her path again. Could I really go back to the cottage on the pretext of telling her that the injured sheep was making a good recovery, or to thank her for rescuing it from the ditch? I mean, I hadn't exactly been polite, had I? Alright, I admit it, I was actually rude to her, but before I saw her and realised how gorgeous she was, I was furious to think that someone would have stolen one of the animals in my care. And, anyway, I was having a particularly crap day.

Seeing her at the Tiffey today was a lucky chance. I hadn't expected to run into her while dog-walking, although I don't know why not. After all, dog owners frequently used the Tiffey river pathway to walk their pets. I was only trying to be helpful, giving her a few tips on how to take command of that exuberant Dalmatian, but she seemed to think I was being a condescending twat.

Well, I probably was, actually.

I hoped that my first aid skills impressed her. That arm of hers was going to be sore for a few days, but the cling film should help, so long as she kept it on.

I went the following morning to Wisteria Cottage, because I genuinely wanted to know if her arm was getting better. I was just approaching the cottage fence when I saw her and an old bloke sitting in the garden. And she was kissing him.

My heart sank.

I turned and got the hell out of there as quick as I could.

34

Hetti

Early autumn, 2018

I sat in a Norwich coffee shop sipping on a Latte that was the best cup of coffee I'd had in a long while. Oscar makes a great cup of coffee, but this was nectar. I'd been in this coffee shop with Daniel a few times but it had recently undergone a makeover, had changed its name and was under new management.

I sat there for ages, in the futile hope that I'd catch sight of Daniel, looking at every young man who resembled him even remotely. I don't know why I thought it was such a good idea to come here, despite the wonderful coffee. Perhaps Oscar was right and it was daft to sit around in coffee shops on the off chance that Daniel might walk in. But I had to try.

I opened my bag and looked at the package I'd bought before I'd headed for the coffee shop. *Clearblue Pregnancy Test. Results in one minute. 99% accurate,* the label read. One minute. Think of it. Just a few moments to discover whether the stopped periods and the sickness really were due to pregnancy. I hadn't put any weight on, but I'd read that some women don't even know they're pregnant until they go into labour.

'Can I get you anything else?' The voice startled me and I looked up at the rotund waitress standing by my table. I quickly shoved the pregnancy test kit back into my bag.

'The sausage rolls are very popular. Really yummy.' She looked like she'd already eaten quite a lot of them herself.

'No, thanks. I'm okay with the coffee.'

'Okay, just give me a shout if you need anything else.'

'Actually,' I picked up my phone and swiped to the picture of Daniel, 'I wondered if you'd seen this chap here at all?' I held the phone up so that she could see the image.

'Oh, we get a lot of people coming in here every day, dear. I couldn't say, really.'

'Could you take a close look, please? It's important that I find him.'

'Sorry, dear. Like I said, we get hundreds of people in here every day. And these young men, well, they all look the same to me.'

She waddled away.

I looked out of the window to the cobbled streets and watched people go by. Young mums struggled to push strollers across the uneven ground, elderly couples slowly walked arm-in-arm. A drunk staggered along, trying to light a dog-end he'd just picked up from the street. Students in twos and threes, smiling and confident, strolled along together, rucksacks on shoulders. I thought about my place at the university. I should have been starting my degree course this year. I might have met those very students on campus. I should have had three years of excitement, adventure and new opportunities and instead I was dog-sitting a crazy Dalmatian, my security money disappeared along with my boyfriend.

How could I have let myself be taken in by Daniel? I'd really fallen for him and when he suggested I move in with him I believed he meant commitment. I'd been over the moon. A sense of belonging that had sometimes seemed fleeting since my parents' death. Oscar did provide some stability and my adorable, if rather batty Auntie Pat in north Norfolk had taken me in as a seven-year-old orphan and provided me with a good home for the next ten years or more. But even so, there was an emptiness that swept across me at times.

A spinster, and the older sister by about twelve years of my father, Aunty Pat wasn't exactly motherly but neither was she unkind or cold. Auntie Pat did her best for me. I really wanted her to meet Daniel, not only because she'd proved herself a cracking good judge of character, but also because I wanted to show him off to her. I knew that, if she liked him, I was onto a winner.

When the rat hadn't wanted to come with me to spend Christmas with Auntie Pat in North Norfolk, that should have set alarm bells ringing, but no, I was a blind sucker and an easy target for a con man. What hurt me most was that Daniel was never interested in me, I now realised, as a girlfriend or partner, a wife even. No, Daniel Jones was only interested in me as a source of cash. What I didn't understand was, why, when he had a good job and a high salary, going by the expensive car and designer clothes he always wore, he needed to steal my trust fund.

I gazed again through the window, at the people happily wandering around. They all looked so carefree compared to how I felt inside. Oscar was right. It was crazy to sit here expecting a sighting of Daniel.

I paid the bill and made for the door. I should get back to the cottage and relieve Oscar of his Dalmatian duties.

I parked the land rover on the driveway, expecting Tosca to come bounding towards me and wash my face with his tongue, but instead there was an eerie silence about the place. There was a huge pile of weeds in the corner of the garden and wisteria clippings in another pile. Oscar must have taken the dog for a walk. Strange, I hadn't seen them on the way home. He must have taken a different route.

Inside, I dumped my bag on the table and put the kettle on. The bag fell onto the floor and contents spilled out. I picked it up and started to fill the bag with things that had fallen out. I stopped and looked at the pregnancy test kit. I knew I needed to wee on that plastic stick, but dare I actually do it? The result was either going to be a huge sense of relief or a source of sheer panic. I placed the kit on the table. After a cup of tea, I'd use it.

The kettle boiled and I made a cup of strong tea. As I sat at the table, drinking tea, I read the instructions on the pregnancy kit. Oh dear. It said not to have a drink before using it. I'd forgotten about that, so I'd have to do it later. I sipped tea; hunger pangs set in and I started to wish I'd had one of those acclaimed sausage rolls in the coffee shop. I'd bought food for dinner but wouldn't start to cook until Oscar got back with the dog. I was rooting around in the cupboards and the fridge for an easy bite to eat when there came a knock on the door.

As I opened the door, Tosca leapt up, whimpering and barking and licking my face and nearly knocking me over. God, hadn't he stopped growing yet? He got bigger every day. Despite myself, I was pleased to see him and stroked his head and shoulders.

'Forget your key?' I said, looking up from the dog.

I gasped, taken aback. Sheep Man/First Aider was standing where I'd expected to see Oscar.

The sinking feeling in the pit of my stomach told me that something was very wrong.

35

Nathan

Early autumn, 2018

I pulled the dog off her and that's the moment I saw panic written all over her well-licked face. She was obviously starting to put two and two together.

'What's happened? Where's Oscar?' So, that was his name. She knew, didn't she, that something was up? Didn't take a rocket scientist to work it out. Boyfriend/sugar daddy had taken dog for a walk and here I was, bringing it back.

I cleared my throat.

'Oscar's on the way to hospital,' I began. She gasped and her hand shot up to her mouth. 'He collapsed on the road. I saw it happen. I was approaching in the car and heard Tosca going mental. Oscar fell on the ground near the grass verge.'

'Oh no!' She palmed her wrinkled up forehead and tears filled her eyes. What was I to do? Tell her I suspected a cardiac arrest? That would scare her witless, but I was ninety percent sure and the paramedics thought so too. The old boy wasn't likely to survive. Prognosis isn't great after a cardiac arrest; I knew that much.

'He's been taken to the Norfolk and Norwich University hospital. I can take you there, if we can sort something out for the dog.'

She was shaking and ashen-faced and I wasn't at all sure she'd taken in what I'd just told her. She looked at me, still rooted to the spot and the dog started pulling on the lead and whimpering.

'I need to see him,' she said, after what seemed ages, but was probably only a moment or two.

'Look, let me tie the dog up, get him some water and I'll take you to the hospital. Best you don't drive while you're in a bit of a shock.'

'What's wrong with Oscar? Oh, I couldn't bear it, if —'

'Come on, let's not jump the gun. Best to see what the medics say.' I reached out and touched her upper arm. It felt warm, but she was trembling now.

On the drive to the hospital, she was very quiet, but agitated. I was deep in thought about Mandy's call a few days ago. I'd sorted out most of the stuff that needed attention before I took off to fetch Ben from Carlisle, but needed to get hold of Matt to come over and hold the fort. I'd do that once I'd got back from the hospital.

'Do you want me to come in with you?' I offered, as I drove into the hospital grounds. I was hoping that she'd say no. Being anywhere near a hospital gave me the heebie-jeebies.

'It's okay, thanks. I'll find him.'

'Cardiology.'

'Cardiology?'

I nodded.

She gasped, jumped out of the car and ran into the hospital. I drove off.

36

Hetti

Same day

They'd put him in a medically-induced coma, the nurse was telling me, as I entered the room. Oscar, normally so full of life, lay still and quiet. There were tubes and monitors everywhere and he had an oxygen mask over his face. Where was the wonderful, vibrant and vital Uncle Oscar in there? My larger than life godfather looked tiny in the hospital bed, with cot sides up to keep him from falling out. My heart broke to see him like that.

'Does he know I'm here?' I asked the nurse, who encouraged me to speak softly to him. She replied, but I didn't take in what she'd said.

It was Oscar; but it wasn't. I'd seen him asleep in a chair before, of course I had, many times, but there was an unsettling stillness and quietness about him that was both eerie and alarming.

Again, fear gripped me and held my stomach in tight knots.

'How long will he be like this?' I asked, afraid of the answer, when a different nurse came to attend to him.

'Difficult to say. Probably twenty-four to forty-eight hours. But it depends on his progress and what the doctor says.

'He's going to be alright, isn't he? I mean, he's not going to die, is he?' There. I'd said it. The 'D' word.

'He's done well to get this far, love,' she said, touching my shoulder, squeezing it, just a little. She was plump, with dimples in her cheeks and very short, blonde hair.

'He's in with a chance,' she continued. 'Let's take it a step at a time and hope for the best.' She smiled; a thin but reassuring smile.

A doctor, complete in crisp, white shirt, sleeves rolled up to the elbows, ID badge clipped to his shirt pocket and stethoscope around his neck, briskly entered the room.

'I'm Doctor James Buxton.' He extended a hand to mine. 'I'm a cardiologist.'

I took his hand and gave it a feeble shake. Doctor Buxton squirted some anti-bacterial sanitiser into his palm and proceeded to rub his hands together,

'Are you a relative?'

'Oscar is my godfather,' I said. 'He was one of my legal guardians after I was orphaned as a child.'

'Are you his next of kin, then?'

What the bloody hell did that matter now? For god's sake, I just wanted him to get better.

'I don't know. Possibly. He has no other relatives, as far as I know. Is he going to be okay?' That was more to the point!

'The man who found him,' he glanced at his notes, 'Nathan Brookes, he performed CPR until the ambulance arrived. The paras used the defibrillator in the ambulance.'

Nathan Brookes. So, that was his name. He certainly seemed to know what he was doing when he gave me first aid for the scalded arm after Dalmatiangate.

'Defibrillator?' My mind came back into the room.

'Electric shock through the chest wall — kick-starts the heart.'

Kick-started his heart? So, Oscar's heart had stopped?

All kinds of horrors entered my thoughts. Stopped heart. Lack of oxygen. Brain damage — brain damage? No!

'So, why isn't he awake?' I was terrified of the doctor's answer; I just didn't want to hear that Oscar was going to be a cabbage. 'Can't he breathe?'

'Oh yes, but his body and mind have been through a lot, so we need to rest him for a day or so and keep him quiet and calm to give him the best chance to recover. And we have also induced hypothermia, using something new called an air flow blanket, to give him a better chance.'

The terminology went over my head. Too much to take in all at once. 'He will recover, then?' I asked. It was the only thing I needed to know.

'Let's just wait and see. One step at a time. To be honest, at this moment in time, I can't promise anything. Nathan acted quickly in performing CPR and calling the ambulance, so he's in with a fighting chance. However, we are not out of the woods yet. As I said, let's take it a step at a time.'

And with that, Doctor James Buxton gave me a thin smile, sanitised his hands again and left the room.

I looked at Oscar lying there and took his hand, shocked at how cold it was. Then I remembered and the doctor's words made sense. Induced hypothermia.

'Come on, Oscar. It's not your time yet. Get well. Get well for me.' I squeezed his hand and kissed it.

'Come back to me, Oscar.'

37

Nathan

Same day

'Matt, mate. Need a favour.'

'What's up, Nate?'

'I need to go to Carlisle.' I put the phone on speaker and started moving around the room, gathering stuff, ready to pack.

'Carlisle? You mean to see Mandy?'

'Well, er, yes. I mean, no.'

'Come on Nathan. That is either a yes or a no. Which is it?'

'She wants me to go and pick up Ben. She's got another baby and isn't coping. She told me to take Ben.'

'Mate, you don't even know the boy.'

'So what? He's my son and I love him. I want him in my life.'

'Yeah, yeah, okay, I get it.' But, of course, he didn't. Matthew was still single and as far as I — or he — knew, childless. Fatherhood was something he could only imagine. The tug at the heartstrings for my son is an emotion I couldn't even begin to describe to Matt.

'So, what's up? How can I help?'

'I can't just leave the place and all the animals for a couple of days. Will you come and hold the fort for forty-eight hours? You'd be doing me a big favour.'

'When're you going?'

'Well, as soon as you can get over here. I've already sorted the practical stuff here. It's just a case of you keeping an eye on things. Will you do it?' I held my breath. Old Jed was no longer up to taking on responsibility for the smallholding, not even for a day or two. 'Please?'

'Nate, you know I'll do it for you. Just need to bung a few things in a bag and I'll come on over.' I breathed a sigh of relief.

'Will you need to organise time off work?'

'Nah, s'alright. I'm off this week.'

'You're a star, mate. Thanks.'

'You owe me one Brookes!' I could almost hear the grin on his face as he said it. He didn't think I owed him anything. 'I'll be there within the hour. Okay?'

'Yeah. Great. I'll need to show you around and give a few instructions. Nothing you can't handle.' Apart from a bloody manic Dalmatian, I thought, but didn't say.

38

Hetti

Still at the hospital

I stayed all afternoon and into the evening. I ate nothing. I drank water but had no appetite for food. How could I even think about eating when my dear Uncle Oscar lay there, hooked up to the machines that were keeping him alive?

Dusk descended. Hours passed. Nurses — a different one each time, it seemed — came gliding in, fixed this, checked that and floated out, barely acknowledging my presence.

Hours became like days. Night time fell and I slept fitfully on the floor next to Oscar's bed. A nurse shook me by the shoulder and I awoke, alarmed.

'Oscar?'

'He's fine, love. But why don't you go home? Come back in the morning?'

'I'm not leaving him. Please let me stay.'

'Is there someone you can call?'

'No. What for?'

'Well, support for you as much as anything, love.'

'I'm okay. I don't want to leave him.' I shivered. It was the fatigue rather than the temperature of the room. And it was the thought that something bad might happen to Oscar if I went away and left him, that made it imperative for me to stay. He deserved my support. He'd always been there for me. I thought of Toby. How could I get hold of him? Would he want to know that Oscar was in hospital? I really didn't know.

The nurse left the room and came back with a small mattress.

'Usually, when a patient is in ICU, we don't let relatives stay. But there's no one else in the unit at the moment, so make yourself as comfortable as you can on here,' she laid the mattress on the floor next to Oscar's bed. 'I'll get you a pillow and a blanket.'

My wild dreams were interrupted, as bright lights rudely flooded the room and a team of medical staff surrounded Oscar like a sea of different shades of blue. Panic paralysed me. I tried to get up from the mattress but my body was stiff, my limbs unyielding.

'Hetti? Hetti? Can you wait outside, please?'

'What's happening?' I stared at Oscar lying there, still wired up with tubes and oxygen mask. 'What is it?'

'Nothing to alarm you, dear. We just need the space to do our job. All routine. Just go and get a cup of coffee in the canteen, and something to eat and by the time you get back, we'll be finished.'

I didn't want to leave him. Didn't want him to wake up and me not be there. Surrounded by strangers. If it were me, I'd be traumatised, waking up in hospital and no one there for me except the doctors and nurses. Strangers. As caring as they were, these people weren't family, were they? I didn't want him to feel abandoned by me, his only relative.

The coffee made me feel nauseous and I was reminded of the pregnancy test kit that lay on the kitchen table at Wisteria Cottage. I couldn't think about it. Not now. The big digital clock in the canteen heralded nine-fifteen and I made my way back to see Oscar.

Walking back to the ward, I passed a woman weeping into a big white handkerchief as she walked slowly along the corridor. Whoever it was that she cried over had obviously lost their particular battle.

'Are you okay?' Daft question, I know, but I couldn't just leave her like that.

She dabbed her eyes with the big white hanky, blew her nose, then turned her gaze to me. A wide smile shone through her tears.

'Yes, love. I'm very okay, thanks. Just had the news that my cancer treatment was successful.' And that's when I noticed. The cotton headscarf tied around her head, the absence of eyebrows.

'I'm so happy for you.'

She smiled again, as she looked me straight in the eyes. 'Live every day like it's your last my dear. You never know.

It might be.' She sniffed and moved on. I stood watching her as she disappeared from view.

'Oscar!'

I ran down the corridor, through double doors and turned right towards ICU. There Oscar lay, peaceful, quiet, still. Oxygen mask in place, tubes doing their job.

Doctor Buxton entered the room.

'Is he —'

'Can't give a prognosis just yet, I'm afraid. But all good so far. Why don't you go home for a few hours? Get some rest and we can call you if —'

'I don't want to leave him.' For god's sake, how many more times? 'I can't just walk out of here and leave him alone.'

'There's nothing you can do, Miss. Why not just leave us to do our job?' He looked to be in his late thirties but sounded like an old man, calling me "Miss" like that.

'I want to be here when he wakes up.'

A sigh. A shrug of the shoulder. 'Okay. Suit yourself.' And off he went, rubbing his freshly sanitised hands together.

I sat on the plastic chair next to Oscar's bed and took his hand in mine. He felt warm. They'd done something with that induced hypothermia thing, obviously. I rubbed his hand gently and kissed his fingers.

'Darling Oscar. Come back to me.'

'Do you think he can hear you?' The male voice coming from behind startled me. I whipped my head around to see Nathan Brookes standing there in the doorway. He wore a blue shirt and his longish black hair was tied back. That battered old panama hat of his sat at the back of his head.

'Sorry. Didn't mean to make you jump. How's he doing?' He stayed at the door.

'Induced coma. Maybe for a couple of days, I think. They don't tell me much.' I looked at the man who had very likely, by his quick, competent actions, saved the life of my godfather. I owed him huge thanks.

'Thank you for — you know — for what you did for Oscar. I can't thank you enough. I'm Hetti, by the way.'

'No probs, Hetti. I'm Nathan.'

'Yes, I know. The doctor told me.'

'I, er, I don't have your phone number, so I had to call in. I tried you at Wisteria Cottage but it's all very Marie Celeste over there. I shut the door and locked it. Key is under the plant pot, where — everyone knows — Olivia keeps it.' A wry, crooked smile. 'The dog is at my place. By the way, I'll neuter him when I get back. Olivia had asked me to before she went on her travels, but I haven't got around to it yet. Doesn't take long. Just to let you know, okay?'

'Oh. Okay.' I hadn't given the house or Tosca a thought since I got to the hospital. Had I really left it open and unattended? I felt in my pocket for my house keys. They were there.

'The keys?'

'Oh, yeah. The spare keys. I know where Olivia keeps them. You'll find them —'

'Under the plant pot, yeah.'

'I'm going away for a day or so. My mate, Matthew, is going to be staying at my place, taking care of things and your dog is with him. Er, Tosca, right?'

'Yes.'

'Matthew'll take care of your dog until you can get home. That okay with you?'

Wow. He'd done all that?

'Thanks — thank you.' My mouth was suddenly very dry. I ran my tongue over my teeth and licked my lips. 'You've — you've done so much.'

'No probs. I've bought some dog food for Tosca. Dalmatians need a careful diet.' Oh, yes. No purines.

Without another word, he stepped away and disappeared down the corridor.

39

Nathan

I couldn't get out of there quick enough. It all came flooding back. The nightmare that, even after all these years I'd failed to come to terms with. My tiny, frail daughter, lying lifeless, in my hand. And Erin. My lovely Erin. I sat in the car, trembling at the memory of the day my world had shattered. Taking a deep breath, I got Matthew on speed dial.

'Hey mate. You on your way yet?'

'Just setting off, Matt. I'm in the hospital car park.'

'Oh, why?'

'The Dalmatian girl. It's her bloke who's in there. You know, had the cardiac arrest?'

'Yeah, yeah, you told me. The old geezer.'

'Yeah. I haven't got her phone number, so I went in to tell her that you had the dog. Look, mate, keep the Dalmatian away from Toff, will you? The first time they met he tried to hump her. Don't need any more problems.'

Matthew laughed. It was a dirty laugh. Straight from the belly. 'I should think it's a physical and practical impossibility for that bloody great Dalmatian to shag little Toffee — but yeah — don't worry. I'll keep them apart. He's a bit lively though, so I can't promise one hundred percent.'

'Are you back at the house, now?'

'Yeah. Sorted out the stuff that needed seeing to, and I'm now sitting in your back garden with a beer. Don't worry about anything mate. I'll look after things for you. Just get back in one piece and for god's sake, don't let Mandy lure you into her bed again!' Another raucous laugh from him and I hung up.

It would be a four-and-a-half-hour drive, one way, from Norfolk to Carlisle and that's not allowing for traffic jams or other reasons for delays.

Ben would probably sleep on a night drive, but a daylight trip would give us the opportunity to chat a bit and get to know each other.

For Chrissake! I'm actually talking about 'getting to know' my own son! Sometimes, in moments like this, I could cheerfully... oh, well, best not go there.

Better, instead, to focus on the anticipatory butterflies-in-the-stomach that fluttered around at the prospect of reconnecting with my son for the first time since he was a new-born infant.

By early evening, I was checking into a Travelodge in Todhills, on the outskirts of Carlisle. It was walking distance to the nearest gastro pub, where I tucked into steak, chips and salad, washed down with a pint.

By nine-thirty, I was strolling back to my hotel room and by ten-thirty I was zonked out for the count.

I hoped she hadn't changed her mind. The emotional turmoil would be too much to bear. She'd done it so many times over the years. Everything would be arranged for me to visit Ben and at the last minute she'd call or text to tell me not to come. My stomach churned at the anticipation of a repeat performance of all those bitterly disappointing occasions over the past five years. I'd seen my son once in his short life. Just once, when he was but a few weeks old. Since then, Mandy would play cat and mouse with me as if it gave her some perverted pleasure to see me suffer psychological distress.

And if she did keep to the script today and let me take Ben, how would the little boy feel about it? As far as he was concerned, I was a stranger — a face he saw on an iPhone or laptop screen once in a while — as his mother would screech and yell at me, red-faced with rage.

Approaching Carlisle, I called into McDonalds for a double-sausage and egg McMuffin breakfast and large coffee. I called Mandy.

'Well?' Charming telephone manner, as ever.

'I'm here. I can be there in about ten minutes.'

I took a deep breath and held it.

'Okay. He's ready.'

I exhaled audibly.

'What?'

'Nothing, Mandy. I'll see you shortly.'

In the flesh, he looked kind of Greek. He'd got my dark eyes and black hair, which, in turn, I'd inherited from my great-grandfather, a Greek fisherman, or so I'm told. I never knew him, obviously. He was gone long before I was a twinkle in my dad's eye.

Ben stood in the hallway of his mother's house, a small blue rucksack at his feet.

'Hello Ben.' My stomach fluttered and churned and I hoped I wasn't going to eliminate my breakfast. I could feel the McMuffin doing its work in my digestive system.

Ben looked down at his feet. He was wearing little blue and black trainers.

I wanted to sweep him up into my arms and hug and kiss him, but slowly does it. Didn't want to overwhelm him and scare him off.

Mandy stood next to him wearing grey jogging bottoms, a sloppy, grey top that hung off one shoulder and a scowl on her face.

'You took your time.'

'Morning, Mandy. Is he ready?'

'I said he was, didn't I?'

'Shall we get going then?' I said, not sure if I was addressing Ben or his insufferable mother. She hadn't changed a bit. I felt revulsion that I'd ever been intimate enough with her to create this beautiful boy.

'Standing there talking about it, you'll be here all day. Go on, get off then.'

I held my hand out to take Ben's.

He flinched.

Had she hurt him? Was he afraid of being hit?

I stepped forward and put my arm around his little shoulders, holding him gently to me.

'Come on, little feller. Daddy's here now,' I whispered softly into his ear.

Lifting him up, and, catching hold of the rucksack as I did so, I backed out of the house. It was a tiny terraced house with no front garden, the door opening straight onto the pavement. A baby's wail rang out and the front door slammed firmly behind us.

I kissed Ben's peachy little cheek. It felt so good to be holding him.

'There's Daddy's car, Ben,' I said, pointing to my Audi. 'We are going on a long car ride to where Daddy lives, in Norfolk.'

A solemn little expression, eyes doleful. Was that confusion? Reluctance? Fear of the unknown? Or me?

We got to the car and then I realised. No car seat for the child.

I put Ben down so that he was standing on the pavement, unlocked the car, dumped his rucksack in the boot and retrieved my mobile from my jacket pocket. There was no way I was going to go back to ask Mandy for a car seat.

Doing an internet search for "Car seats. Children. Carlisle" plus Mandy's postcode, I found, to my enormous relief, that there was a suitable store in the next street. Taking Ben's hand, I set off on foot. One hundred and thirty quid later, we walked back to the car. I fixed the smart black seat into the back of the car and safely secured my son into it. I kissed his little cheek. Moments later I was sighing in huge relief as we headed off towards the motorway.

40

Hetti

Hospital

I sat by his bed all day, not even thinking how I must have stank after all that time without access to a shower or a tooth brush. It was as though by staying there with Oscar, he couldn't slip away into the oblivion of death while I wasn't looking. Don't you dare die, Oscar!

In the evening, I went to the canteen and ate something, and, if you'd asked me five minutes later, I wouldn't have been able to tell you what it was. I was on autopilot. Sitting holding Oscar's hand, gently, softly speaking to him every now and then, and willing him wake up and be well.

After several days — I'd lost track of time — the cardiologist and his team came into the room. I sensed they had news for me and I was right.

'We're going to bring him out of the coma now, Hetti,' said Doctor Buxton.

My heart leapt in relief and anticipation. That is, until I realised the grave expression on the face of the doctor.

'What? What's wrong?'

'Nothing. So far, so good. But you need to be aware that lack of oxygen at the time of the cardiac arrest can lead to brain damage.'

So, I'd been right. 'Brain damage? What kind of brain damage?'

'Okay, let me explain,' said the cardiologist. 'When a person suffers a cardiac arrest, they will lose consciousness very quickly, once the heart stops. This is a matter of seconds. Half a minute at the most.'

I sat there, holding my breath, unable to move or speak. The thought of Oscar's heart stopping was terrifying. He had the biggest of hearts and it must never stop beating.

The doctor was speaking again. 'When cardiac arrest occurs, the blood fails to circulate around the brain and this is what causes brain damage.'

Those two words again. Brain. Damage. I just could not imagine Oscar not being Oscar. What would we do? Would I be able to take care of him? If not me, who, then? Not one of those awful care homes I'd heard about. Never!

I was brought back to the doctor's explanation, 'we are hoping that,' he glanced back to his notes, 'Nathan, the chap who found him, started CPR quickly enough, so that damage, hopefully, will be minimal or, best case scenario, zero.'

'Hopefully?'

'Yes. I'm hopeful but there are no guarantees, I'm afraid. You see, the longer the brain is deprived of oxygen, the worse the damage is likely be.'

41

Nathan

Leaving Carlisle

I could see his bewildered little face in the rear-view mirror.
'Alright, Ben?'

He nodded his little head. I still hadn't heard him speak a word since I picked him up. Not ever in his life, actually.

'You let me know if you need anything, okay?'

Another nod of the head.

'Are you hungry?'

A shaking head.

'Need a drink?'

More head shaking.

'Okay, Ben, my little man. Just tell me if you need anything.'

A nod.

We were about an hour from home and I didn't know about Ben, because verbal communication was, it seemed, not exactly his forte, but I needed a bathroom break and a drink. I pulled into a service station and parked the Audi.

I freed the boy from his safety seat and kissed his cheek as I lifted him from the car. He touched the area where I'd kissed him and I didn't know whether he had an itch or if he was rubbing the kiss away.

'Alright, Ben?'

A nod.

In the service station, I chose a sugar free cola and asked Ben what he'd like to drink.

He just looked up at me with those huge dark eyes and said nothing.

I tried to help him out.

'Juice? Water? Milkshake?'

Nothing.

'Okay, I'll choose for you,' I said, and picked up a banana milkshake and a bar of chocolate.

I filled the petrol tank and we started on the last leg of the journey.

Glancing in the rear-view mirror, I saw a snoozing five-year-old with chocolate all over his little mush.

42

Hetti

Hospital

'Hetti, darling.' Oscar's words were croaky and weak.

'Oscar!' My heart leapt into my mouth and I couldn't tell whether it was due to sheer joy or anxious anticipation. The sound of his voice was music to my ears.

I kissed his face all over and smiled through my tears. I squeezed his hand, stroked his bewhiskered cheeks and ran my fingers through his wavy, baby-soft white hair.

Nurses and doctors worked around us, doing their necessary tasks with cool efficiency. Tubes removed. Plugs unplugged.

Colour flooded Oscar's cheeks. Blood pressure taken. Pulse monitored.

My own heart pumped with irregular beats, fast and furious.

To see Oscar's warm smile again after seeing him lying there comatose for so long was enough to convert an atheist to believing in any deity you care to name.

'Step back, if you will, please, love,' a nurse gently guided me towards the door.

My eyes remained on Oscar. Signs of brain damage? I was scrutinising his demeanour. Was this still my own dear Uncle Oscar?

'He's fine. You can take him home, Hetti.' The doctor's smile was a mile wide and so was that of the nurse, who squeezed my shoulder as she walked by me on her way out of the room.

'No, er, no problems?' I could hardly dare to ask the question, but I needed to know.

'Well, the defibrillator we've implanted into his chest will do the trick and he'll need some rehab — physio and the like — and we'll arrange for the occupational therapist to see him — but medically, he's fit to go home.'

'Ahem. Excuse me. I am in the room and compos mentis, you know,' Oscar faked indignation but had that old twinkle in his eye that I'd always loved so much.

'Shush, you!' I gave his shoulder a little shove and we both laughed. Looking at the doctor, I asked him, 'what exactly does the defibrillator do?'

'Well, a defibrillator is a device that is operated by a battery and keeps track of the heart rate. In the event that an abnormal heart rhythm is detected, for example, if the heart is beating too fast, the device sends an electric shock to bring the heartbeat back to normal.'

'So, doctor, Oscar is going to be alright, with this thing implanted in his chest? No more cardiac arrests?'

'We are very hopeful, yes.'

'Don't you ever scare me like that again!' This time I hugged him tight. 'Oh Oscar, I'm so happy!'

'Not half as happy as I am, my love.' Looking down at his chest and the small bump of the defibrillator underneath the skin, his eyes twinkled. 'Look! I'm a bionic man!'

It was so good to hear Oscar's old voice. At first, he'd sounded croaky and not quite himself, but gradually the natural timbre of his voice returned and it was clear that, as the doctor assured us, there was no brain damage. One of the nurses called it a miracle but the doctor was more pragmatic in his approach. 'The man — Nathan — who performed CPR on the roadside, effectively saved your life,' he said.

'Yes, Mr Brookes was your guardian angel that day,' said the nurse.

Everyone in the room was laughing at this point, but the sound faded out as I thought back to Nathan. It was true that I'd not taken to him at all — certainly not on our first meeting when he all but called me a sheep thief. Then our later altercation by the River Tiffey, over Tosca's behaviour. Oh, but yes, he did the first aid gig when I scalded my arm during the Dalmatiangate incident. I shouldn't forget that. Nathan had shown himself up to be an arrogant so-and-so that day, but even so, now I was in his debt for saving my beloved uncle's life.

'I need to phone Toby, my dear.' Oscar's words jolted me back from my contemplations over Nathan.

'What?'

'Toby, Dear One. I should get hold of him.'

'Oh, right.'

Actually, Toby had been conspicuous by his absence throughout the whole cardiac arrest episode, but to be fair, given that he had no idea about what had happened to Oscar, it was perfectly unsurprising that he had not shown up at the hospital. But even though rationally, I knew that Toby had a very good reason for not showing up at the hospital, that is, he didn't know that Oscar was in it, I still had a bad feeling about him. I just couldn't bring myself to trust him and I was dubious about his motives.

'Okay, so, where's your phone?'

'I don't know. Is it here?'

I looked in the bedside locker but all I could find were the muddy, crumpled clothes that Oscar had been wearing on the day of the cardiac arrest.

43

Nathan

Back in Norfolk

I looked in the rear-view mirror as I pulled into the yard and Ben was slumped sideways, still fast asleep.

Toffee ran towards me as I parked the car, always good for a welcome home. The front door opened and Matt stood there, can of beer in one hand and a slice of pizza in the other.

'Alright, mate? How'd it go?' He smiled and took a bite of pizza.

'Better than anticipated. With Mandy, that is. I couldn't let myself believe that she'd let me take him, until I'd actually got him in the car and on the motorway.'

'How's the boy?'

'He's very quiet. Not said a word, yet.'

I opened the boot and removed our luggage. I looked at Ben's small bag. One small rucksack wasn't much for a five-year-old boy's entire worldly goods. Poor little mite.

The sound of the boot closing woke him up and he looked alarmed.

'Hello Ben. Welcome home. It's alright. We're at Daddy's place now. Daddy and Ben live here now.'

I reached for him and he flinched, just as he had back at Mandy's.

'It's okay, little man. Daddy's never going to hurt you.' I unbuckled his safety belt and lifted him out of the car. 'This is my friend, Matthew. Are you going to say Hello?'

Ben regarded Matt.

'Hi mate,' Matt tried, but Ben was reticent.

I led my son into the house and sat him on the couch. Matt had carried in Ben's rucksack and he put it on the couch next to the boy.

'Would you like a drink, Ben? Something to eat?' He just looked at me with an uncertain expression in those big, dark eyes. No DNA test was necessary to prove that this was my son.

I gently removed Ben's jacket and trainers and sat down next to him, stroked his head, kissed his cheek and gave him a little hug. 'I'll get you a sandwich, shall I? And some milk? Would that do?'

Ben nodded. At least it was some form of communication and I preferred it to nothing at all. I did worry, however, how long it would take for me to break through that barrier and actually hear spoken words coming from my son.

'Wait there, then, and I'll be back in a sec, okay?'

Ben nodded again.

I indicated to Matthew to follow me into the kitchen.

'Everything okay here, Matt?'

'No probs, mate. The injured sheep is ready to join the others, I reckon. No sign of the leg injury now.' This was good news.

My mind wandered to flame-haired Hetti and the way I'd just about accused her of stealing the sheep that day when in fact she'd rescued it. What a prat I'd been. The very thought of her triggered that certain stirring again and I quickly dismissed it. She was, undoubtedly, a no-go area.

I made a marmite sandwich for Ben and poured some milk into a mug, then went back into the living room.

Ben took the sandwich and started to eat. Well, that was something. At least he had an appetite. Maybe, once he'd settled in, I could take him out to eat. A day out and dinner. Father and son bonding session. There were lots of things that we could do together and I couldn't wait.

He still had chocolate on his face when I carried Ben and his rucksack upstairs to the bathroom and started to run a warm bath. It occurred to me that there were no bath time toys for my boy to play with and I made a mental note to put that right.

'Okay, Ben, shall we get you into a nice warm bath and into your pyjamas?' I hunkered down and held him close. 'I'll tell you a story once you're nice and clean and tucked up in bed. How does that sound?' I didn't even know when his usual bedtime was, but he was obviously worn out by the journey, despite his long sleep in the car.

He treated me to a barely perceptible nod of the head.

'Right. Let's get your things off then and pop you into the bath.'

He didn't put up any resistance, but he didn't help either. Just stood there and let me remove his clothes and lift him into the water. I took the soap, lathered a soft flannel and started to wash my son for the first time in his and my life.

44

Nathan

Norfolk

'Er, Matt — where's the dog?'
'Which one?' He took another swig of his beer and carried on watching the rugby.

'Well, both, actually. There's not a sign of either of them.'

I'd bathed Ben and put him to bed and he'd fallen asleep in a nanosecond. Didn't even get to tell him the story I'd promised and that he'd actually seemed eager to listen to. Never mind. Plenty of time for stories. There was no way that I was ever going to let Mandy have Ben back. I'd looked in his rucksack to find very little. One pair of PJs which, when I tried to put them on the boy, turned out to be on the small side. I took out my smartphone and started dictating into it a list of clothes and toys my son would need. There wasn't even a single book, teddy bear or any other toy in his rucksack and my heart shattered for him. Call me naïve, but what exactly I did expect? Well, alright — I don't know why — but I did expect to find a children's story book, at least. I found a spare tee-shirt and a pair of shorts, both of which, like the PJs, looked on the small side for a five-year-old boy. There was one pair of socks, one pair of underpants and that was it. Nothing else. I'd change all that tomorrow, but right now, while Ben slept, I needed to check on things with the small holding. And that is the first time it dawned on me that the dogs were missing.

'Christ, Matt! You were supposed to be looking after things here for me. Instead you've lost two dogs while you lounge around guzzling beer!'

I was knackered. I'd driven for two days and had to cope with the emotional turmoil going on in my head and the fear that Mandy would live up to her Bitch of the Year persona, change her mind and refuse to let me have my son. Ben was worryingly quiet — still hadn't uttered a word — and I wondered if he had something wrong with him or if his silence was due to the strangeness of everything new. After all, he didn't really know me from Adam and he was only five. How does a kid of that age manage to process everything that had happened to him in the last two days?

Matthew turned off the rugby, got up from the sofa, threw the remote onto the coffee table, went to the front door, opened it and whistled.

Toffee came hurtling towards us, ran past Matt and jumped straight into my arms.

It was good to see her; even though I'd only been gone a couple of days, I'd missed her.

'Hello, Toff! How's Daddy's girl, then? You missed me?' I patted her back and ruffled her ears and she panted and licked me. 'Good girl. That's a good girl.'

Matt snorted, turned around and sauntered back to the sofa. I followed him in, Toffee at my side.

'What about the Dalmatian, mate?'

'Oh, he'll be back.'

'Jeezus, Matt. You're losing all sense of responsibility. What's got into you? I thought I could trust you to take care of things around here.'

'Everything's cool, Nate. The sheep are all okay in the field, the injured one is better and the other dog will come back when he's hungry.'

'I'm supposed to be looking after him while his owner is at the hospital. You can't just let him run off wild like that.'

'Sorry mate. I'll go out and look for him. You hang on here.'

'Just make sure you come back with the friggin Dalmatian!'

'He's likely to be over at Wisteria Cottage. I found him over there this morning after he'd wandered off. Probably missing his owner. Don't blame him. She's a cracker.'

Hetti? Matt had met her? I felt a stab of jealousy strike through my heart.

'You mean Hetti?'

'Don't know her name. Tall, skinny babe, masses of crazy red hair.'

It was Hetti alright.

'Wouldn't mind a night in the sack with her.'

'Matthew, you get worse. It's time you grew out of that juvenile talk. You're worse than when we were at uni. And anyway, she's got a bloke and she's likely pregnant.'

'Didn't look preggers to me. Skinny as a rake.'

'Probably because it's early days. But I saw a pregnancy test thing on the kitchen table that time I had to secure the cottage after the old boy was taken into hospital.'

'The old boy? You mean, the one that had the heart attack, that's her bloke?'

'Looks like it.'

'No way.'

'Yeah. So back off.'

45

Hetti

Hospital

There was absolutely no way that I was going to take Oscar home in those dirty, crumpled up clothes.

'Hang on a sec,' I said to Oscar and went off in search of a senior nurse. There was one at the nurses' station just outside the ward.

'When does Oscar have to be out by? I mean, the clothes he was wearing are absolutely not fit for him to go home in, so I need to go and get him something decent.'

She looked at the computer screen.

'No worries, m'dear. He can stay and sit in the chair because we'll need the bed later. And we'll give him some lunch, by which time, hopefully, you'll be back with some clothes for him and — may I say — it'll give you a chance to freshen up yourself while you're at it?'

Bloody cheek. Well, okay, so I suppose I must have ponged a bit, but I'd only been home twice since Oscar had been brought into hospital. What did she expect? My concern for Oscar was far greater than my need to see to my personal hygiene.

'Thanks,' I said and nipped back into the ward.

'I'm going home to get you some clean clothes, Oscar. And then I'll take you home. The nurse said you can stay for lunch, but you need to be in the chair, not on the bed, because they need to get it ready for the next patient. See if you can take a shower before lunch, then you'll be nice and fresh to get into your clean clothes.' I hardly drew breath as I listed my plans for him.

Oscar gave a cheeky grin and a very camp army salute. 'Yes, ma'am!' Then he tickled me under the chin like he used to do when I was a small child. I blew him a kiss as I grabbed his dirty clothes and left.

I stopped off at the supermarket and did a week's shopping. Back at Wisteria Cottage, all was quiet. I unpacked the groceries and filled the fridge and the kitchen cupboards. I'd bought some fresh salmon, new potatoes and asparagus for dinner and a bottle of white wine. I shoved Oscar's clothes in the washing machine, added soap powder and conditioner and switched it on.

The pregnancy test kit was still on the kitchen table where I'd left it the day that Oscar had had the cardiac arrest. With all the resolve I could muster, I picked up the kit and skipped up the stairs, two at a time.

In the bathroom, I stared at the words: *Not Pregnant.*

A long exhalation of breath and I looked at the plastic stick again. The words hadn't changed. Not Pregnant.

I jumped up and down on the bathroom floor, whooping and yelling. That was pretty certain, wasn't it? Two tests showing negative, had to mean that I was not pregnant with Daniel's child, but if I was not pregnant, then what was causing the lack of periods and the nausea?

Turning on the shower, I whipped off my clothes and jumped in, luxuriating in the Niagara effect of the warm water cascading over me. My hair was matted through lack of washing. I rubbed shampoo in, enjoying the feeling of cleanliness, the bubbles multiplying as I massaged my scalp with fingernails that had become long and unmanageable through neglect. I sang to my heart's content, any old rubbish song that came into my head. Oscar was well, he wasn't going to die, I wasn't going to have a baby any time soon and life was worth living again. There was just the little matter of the absent periods and occasional nausea to deal with, but that could wait a few more days. And, of course, the money that Daniel had stolen from me. I still needed to get that back. But for now, at this very moment, nothing mattered except that Oscar was coming home today and there was no baby in my belly.

I rinsed my crazy tresses and stood with my head tilted backwards as the water splashed onto my head, my face and down my body.

46

Nathan

Same day

I nipped upstairs to check on Ben and found him sitting up in bed, looking bewildered.

'Hi little feller,' I said with a huge smile. It was so good to have my boy with me, even though we hadn't had a conversation yet.

He looked at me and I tried to read his mood as I walked over to the bed and sat down next to him.

'Feel better after your nap?' I ruffled his hair and stroked his head.

No response.

I couldn't leave him alone with Matthew, now that he was awake. And anyway, if he should wake up while I was away, who knows how scared he'd be?

'I'm going out to check on the sheep, Ben. I've got lots of sheep in a big field down the road. Would you like to come and see them?'

A nod of the head.

Good. This was a positive sign.

'Okay little man. Let's get you dressed and you can come with Daddy to see the sheep. There's also a big dog that I'm supposed to be looking after for someone and he's run away. We need to look for him. Okay?'

He seemed to think about this for a moment before nodding his head again.

I drove down to the sheep field to check on things and to make sure the Dalmatian wasn't there and up to no good. It was still daylight and I unbuckled Ben from his car seat and lifted him out. Taking his hand, we wandered around the field, as I checked each individual animal. All was well. At least I could rely on Matthew to look after the sheep, even if he was hopeless with the Dalmatian. That man had never changed since our university days. He was so laid back he was horizontal. Matthew had a good heart and was a smart, intelligent bloke, so why couldn't he take charge of a dog for a couple of days without losing it?

Ben stood there, gazing out across the field and it occurred to me that he probably hadn't seen a real sheep before.

'Do you like the sheep, Ben?'

A tiny smile and a nod of the head.

'Come a little closer and touch this one.'

Without a sound, my son moved towards the sheep and tentatively reached out to feel its wool.

Stroking gently at first, he went on to rub his hands all over the back of the animal, burying his tiny fingers into the tangled wool.

'Do you like her, Ben?'

He placed the side of his face against the sheep and hugged it.

'Good boy.'

A little smile, still tentative, but detectable.

'We can come to see the sheep every day, if you'd like that, Ben.'

Another little smile, which I took to mean a yes.

We walked back to the car and I clipped the boy into his seat. I sat at the wheel for a moment, thinking about Ben and the journey down from Carlisle. Why didn't he speak and what was with the flinching every time I went to touch him? Mandy was a hard-faced woman, but would she really hurt him? And who was the father of her new baby? Was he still around and had he hurt Ben? My mind was in turmoil, wondering what kind of life my little son must have had in his five short years. I resolved to give him everything he needed, which included heaps of love.

'Alright, Ben?' I said, looking through the rear-view mirror.

A nod of the head again.

'Okay, let's go and look for that dog, shall we?'

Another nod.

I turned on the engine and drove slowly along the lane, looking out across the expanse of surrounding fields for the Dalmatian. That animal was like an unruly adolescent but in the few days before I'd left for Carlisle, I'd managed to calm him down somewhat, with a bit of strict training. Obviously not enough training though, because Matthew had managed to let him run off. A couple of dog walkers moved to the edge of the lane to let me drive by. I slowed right down and asked them if they'd seen a spotty dog on the loose. They hadn't.

I waved my thanks and carried on down the lane, heading towards Wisteria Cottage.

The light breeze was cooling down the day as I drove along with the window down. A flight of birds on the wing moved in formation across the sky like one animal.

Across a field and on the horizon, I spotted a white and black animal tearing around. It had to be the Dalmatian. I hit the accelerator pedal and drove towards the field where I saw, for sure, that it was Tosca running up and down a hedge row. The dog stopped momentarily, looked over at me from some distance, then made off in the opposite direction. I drove after it and could see that it was heading in the direction of Wisteria Cottage.

47

Hetti

Same day

Downstairs, I reached for Oscar's holdall and searched through it for some clean clothes. Everything was creased, so I took the ironing board out from the cupboard under the stairs and the iron from under the kitchen sink. I put on some music and ironed out the creases from a pair of beige Chinos and an electric-blue silk shirt, singing as I worked. Placing the clothes on hangers, I hung them on the back of the door and dug around the holdall for some underwear. Oscar's man bag hung on the back of one of the kitchen chairs and I looked through it, hoping to find his mobile phone and there it was, dead as a door nail.

'Blast.' I cursed aloud and rooted around some more, hoping to find his charger. Nope. Nothing in the man bag and it wasn't in the holdall either. I looked around and found the charger plugged into a socket next to the fireplace in the sitting room, the cable trailing on the floor.

With a sigh of relief, I plugged the phone into the charger and it sprang to life. I could see messages coming through but, not having his security code, could only read the previews. Anything from Toby?

My heart sank when I realised that there was no text from Oscar's lover. Was there not one single man, other than dear old Oscar, that could be trusted?

I threw the phone down on the end of the sofa and left it to charge.

The washing machine cycle had finished and I opened the door to find the clothes torn up. I pulled everything out of the machine and inspected the clothes. Every item was ruined. Olivia's note about the washing machine came to mind. It might have been playing up for her but it had been working fine for me until now. I rooted around in the kitchen drawer for her note with the mechanic's name and phone number.

My hair was still wet and wrapped in a towel when I heard barking and whimpering and scratching at the door. When

I opened the door, there was no one there but Tosca was jumping all over me, licking my face in his own inimitable manner.

A grey Audi pulled up on the lane outside the front gate and Nathan Brookes jumped out.

He put a hand on the gate post and did a scissor style sideways leap over it.

'Wouldn't it have been easier to just open the gate?' I asked and realised it was probably the first time I'd ever smiled at the man.

'Yeah, whatever. Sorry about the dog. Matthew isn't always as reliable as I'd like.' My smile wasn't returned.

'I think Tosca just likes to visit the cottage sometimes. Your friend came looking for him while you were away.'

Tosca carried on enthusiastically jumping up to me and I nearly toppled over.

'Tosca! Down!' Nathan's command was immediately obeyed as the dog sat down. 'Tosca, here, boy!' And the dog obediently moved over to sit down next to Nathan.

I was impressed and annoyed in equal proportions. I had to admit that Nathan certainly had the dog under control, but felt envious that he was able to do this whereas I had obviously failed miserably. But nothing was going to faze me today. Oscar was alive and as well as he could be and I was going to bring him home today.

'Er, wow. That's pretty impressive,' I managed to say, trying to sound like I meant it.

'The dog needs training,' he said, still unsmiling. 'I've made a start, but there's a way to go. Is this you, home now? I mean, how's Oscar?'

'Oscar's recovering really well. He's being discharged today. I'm just fetching some clean clothes for him.'

'That's, er, that's good. By the way, as the Dalmatian needs a special diet. I've got some dog food appropriate for the breed. It should also help with his behaviour.'

'Oh, er, thanks. That's really kind. I must settle up with you.'

'No need for that. I'll hang onto the dog for a while, if you like?'

'Well, if you're sure? I'll need to look after Oscar for a while.'

'Okay. I'll be off then.' He took the dog by his collar and started to walk towards the gate. 'I'll neuter him, now I'm back. Just need to find the time.'

'Oh, okay, thanks.'

'No worries. I'll hang onto him while he recovers. He should calm down a bit after the op.' Wow.

'Er, Nathan?'

He turned back, still holding onto the dog's collar. 'Yeah?'

'I never thanked you properly. I mean, you know, for saving Oscar's life. The doctor told me that your quick action was crucial to his recovery. I don't know what I'd do if anything happened to him. He means the world to me. So, er, so, thank you, thank you so much.'

'No probs.' His expression inscrutable, he made once more for the gate, this time opening it rather than leaping over it.

I stood there, watching him opening the back door of the car, commanding the dog to get in. And that's when I saw the child. So, Nathan had a child. And a wife, presumably. So, what was he doing trying to flirt with me while administering first aid to my scalded arm at the Mad Hatter's that day? I watched him jump in the driver's seat and move off with an audible whoosh down the lane.

After dinner that evening, as Oscar and I sat together on the sofa, he took my hand and squeezed it.

'How are you feeling Uncle Oscar?' He looked remarkably well, considering what he'd gone through, but I needed all the reassurance I could get.

'Jolly good, Hetti my love. Jolly good indeed.'

'Have you any messages from Toby?' I knew the answer already.

A sigh. 'No, dear. I guess he's busy.'

'Right.'

The rat.

48

Nathan

Same day

In the car, Tosca licked Ben's face. The boy put his little arms around the dog's neck and hugged him tight.

When we arrived home, Matt was shoving his stuff into a bag.

'You off, mate?'

'Yeah. Thought I'd head off. You're all sorted here now, aren't you?'

'Sure, but you don't need to bugger off just yet. Stay and have something to eat.'

'I don't know. I ought to get back. I've got things to do back at my place and I'm back at work after the weekend.'

He'd had at least three cans since I'd got home from Carlisle and I didn't want him taking a chance behind the wheel of a car.

'Come on, mate, stay. Have some dinner, stay the night and head off in the morning. We could have a takeaway if you like I just need to make something for Ben.'

I moved over to the kitchen door. 'Not sure what I've got in the fridge by way of a meal.'

'I ate most of it, Nate.' He gave a little, almost embarrassed laugh.

'No worries, mate.' I picked up my mobile and scrolled through the takeaway apps. 'What do you fancy? Indian? Chinese? Thai? We can get it delivered.'

'Okay, you've twisted my arm,' he said with a grin. He dumped his bag on the floor, flopped down on the couch and started scrolling down the takeaway app on his phone.

I found one egg and a potato in the fridge.

'Egg and chips, Ben?' I used to love egg and chips as a kid.

No words, but a nod and a little smile.

It was a start.

The following morning, Matt headed off early and I busied myself with jobs on the smallholding. Ben woke up late.

He was still very quiet and I worried that he might not be happy, even though he didn't seem unduly upset about his new situation.

I went out to the chicken coop and collected six eggs. Back at the house I boiled an egg for Ben and made toasted soldiers. He sat there quietly eating his breakfast. I made myself an omelette.

'We've got a busy day, today, Ben', I began as we sat at the kitchen table eating breakfast. 'We need to go shopping and buy you some new clothes.'

He just looked at me, silently.

'And we need to check on the sheep. Would you like to come with me to see the sheep?'

Ben dipped his toasted soldier into his egg and the yoke ran down the sides and onto the plate. He looked at me and nodded, before taking a bite of toast and egg.

'Had you ever seen a real sheep before yesterday, Ben?'

A little shrug. He was more interested in his breakfast.

It was a dry day, so I left the car in the yard and we strolled along the lane to the field where the sheep grazed. The sun peeked through white, fluffy clouds with the promise of good weather to come. Ben let me hold his hand and seemed relaxed, despite his obvious reluctance to speak.

At the field, Ben stood in wonder at the sight of a flock of sheep busily munching grass.

'Come closer, Ben. They all look the same from a distance, but when you get close up, you'll see they are all different, just like people are all different.' I led him over to the sheep. I took his hand and held it to the wool of one of the ewes. He ran his fingers through the coat. The ewe bleated. Startled at first, at the sound, Ben stepped back momentarily, then moved closer again and felt the wool of another sheep.

I wandered around, checking each individual ewe. There were no immediate issues, but they needed careful monitoring to make them ready for the upcoming breeding season.

On the walk back to the house, despite Ben's lack of response, I chatted to him, pointing out rabbits hopping in one field, geese flying overhead, a pheasant scuttling across the lane.

After lunch, we headed off into Wymondham in search of new clothes for Ben. I also took him to *Kett's Books* and bought some bedside stories and other reading material for him, before calling into *Waitrose* on the way home.

By bedtime, Ben had still not spoken a word.

49

Hetti

I found Jack, the washing machine mechanic's number and gave him a call. At eight-thirty the following morning, he was knocking on the door.

'Not too early, am I?' He had ginger hair, freckles and an enormous white smile that seemed to reach from ear to ear. Resplendent on his upper arm was a tattoo of a buddha's head, that moved around with the flexing of his muscles.

I'd been sleeping on the sofa cushions on the sitting room floor and my bones ached.

'Not at all,' I said, aware of the mess I must have looked, with my wild, 'bed hair', crumpled pyjamas and bare feet.

Minutes later, I was making tea and being told by Jack that the washing machine would cost more to fix than the price of a new one.

Great. Now I'd have to find the money to replace a washing machine that actually belonged to someone else. Anybody would think I was loaded with money. Oh well, I suppose that's what credit cards are for.

'So, how long have you lived here at Wisteria Cottage, then? I thought it belonged to a woman called Olivia.' Jack sipped on his tea.

'A few months. Actually, I'm housesitting for Olivia. And supposedly taking care of her crazy dog.' I explained about Oscar's illness and that being the reason that the dog was not here and that Nathan Brookes at the small holding was taking care of it.

'Oh, yeah. I know Nathan. Really bad, what happened.'

'Oh?'

'Yeah.' He finished his tea, got up and took his mug to the kitchen sink. 'Some years ago, it was now.'

Just then, Oscar walked in, scratching his head.

'Morning dear. Oh! And a jolly good morning to you too!' Oscar's eyes did their twinkling gig as he noticed Jack, all hunky and tattooed, standing there.

'Er, yeah, morning, mate.' Looking at me as he moved towards the back door, he said over his shoulder, 'No charge for today. Sorry the washing machine is knackered.'

'Not your fault. Thanks for coming out. I'll have to go shopping for a new machine.'

At the door he turned and said, 'I might be able to get hold of a reconditioned one, if you like? People get rid of good machines just because they've had a new kitchen or utility room fitted and want matching washers. I'll let you know, shall I?'

'That would be a big help, if it would save me some money.'

'Okay, leave it with me.' He squinted at me for a moment, then said, 'haven't I seen you somewhere, before?'

'I'm not sure, Jack. Where could we have met before?' He certainly didn't look familiar to me.

'Dunno. Perhaps a friend of a friend? Dunno.' He shrugged and turned back around to walk towards the door.

'I know,' he turned back to me. 'Danny Jones. You're his girlfriend, aren't you?'

'Not any more. Do you know him well?'

'Not really. He used to hang out with some guys I knew. Haven't seen him in ages. Don't want to either.'

'Really?' I needed to know more. 'Why's that?'

His mobile rang out and he took the call, turning back towards the door.

'Sorry. Gotta go. Bye then,' he said, looking back at me and with that, he was gone.

The following day Oscar and I decided to take a trip into Norwich to look at washing machines. The linen basket was starting to overflow, I was running out of clean clothes and what Oscar had with him had been ripped to shreds in the faulty washer.

'Shall we pop into my place first and check the mail, pick up some fresh stuff for me?' Oscar suggested as I drove along the A11 into Norwich.

'Sure thing,' I said, and turned off towards Oscar's house. As I drove along Bluebell Road, the university ziggurat buildings loomed and I thought again about my lost opportunity to start my studies. My feelings for Daniel were still mixed. On the one hand, I despised him for what he'd done to me, yet at the same time, as much as I hated to admit it, even to myself, I missed him terribly. Jack's words came back to me; he hadn't seen Jack for a long time and *didn't want to*. What did he know about Daniel that I didn't? I wished I could hate Daniel; perhaps that would be a healthier emotion than wishing we were back together, but that was easier said than done.

Oscar picked up on my change of mood.

'You'll be starting university next year, Hetti and all the bad times will be behind you.

'I've still lost my hundred-thousand pounds, though and it looks like I'll never get it back.'

'Don't give up hope, dear. All will be well, you'll see.'

I pulled into the kerbside in front of Oscar's house and stopped the car engine.

The next-door neighbour, an elderly university professor, with grey, wiry hair brushed back off his forehead and a ruddy complexion, came out of his house and walked towards Oscar, offering his hand to shake. As I locked the land rover, I heard the professor remark how very pleased he was to see my uncle, as everyone in the street had been worried by his absence.

'Your friend, the young fellow, he was here a couple of times,' he said, 'asking if we'd seen you, Oscar. I told him we hadn't. But that was some time ago.'

Oscar quickly explained about the 'little health issue', as he described it, and we let ourselves into the house.

'I really must get in touch with dear Toby. He'll be worried.'

Personally, I didn't think so.

I picked up the post from the front door mat and went into the kitchen to put the kettle on. Oscar listened to his answer machine.

There was a message from Toby, then another and another, all demanding to know where the hell Oscar was.

50

Nathan

September 2018

The new school year was about to begin and I got Ben into the local primary school. He was his usual reticent, unspeaking self as we met the head teacher, who said it would be a pleasure to have Ben join the school.

We went school uniform shopping a few days before the start of term and came back with two pairs of dark grey trousers, three pale blue shirts and two bright blue sweaters sporting the school logo. An overcoat, socks, underwear and black shoes completed the day's shopping. Trying on his new uniform when we got home, he smiled at his reflection in the bedroom mirror. A lump shot up into my throat and tears of pride pricked the backs of my eyes.

'You look great, Ben,' I said, 'very smart!' His reply came in the form of a tiny, shy smile.

'You'll meet some new friends once you're in school and maybe you could have one or two of them back here for a playdate. How does that sound?' Since Ben had arrived in Norfolk, he had met no other children but his attachment to the dogs and the sheep grew each day.

Now he looked at me anxiously.

'It's okay, little man. You'll have a great time at school. Did you like your school in Carlisle?'

No reply. Not even a nod or a shake of the head.

I did wonder about his schooling in Carlisle. Wondered if Mandy had even taken him to school. Of course, during Skype calls and on text messages I'd asked such questions, but according to Mandy, it was none of my business. Sure, Mandy. I wasn't really the boy's father; merely a source of income for you!

'Come on, let's get you out of your smart new uniform and into your play clothes. Shall we go and see the sheep after lunch?'

A rigorous nod and a big smile.

'Okay. Come on, mate. Lift up your arms and let's get you out of this jumper.' He dutifully did as I'd asked and I tickled his armpits. Couldn't resist.

And that's when it happened. For the first time in his life, I heard my son giggling. I tickled some more and he giggled uncontrollably, a wide smile on his face. Then I hugged him close to me and ruffled his hair.

'That's my boy,' I said, 'that's my beautiful boy.'

It didn't take long for yummy mummies at the school gate to figure out that Ben's daddy was a single one and the offers of help in the form of washing, ironing, shopping, cooking, came flooding in. No, thanks, ladies. I am quite a capable dude, believe it or not!

I mean, seriously! Would they be making such offers to a newly single mum, I wondered? I didn't think so. Women are presumed to be already schooled in such tasks. It's expected of them to just get on with it, when it comes to domestic issues and child care. Yes, even in this day and age. And yet, when it comes to a bloke taking full responsibility for a kid, it's assumed that he's useless and needs help. Or perhaps I'm being a little ungracious here. Maybe these lovely ladies were just good-hearted and community-spirited and really did want to help. I wasn't entirely convinced that this applied to all of them, however. Especially the one who turned up on my doorstep one afternoon on the pretext of bringing a vegetarian moussaka for our dinner (said she'd made too much and didn't want to waste it), which turned out to be an excuse to try and fit in a romp in the sack before the afternoon school run. I kid you not!

End of September approached and Ben's sixth birthday loomed large. I was giving some thought as to how we could celebrate the day, but it wasn't easy to get information out of a boy who rarely uttered a word. He hadn't really spoken since I'd collected him from his mother back in the summer, although the odd 'yes' or 'no' along with the nod or shake of the head could be seen as some progress, I suppose. One day, not long after the start of the school year, Ben's teacher, Miss Abbot, a mousy woman in her mid-to-late thirties, called me to one side and asked me, in hushed tones, if my son was quiet at home, because, she said, he hardly made a sound at school.

'He's only been living with me since the summer,' Miss Abbot. Ben was born in Cumbria and was living with his mother until recently. I only saw him once in his life before I went to pick him up and bring him home with me. Like I said, only a few months ago. His mother, well, she's got another baby now — er — not mine, obviously — and well, she wasn't coping.'

'So, you didn't know each other, before this summer, then? You and Ben?'

'Well no. But not for want of trying on my part. What exactly are you getting at, Miss Abbot?'

'Well nothing, except that perhaps Ben is pining for his mother? Have you thought of that?'

At this — sorry, I just couldn't help it — I gave a snort. Miss Abbot seemed taken aback.

'I doubt it,' I managed to say. Bloody hell. Ben missing his mother? The very thought was laughable. The woman was a harridan and I still suspected that she — or one of her boyfriends — had hurt him in the past. No child flinches the way he did without good reason.

'But surely,' Miss Abbot continued, 'I mean, she's his mother and a little boy needs his mother.'

Anger welled up inside me. Who was this bloody teacher to assume she knew anything about Ben? She'd only known him a fortnight.

'Ben is doing just fine with me, thank you very much, Miss Abbot. He just needs time to settle down and get used to things. Now, if you don't mind, I'll take him home. And in future, please keep your prejudgements to yourself. You're here to teach my son, not try out your amateur psychoanalysis on him.'

She stood there with her mouth open and eyebrows raised. I had to walk away there and then. I could have said more, but it wouldn't have been wise; after all, I wanted Ben to have a good relationship with his teacher and one not tainted by a row between her and his dad.

51

Hetti

It was unseasonably warm for late September and while Oscar sat tucked up in a blanket on the sunbed, I pottered in the garden.

The wisteria was past its best but small pockets of colour managed, defiantly, to burst through.

I suddenly had that same feeling, like I'd had some months ago, that someone was watching me.

Standing up straight I rubbed my sore lower back. What with sleeping on the floor on sofa cushions and working in the garden, my body was complaining bitterly.

The sun was low in the sky and I shielded my eyes with my hand, as I looked around, wondering who might be watching me.

I looked over towards the old house, a holiday home, that was the nearest neighbour and heard a rustle in the vegetation, but saw nothing. Shivering, again as though someone had 'walked over my grave', I picked up the hoe and carried on working.

I glanced over at Oscar. He'd nodded off, his book fallen to the ground and the sound of gentle snoring emanated from his nose.

Even after all these weeks, I still worried about him. Watching him sleep reminded me of the days that I sat by his side, day after day, night after night, anxious and scared that he'd never come back to me. Now, it was a different story. Oscar had good colour. He'd lost weight, as advised by the doctors, and his physio regime was proving successful.

That rustling in the bushes again. I moved in its direction and I thought I saw a lone figure scurrying off. Who had been watching me?

'Oscar! You're awake!'

'Well, don't sound so surprised, Dear One! I don't sleep twenty-four-seven, you know,' he said, with that familiar twinkle in his eye.

I'd finished all I'd wanted to do in the garden and the sun was beginning to fade. It was time to start thinking about food.

'What would you like for dinner tonight, Oscar?'

'Ooh, now, let me think, what's on offer?'

'Need to shop for dinner — so anything you fancy, really. I can easily nip into Waitrose or Morrison's. What would you like?'

'What would I like? I'll tell you what I'd like. I'd like to take my darling goddaughter out to dinner.'

'No need, Oscar. I'm happy to shop and cook.'

'I'm sure you are, Dear One, but it's Friday and I think a night out is in order.'

'Ah, that's so sweet. Okay, then. Where shall we go?'

'Well, I thought we might try that new Thai place in Wymondham that I've been reading about in the local paper. The *SathuDee*, I believe it's called. Got some very good reviews on TripAdvisor.'

'Okay, if you're sure you're feeling up to it. Don't want you overdoing things. And remember, only one glass of wine is allowed – doctor's orders.'

'Killjoy!'

As we walked into the restaurant the three waitresses and the one waiter placed their hands together in prayer position and bowed their heads. They all smiled sweetly. Oscar asked if they could squeeze us in and the manager took us to a small table at the window and told us that someone would be over in a moment to take our order.

A young Thai man, dressed in traditional Thai costume, came over to our table. '*Sa wat dee krup,*' he said and I had no idea what that meant. Presumably it was some kind of greeting, so I nodded and smiled.

'I am Chaiyuth, your waiter for this evening. Welcome sir, welcome madam.' He nodded at Oscar and me in turn. 'Can I get you some drinks?'

'Could we just have a jug of water, please, and then a glass of wine with our meals.' I looked pointedly at Oscar and he knew I meant business. Doctor's orders: one glass only.

'Of course, madam,' Chaiyuth replied, smiling sweetly, 'and I will bring the menus for you.' He turned away from the table. Watching him walk towards the bar I saw that his long hair was tied back and twisted into a knot.

During the meal, Chaiyuth returned to the table to ask if everything was to our liking. The food was delicious and beautifully presented with ornately carved raw vegetables that garnished each dish.

Oscar smiled at the young Thai man. 'How long have you lived in England may I ask? You speak very good English.'

'Thank you, *krup*. Nearly three years. I am studying law at the University of East Anglia. I will finish next summer, *krup*.'

'Jolly good for you, young man!'

'Thank you, *krup*.'

As the evening progressed, we heard more about Chaiyuth and his family back in Thailand. He spoke softly as he answered our questions, the smile never once leaving his face. He told us that he was the eldest of four sons, and that from the age of fourteen he had worked after school and on Saturdays in a music shop to help his family and save the money for his studies in England. Throughout his degree he had worked evenings and weekends serving in a Thai restaurant in Norwich and more recently moved to the *SathuDee* when it opened in Wymondham.

As he paid the bill at the end of the evening, Oscar pushed a folded up ten-pound note into the hand of the waiter. He winked, saying, 'just for you, young man. You've done an excellent job this evening. Keep working hard and one day you will be a great lawyer.'

'Thank you so much, *krup*.' With a very broad smile on his face, Chaiyuth placed his hands together in prayer position and bowed his head.

52

Nathan

At home, after getting him out of his school uniform and into his play clothes, Ben climbed up to the kitchen table and I fed him a snack and some milk. The day was still mild and dry and I asked Ben if he'd like to come and see the sheep after he'd finished his snack. The dogs were bouncing around and I thought that together we could walk them over to the field. Tosca wasn't quite so keen on humping Toffee since I'd neutered him. I needed to spay Toff at some point, but it was a bigger procedure with a female dog and recovery was longer than for a male. Also, she needed to be a bit older, I thought, despite what some vets advise.

My quiet little son merely nodded his silent agreement at my suggestion and we got into our Wellington boots, collected the dogs' leads and headed off.

We were wending our way back to the house when a familiar looking land rover approached and I took Ben's hand and pulled him and the dogs over to the side of the lane. Hetti stopped the car and I saw that she had her bloke in the passenger seat. It was the first time I'd seen him looking alive and not collapsed with a cardiac arrest or wired up in hospital.

Tosca leapt up to the car window, whimpering and barking and licking Hetti enthusiastically.

'Tosca!' She leaned out of the car window and ruffled his ears and patted his back.

'Hello Nathan.' She smiled and glanced down at Ben. 'And who's this lovely boy?'

'He's my son, Ben.'

'Oh. I see.' The smile faded somewhat. What? Didn't she like kids, then?

I looked at Oscar, who, at the sound of my name, was getting out of the car and approaching me with an outstretched hand.

'Nathan, dear boy!' A huge smile spread across his face. 'You're the hero. You saved my life. How can I ever repay you? Many, many thanks, dear boy.'

'Er, no probs, mate.'

I was still holding the dogs on their leads but had let go of Ben's hand. Oscar was holding my one free hand with both of his and squeezing it tightly as he shook it.

'No, no, dear boy. Don't be so modest. Hetti and the doctors told me how important it had been to my recovery that you were there on the scene and acted so quickly. I cannot thank you enough.'

'We'd best be getting off, then,' I said, letting go of the old man's hand and taking hold of Ben's. I must say, I was a bit surprised at how effeminate this Oscar bloke came across in real life. I mean, like, I'd only ever seen him either having a cardiac arrest or lying comatose in a hospital. I'd — obviously — never heard him speak before. Perhaps that's how Hetti liked her men. A bit girlie rather than Alpha Male. And what was with all that 'dear boy' stuff? I mean, who talks like that these days? What does she see in him? Oh, well, no accounting for taste, I suppose.

I waved goodbye and walked on with Ben and the dogs. Tosca wanted to go back to Hetti, but one command from me to 'Heel!' and he behaved himself.

The land rover overtook us and the old boy waved at us enthusiastically as they drove by.

Like I said, no accounting for taste.

53

Hetti

The Thai meal and the excellent service certainly lived up to all the five-star reviews on TripAdvisor and as we made our way to the car park, we agreed that we'd definitely go back again. A solitary figure stepped into the darkness of a shop doorway and I shivered. I didn't say anything to Oscar, but it was the same feeling that I'd got in the garden, a number of times now, like someone had walked over my grave.

On the way home, Oscar was quiet and seemed deep in thought.

'Alright, Uncle?'

'Yes, my dear. I was just thinking about that sweet boy who served us in the restaurant. He's a shining example, isn't he? Hardworking, intelligent, humble, exquisite manners and no false sense of entitlement. Our encounter with him will stay with me for a long time, I think.'

I had to agree. Chaiyuth had inspired me and fuelled my determination to take up my place at university next year, no matter what.

The following morning, we sat at the kitchen table having coffee when Oscar's phone pinged with a message.

'Toby wants to meet me for lunch in the city, darling,' Oscar said, looking up from his mobile phone, with a happy smile sweeping across his face. It crossed my mind, given that Oscar had returned from near death, that Toby might more appropriately have come out to visit, with flowers and chocolates and other goodies. But no, that would involve being a thoughtful, caring boyfriend, not the selfish so-and-so that Toby was. But I didn't say so. Of course, I didn't.

'Er, okay, I'll drive you in, then.'

'No, no sweetness, that's okay. I'll take the train. Just drop me off at Wymondham station, if you would?'

'Oscar, have you seen Wymondham station? When you get back from Norwich, you'll have to climb at least thirty steps to cross the bridge. With your heart, I am not allowing you to do that. No way!'

'Darling, are you forgetting that I'm bionic now?' Oscar's grin was infectious and I had to laugh, despite my anxieties about him wanting to exert himself. 'You heard my physio. I must exercise.'

'Yes, but not that much. Gosh, those stairs could kill off the fittest person. I'm driving you in and that's that. Anyway, we still haven't got a washing machine. It'll give me a chance to look around on my own while you're with Toby.'

I'd handwashed a few essentials and hung them on the line, dripping wet. It would take days for them to dry, now that the summer weather was more or less behind us, but heigh-ho!

'Why don't you order a machine from the internet darling? It's the way everyone does it these days. No need to go traipsing around the city.'

'Yes, I know I could do that, Oscar, but I want to see before I buy.' I was also very wary these days about money. Getting my fingers burned again wasn't something I was going to let happen any time soon. Daniel's face sprang into my mind and I shook it away. The pain of betrayal would never fade. Neither would the feeling that I was a complete and utter fool, not to mention a really crap judge of character. Oh, well, I'd learnt my lesson. I would never in a million years trust a man again.

'I've looked on the Argos website and they've got a machine for under two hundred pounds. I can go in and order it and ask questions if I need to. And I'd rather pay in the shop than online.'

'Well, okay then, drop me off in the city and then go to Argos. But I hope a two-hundred-pound washing machine doesn't conk out on you in six months! Cheapest isn't always the best.'

'Well, I can't afford any more than that. And anyway, so long as it lasts me until my year in this place is up, I don't care.'

We headed for the city and the magnificent spire of Norwich Cathedral loomed ahead. Even in the grey of a cloudy day, it gave weight to the long-held maxim that Norwich is, indeed, a fine city.

I parked in a multi-storey carpark and Oscar inserted coins into the pay machine. He took the ticket and, as he walked back towards the land rover, it seemed as if something had caught his eye. He hesitated for a moment then stood there, looking at something that was out of my vision.

'Oscar?' I looked around but was unable to see what had distracted him.

'Oscar? Are you coming?'

His head snapped around to my direction. 'Yes, dearest. I'm coming.'

As he approached me, I noticed a puzzling expression on his face.

'What is it, Oscar? What were you looking at just now?'

'Oh, nothing, dear. Just thought I saw someone I recognised. But I was mistaken, I'm sure.'

54

Nathan

Late September, 2018

Ben's birthday fell on a Saturday and, as he seemed to have no friends as yet, it was up to me to entertain him with some sort of celebratory event.

After breakfast, I took him by the hand and led him outside to the barn, where I'd hidden a box, wrapped in brightly coloured birthday paper and with a big blue bow tied around it.

'Happy Birthday, Ben! I hope you like what Daddy's bought for you.'

Tentatively, he stood there and I wondered if I'd done the right thing. It was hard to know what Ben would like for his birthday. I'd asked him, of course I had, but he'd just looked at me with those big dark eyes of his, as if afraid to answer.

'Come on, let's see what's hiding inside all this wrapping paper, shall we?' I took hold of his hand and encouraged him to move towards the brightly wrapped box.

The box was bigger than the boy.

'It's for you, Ben. Go on, open it.'

Slowly, carefully, he started to tear at the paper. Little ripping sounds at first, then louder tearing and on the box the picture of the shiny blue bike was revealed. Ben's expression, first unsure, then sheer delight.

'Come on, Ben, let's get the rest of the paper off.'

A wide smile spread across his face, as, cautiously at first, then when I nodded my encouragement, he excitedly grabbed the paper and tore the rest of it off the box until the blue ribbon was on the floor, along with the brightly coloured wrapping paper. I'd never seen my boy so animated.

The box was tightly sealed. I took a Stanley knife from my toolkit on the workbench against the barn wall and started to slash at the heavy-duty cardboard.

Finally, the bike was out of the box.

He touched it with the very tips of his fingers, as if afraid to damage the bike.

'So, what do you think, Ben?'

The grin on his face told me everything I needed to know.

'Like it?'

Energetic nodding of his little head.

'Okay, let's wheel it into the yard, but before you ride it, there's another present waiting for you in the house.'

In the yard, Ben held tight onto the handlebars of the bike as if he had no intentions of letting go.

'Come on, no riding yet. Come inside. It won't take long, but it's important.'

Reluctantly, he handed over the bike to me and I parked it next to the front door.

Inside the house, I took Ben to the under-stairs cupboard, where I'd hidden the safety helmet, his second birthday present.

'There you go, little man. See what's in the box.'

He ripped off the paper and took out the helmet.

'Okay, now, listen very carefully. You must never get on the bike without first putting on the helmet, right?'

An expressionless glance at me.

'Promise me, Ben. It is very important, for your safety, that you always, always wear the helmet when you're riding your bike, right?'

Big eyes looked at me.

'I need you to promise me, Ben. If I ever find you have ridden your bike without first putting on your helmet and fastening it properly, then you will not be allowed to ride your bike again.'

A vigorous nod of the head and I tussled his hair and hugged him close to me.

'Okay, let's get you into this helmet and then you can have a go on your bike. But you can only ride it in the yard, okay? Don't go out onto the lane without me. Do you hear me, Ben?'

A tentative look. Then a slight nod of the head.

'I want you to promise me, Ben,' I said, holding his chin in my hand and looking him straight in the eye. 'You can't ride your bike until you promise me that you won't go out onto the lane.'

That look again.

'Well?'

A thoroughly good nod of his head. I hugged him tight then secured the helmet in place.

Outside, I checked over the bike, and held onto the back of the seat as Ben peddled around the yard. Slowly at first, then he picked up speed, meaning I had to run behind him as I held onto the seat.

I let go and off he sped, circling around the yard like it was a circus ring. A look of sheer joy spread over his face.

'That's my boy,' I whispered to myself, as I watched him through tears of pride. 'That's my beautiful boy.'

All those years of never seeing him. I vowed there and then that I would make up for every single day of those missed years.

Tosca, scratching on the shed door brought me back to the moment and I went to let him out, as Ben carried on peddling as fast as his little legs would allow.

55

Hetti

I left Oscar at the Italian restaurant in Tombland, a historical area of Norwich, where he and Toby had arranged to meet and made my way to Norwich market. I could take as long or as little time as I felt like, because Toby had promised to drive Oscar back to Wisteria Cottage.

The delicious smell of fish and chips assaulted my nostrils and I headed for the queue at the stall.

Sitting on a circular bench that surrounded a tree in the cobbled area of Gentlemen's Walk, I luxuriated in devouring the first meal of fish and chips that I'd eaten in a long time. Even this cool, grey day didn't detract from my enjoyment.

I finished the meal and headed for a coffee shop opposite and ordered a large cappuccino. Sitting at a window seat, I people-watched as I sipped on my coffee. After coffee, I would wander around Norwich Lanes, window shop, maybe treat myself to something nice from *Neal's Yard*. Or maybe not, as money was tight and I had a washing machine to buy. Oscar had offered to pay for the washing machine and to give me a bit of money to live on until I found a job, but I'd refused. It was good to know that I had that option though. Later I would pop into Argos before heading home. Thank goodness I didn't have Tosca to worry about, but I should get him back soon. Couldn't expect Nathan to have him indefinitely, and anyway, Oscar was looking much better.

Gazing through the plate glass window of the coffee shop, my world suddenly started to rotate in very slow motion. And why was it spinning clockwise? Wasn't it supposed to go anticlockwise? Something was terribly wrong. The cup broke as it hit the deck, dregs of coffee spreading across the floor. The room fell into stunned silence.

No. It couldn't be. Why would —?

I moved to stand up, drowning in a sea of turmoil. A woman stood over me as I slumped over the table.

'Are you alright, lovely?'

'Can you hear me, love?'

'She looks very pale.'

'Have you eaten today, dear?'

'Oh, these young girls, they don't eat enough to keep a sparrow alive, do they?'

'You're right there. Look at her, she's as skinny as a rake.'

The words came through a tunnel.

Blackness.

*****

'Hello, Henrietta. How are you feeling now?'

I blinked. Who was this calling me Henrietta? I hadn't been called that since I was a kid at school.

'I'm just going to check your blood pressure again.' She moved towards a machine next to the bed. After that she took hold of my wrist and looked at her watch.

'What happened? Why am I here?' My voice was not my own.

'You apparently had a funny turn in a coffee shop in Norwich. They called an ambulance and here you are. Don't worry, Henrietta, so far we haven't found anything too worrying.'

'How do you know my name?'

'The ambulance crew checked your handbag for ID and found your driving licence.'

'Oh. My bag. Where is it?' Panicking, I tried to get up. 'Who's got my bag?'

'Stay there, now. Don't get up. It's okay, my love. It's safe, right in here,' she said, indicating the locker next to the bed, and gently pushing me back down to lying position. I wasn't objecting. The room was moving like a tiny boat bobbing about on a stormy sea.

'How long have I been here?' I asked, looking down to notice for the first time that I was wearing a hospital gown.

'Oh, couple of hours. You're okay. We can probably send you home soon. But not before the doctor has asked you a few questions.'

The curtain swished open and in walked a tall, muscular man in blue scrubs, a stethoscope and ID tag around his neck. He was carrying an iPad.

'Hi Henrietta. I'm Duncan, one of the doctors.' He extended his hand and gently shook mine. 'How're you feeling now?' He had a Scottish accent a mile wide, somewhat unsurprisingly, with a name like that.

'I need to go home.'

'Whoa. Steady on. Of course, you can go home, but not before we find out what made you pass out in the city today. Now: I need to ask you a few questions. Okay?' He tapped on the iPad.

I nodded.

'Where do you live?'

'Wymondham.'

'Anyone at home right now?'

'Well, my godfather, Oscar, might be home by now.' I looked around for a clock. It was getting on for four. 'He was meeting a friend for lunch in the city, but that was at about twelve.'

'Okay. Your godfather.' He tapped into the iPad. 'You're not married, then?'

'No.'

'Do you have a boyfriend?'

And then I remembered.

It was him, I saw, strolling through Gentleman's Walk like he had not a care in the world. Daniel.

'Daniel! I need to go. I have to —' I made to get off the bed but my body was in no mood to cooperate.

Doctor Duncan placed a hand on my forearm. 'You can't go yet, but do you want us to call your boyfriend?'

'I haven't got a boyfriend.'

'Er, right. So, who is Daniel?'

And the floodgates opened. Duncan and the nurse, called Sue, had to listen to me blurting out the whole sorry tale about what Daniel had done to me, deceived me, betrayed me, stolen all my money and made off without even a goodbye, leaving me homeless, etcetera, etcetera and I'd seen him in the city this afternoon, sauntering along like someone walking on a sunny beach. What the hell was he doing in Norwich? And had he no conscience? Or sense? I mean, he'd done a runner with all my life's wealth. Surely, he needed to stay well away from the scene of the crime?

And the tears came. Soaking my face and dampening the hospital gown and the bed cover and the pillow. Sue tore off a strip of blue paper from a roll near the sink and handed it to me. Snot ran out of my nostrils over my lips, sliding down my chin.

Duncan walked away.

'It's a man thing,' said Sue. 'Can't bear to see a woman cry.'

And she smiled as I dried my tears, only for more to come.

56

Nathan

I commanded Tosca to sit and to stay away from Ben on his bike. I fed the dogs and prepared some breakfast for Ben and myself. Parents had been informed that the kids would be having swimming as part of their sports curriculum and it crossed my mind that it was unlikely that my son had ever been near a pool in his life. Sure, we'd been to the beach a number of times since he'd arrived in the summer, but he hadn't shown any interest in going in the water. I hadn't wanted to push it. Slowly does it. Slowly, slowly.

So, today, I thought, it might be a nice idea for us to take a little trip to the swimming pool. A birthday activity. There were several pools to choose from so after breakfast I put the idea to Ben.

'So, what do you think, Ben? Have you ever been to the swimming pool before?'

He shook his head.

'It's fun, Ben. Daddy will be with you all the time and we can have a lot of birthday fun in the water and then go for a special lunch with birthday cake. What do you say?' Daft question, I know, asking him what he'd say. The boy never spoke.

But he did nod and shake his head by way of reply and this time he answered with a nod. Great. Now we needed to kit him out with some trunks and gear.

We approached the side of the pool, which luckily was not very busy. Only a handful of kids were there with a parent so it was relatively quiet for a Saturday. I held Ben's hand.

'Shall we put your goggles on, Ben? And you can pop into your rubber ring, too.'

He didn't nod and he didn't shake his head either, so I gingerly, while trying to come across as confident and in charge, lowered the swimming ring so that he could step into it, which he did. So far, so good. Then I went to put the goggles over his head and that's when he protested, shaking his head, waving his little hands around. Okay, so he didn't want goggles. Fine.

Holding hands, we stepped closer to the edge of the pool and I checked Ben's reaction. It was hard to read his expression.

'Ready to give it a go, Ben?'

Not even a nod or a shake of the head. Nothing.

'Come on, big boy. Let's go.'

I gently pulled on his hand and he followed me to the steps of the pool. I went first, taking the steps slowly, while still holding firmly onto his hand. I turned to face him.

'Ready?' I tried to sound encouraging and confident and as if I was thoroughly enjoying the experience, but I'm not sure I was fooling anyone, let alone Ben.

A kid approached the side of the pool and dive bombed straight in, drenching me.

I wiped the water from my eyes with a fake expression of shock and exasperation. Ben started to giggle. Just a little at first, then his shoulders shook up and down and now he was in full flow, laughing his head off.

I reached for him and lifted him straight into the water with me. He beamed, his face lighting up like a warm, summer's day.

'That's my boy,' I said. 'That's my beautiful boy.'

It was hard, in the end, getting him out of the pool. He splashed around and I tried to teach him to kick his feet while I held his hands and walked backwards. The pool was thinning out of swimmers now and there were only two or three others apart from us. The goggles lay, abandoned on the poolside and later, much later, I wondered what it was that made my beautiful son so averse to wearing them. And was it at all connected with his reluctance to speak?

With hair still damp, we drove along the narrow, winding country road to Wymondham town. Life felt good. I had my son, he'd enjoyed his birthday bike and the swimming, the sun was shining now, despite the September chill in the air and white fluffy clouds danced across the wide, east Anglian sky. I slowed down as a pheasant darted across the road in front of me. Ben sat contentedly in his car seat and gazed at the views as we travelled along.

I parked in Wymondham's central carpark, took his hand and we walked up to *The Mad Hatter's Tea Shop* for the birthday cake that I'd promised Ben.

'Hello my man!' The rotund owner smiled from ear to ear as we walked into busy the shop. She came across as a woman very happy and satisfied with her lot in life and as the proud proprietor of the best tea shop in town. 'You're the chap what did the first aid on that girl that day, aren't you? I never forgets a face.'

'Hi there. Yes, that's me,' I said with a grin. 'Can you squeeze us in? It's my son's birthday and I've promised him a slice of the best cake in Wymondham.'

'Course, we can!' She looked at Ben, her smile still spread across her dimpled cheeks. 'Happy birthday, my man! And what's your name, eh?' Awkwardly, I answered for my son, hoping to avoid an embarrassing situation. He didn't speak to me, so he was hardly going to speak to a stranger, was he?

'Well, now, Ben, Happy Birthday! Now come you here and sit you down and let's see what cakes we can offer a boy on his special day.'

We ordered drinks and these were delivered to our table, followed by two huge slices of chocolate cake, one with a lit sparkler stuck in it. The other tea shop staff approached from behind the counter, all singing 'Happy Birthday' to Ben, who looked a little startled at first, but soon forgot himself and his little face portrayed sheer delight at the special attention. The rest of the tea shop customers joined in singing the birthday greeting and I felt a lump in my throat and that familiar prick of tears of pride at the back of my eyes.

That evening, as I tucked Ben into bed and read him a story, he looked at me with those big, dark eyes of his and held my gaze.

'Okay Ben? Did you enjoy your birthday?'

He nodded his head and smiled. 'Yes, thank you, Daddy.'

And that, on his sixth birthday, was the first time in his life that I'd heard the sound of my son's voice.

57

Hetti

Hospital, same day

'Feeling better?' The doctor whose name was Duncan closed the curtain behind him, pulled up a chair and sat by the bed.

'Mmm.'

'Okay if I ask you some questions now?'

'Mmm.'

'Right. When was your last period?'

'Don't remember.'

'When was the last time you had sex?'

'What?'

'Sex, Henrietta. When was the last time you had sexual intercourse?'

'Ages ago. I don't know. In the summer.' And he'd said he loved me at the time!

'Okay.' He typed something into his iPad.

'It's just that when you arrived, you were losing a lot of blood from down below.'

'Down below?'

'Yes. And quite a bit more than could be expected from even a heavy period.'

So that was why I'd been stripped off and humiliatingly dressed in a hospital gown that was definitely not what a stylist would call 'bang on trend', paper knickers and a large sanitary pad.

'I've been nauseous for a while. Well, since Daniel — you know —and I didn't have my period. But I'm not pregnant. I did a test.' He tapped on the iPad.

'Have you seen a doctor about your nausea and missed periods?'

'Er, no.'

'And why was that?'

'What?'

'Why didn't you see your doctor?' More typing onto the iPad.

'I was busy.'

'Busy?' He looked up from the iPad.

'Well, yes. You see, I had nowhere to live and I had to find a housesitting job and then Oscar had a cardiac arrest and I was up here for weeks while he was in intensive care and all that and I've been looking after this bloody demented Dalmatian that isn't even mine and — oh, I don't know — the time just goes.' I didn't even draw breath, as I spilled it all out.

'And Oscar is—?'

'My godfather.'

'Oh, yes, of course.'

My mouth was dry. I asked for a drink of water. Duncan stood up and brought a drink from the water cooler in the corner of the room.

I gulped it down.

'I'm going to get another doctor to come and see you. A gynaecologist. A specialist in women's problems.'

'I know what a gynaecologist is, thanks very much. I fainted. That's all. Doesn't mean I'm senile and it doesn't mean I'm stupid, either.'

As if I hadn't spoken, the doctor continued, 'We need to find out what's going on with the old missed periods and why you've been feeling sick. You need to stay here for a while longer.' And with that, he was away.

She looked young, I thought, to be a senior consultant. Tall, skinny, very pale complexion and long, straight, platinum blonde hair. She held out a cool hand and I shook it lightly.

'I'm Miss Nilsson. Sigrid. I'm a consultant gynaecologist.'

She had a heavy accent to go with the look and the Scandinavian sounding name.

After many questions, a thorough examination, and some more blood tests, Miss Nilsson — Sigrid — told me that all the emotional upset of recent events had more than likely caused the failure of my periods to appear and also could account for the nausea. She would do a few more blood tests and contact me when she had the results, but for now, there was nothing to worry about.

'So, can I go home?'

'Yes, you can. Is there someone with a car who can come and pick you up?'

Car?

Car!

I'd left the bloody land rover in the multi-storey car park, with only a couple of hours on the ticket. It had been there for hours and hours. Would it have been clamped? Towed away? A hefty fine left on the windscreen? Oh, god, this was all I needed.

I reached down to the bedside locker and pulled out my bag. The phone had run out of juice when I'd tried to call Oscar earlier, so he still didn't know where I was.

A ward assistant walked into the room.

'Excuse me,' I pleaded. 'My phone is dead. And I need to call my godfather to come pick me up.'

'No worries, love. I'll bring you the payphone.' She walked briskly off the ward and returned wheeling a trolley.

'There you go, my lovely. You can use this.'

And, of course, without looking at the contacts list on my iPhone, which was well and truly dead, I had no clue what the bloody hell Oscar's phone number was. Priceless.

I could've have taken a taxi home, were it not for the big blood stain on the seat of my white jeans.

58

Nathan

He spoke. He actually spoke to me.

That September was eventful, one way and another. Not only did Ben start school and have his sixth birthday, but he spoke to me for the first time, ever. I was ecstatic. I'd been reading a little about selective mutism and hoped with all my being that this silence from Ben was merely some mild form of that and nothing more serious. I couldn't bring myself to dwell too much on what kind of a life Ben might have experienced with his mother. She had not once sent a message or phoned since the day I'd picked him up. I'd texted her to let her know that we had arrived safely home and that Ben was okay, and received one word — 'fine' — back from her. Since then, nothing, not even a card on his birthday. It spoke volumes to me, but Ben seemed none the worse for it. His teacher's words came back to me, a boy needs his mother — yeah, right! We were doing very well without her, thank you very much.

September was also the time of year for me to examine the sheep to check that they were the right weight — not too fat and not too thin — for them to be introduced to the ram for mating. I took Ben out with me on the Sunday morning; he rode his bike on the lane alongside me as I walked to the field. He looked happy and confident on his bike. Again, I felt that overwhelming sense of pride in my son.

Once in the field, I took hold of one of the ewes.

'Look, Ben, watch how I check that this sheep is ready to start a baby with a daddy.' Was I really giving my six-year-old a lesson in reproduction?

To gauge the size, I pressed my hand along the loin area, on the backbone of the animal, just behind the ribs. Being too fat or too thin meant they were unlikely to conceive lambs, or — worse — raise their offspring successfully.

'You want to try, Ben?'

He gave me a look so difficult to read that it was impossible to know whether he wanted to try or not. Then, a tentative step forward and a little hand reached out.

'That's it, Ben, come and feel the sheep. Is it too fat, or too thin? What do you think?' He grabbed the animal and ran his fingers through the wool.

'Here, look, take hold of her here,' I moved his hand to the loin region and guided it to feel the size. 'It mustn't be too fat and it mustn't be too thin, otherwise it won't be able to be a mummy.'

Ben looked deep in thought, as if weighing up a mathematical or scientific problem, then shrugged his shoulders.

'Well, I think she's just right to be a mummy.' I put my hand back onto the animal and squeezed gently. 'You see, she feels just the right size. She's been eating well enough but not too much. So, I think we can let her have a baby soon.'

A huge smile and an enthusiastic nod of the head spoke his thorough approval and I moved around the field to check the rest of the ewes.

'Okay, Ben, now we have to take a look at the ram. Ready?' I held out my hand and he took it. At the roadside, I secured his safety helmet and he hopped on his bike. We meandered companionably, silently, back to the smallholding.

The ram was in fine fettle; fit as the proverbial fiddle. I checked its teeth, its feet and its testicles, which were all in good working order. He would service the ewes well, I was sure. Weight-wise, he was just right. A ram needs more weight on it – fat – than the ewe to prepare it for the strenuous task ahead. I thought in wonder about the life of a ram. All it needed to do was eat, sleep and copulate. Alright for some!

I looked down at Ben, who had been standing with his bike, watching me carry out the examination.

'Hungry?'

A smile.

'Okay, come on. Let's get cleaned up and go out for a Sunday roast. Yeah?'

'Yeah!'

'That's my boy!'

59

Hetti

Hospital

I found my cardigan and top in the bedside locker along with my bloodied white jeans and knickers in a hospital plastic bag. The doctor wasn't kidding when he told me I'd bled a lot. I didn't know whether to take a taxi to the carpark to retrieve the car or go straight home. Thinking about Oscar helped me make up my mind. He'd be worried, I knew he would. But did I have enough for a taxi?

Rummaging through my bag, I found that I was down to my last twenty-pound note. That should be enough to take me to Wymondham.

With my cardigan wrapped around my waist, the sleeves tied in a knot, hopefully hiding the glaring red evidence of a heavy bleed on the seat of my white jeans, I took a taxi to Wisteria Cottage, where I found Oscar in a state of extreme agitation.

'Darling! What happened to you? I've been frantic with worry. Why didn't you answer my calls?' His words strung together without a moment to draw breath.

Shoving the fare into the palm of the taxi driver's hand I took Oscar by the arm, led him into the cottage and proceeded to tell him the whole sorry tale.

After a long, hot shower, a change of clothes and a good meal inside me I felt better than I had for a long time. Oscar handed me a cup of tea when I came down from the bathroom. 'So, you thought you saw Daniel in the street, and that's what made you faint?' Oscar's expression was difficult to decipher.

'Well, yes, but the hospital doctor said that my passing out was probably caused by a combination of the shock of seeing Daniel and the menstrual issue. But maybe it wasn't him. Maybe it was someone who looked like him.'

'I think it was him, Hetti.'

'Why? What makes you so sure?'

'Well, I myself saw him. In the carpark that very day.'

And that's when I remembered. Oscar's face as he returned to the car with the pay and display ticket. I knew that he'd seen something. He'd had that look on his face and I knew something was bothering him.

'I must tell the police, Oscar. They've done bugger all so far, but that's two of us who saw him on the same day. They need to get out there and find him.'

'Facebook, darling. Put his picture on Facebook. We know that he's still in the area, so we can ask if anyone has seen him. And we can also ask everyone to share the post. He's stolen a hundred-thousand pounds of your money and he needs to be caught and punished. And you need to get your money back!'

'But what if he sees it on Facebook and comes after me? If he's capable of deceiving me and stealing my money like that then who knows what else he could do?' Was I finally starting to see Daniel for what he really was? A thoroughly nasty piece of work? Was I actually falling out of love with him after all these months? I really hoped so.

'If the police are aware, darling, they will do their job of protecting you. Come along, let's get on Facebook. And I will also post on mine. Now, where are your photos?'

The following morning, we took the train into Norwich, found the land rover still parked where I'd left it, with a parking penalty stuck on the windscreen. I would later send off a letter of appeal, with the hospital report attached and, no doubt after loads of totally unnecessary bureaucracy, the fine would hopefully be cancelled.

60

Nathan

It had been ages since I'd had a decent Sunday roast and the aroma of enticing food cooking hit me as we walked into *The Queen's Head*. The gastro pub had recently been refurbished and was now a really great, upmarket business that was a credit to Wymondham. I was thankful that such establishments were now suitable for children and held Ben's hand as I approached the bar.

'Got a table for two, mate?' I asked the bartender, a tall dude with chiselled bone structure and long, mousy brown hair tied into a man bun. He had a badge with 'Tim' on it pinned to his tee-shirt.

'You're in luck,' said Tim. 'We've just had a cancellation. There's a small table over there in the corner, if that's okay for you?'

'Yeah, great.' My gastric juices were already working overtime in anticipation of the good meal I looked forward to.

'Someone will be over in a moment to take your order for drinks. In the meantime, here's a couple of menus.'

'Only need one, thanks,' I smiled. Ben's reading skills were not yet sophisticated enough to be reading a menu. I led him over to the table and settled him into a chair, then sat opposite him.

'This is nice, isn't it, Ben?'

A very tiny voice replied, 'Yes, Daddy,' and my heart soared.

The drinks waiter arrived at the table.

'Have you had a look at the drinks or do you need a little more time?'

'Well, I'd like a ginger beer, please.' I looked at my son. 'Ben, would you like some orange juice?'

A little nod of the head and the waiter made a note and walked away, saying, 'Back in a minute.'

'Okay, Ben. Let's see what's on offer for lunch.' I perused the menu card and my eyes rested on the roast pork. My mouth watered. I knew what I was going to have, but what about my boy?

'I'll read out and you tell me when you hear something that you fancy, okay?'

An enthusiastic nod in reply and I began reading. It was all very grown-up food – not a fish finger insight - but that was good because I wanted my son to develop a taste for decent grub. Egg and chips and burgers were all very well and good now and again, but a healthy, wholesome diet was important.

We settled for ordering the same for both of us. Slow roast pork.

Our drinks arrived and I placed the lunch order.

'The portions are quite big. Shall I get chef to make a smaller portion for the boy?'

'Might be a good idea, thanks. But give him everything on his plate that I get on mine, okay?'

'Sure thing. We're a bit busy, as you can see, so there might be a little bit of a wait. Would you like some complimentary olives to keep you going while the food is cooking?'

'Please.'

Ben had never had olives before. Well, why would he have? He was six. I watched his little nose wrinkle as the olive hit his taste buds.

'They're an acquired taste, Ben,' I said, laughing gently with him but not at him. He struggled to chew on the thing and swallow it, but refused the offer of more.

'Well, hello there! It's Nathan, isn't it?' A loud voice boomed out. 'How are you dear fellow?'

Oscar approached the table and Hetti, looking a little pale, followed in his wake.

I stood up and shook Oscar's hand.

'Me? Oh, I'm fine, thanks, mate. What about you?' I replied, glancing beyond him at Hetti.

'Splendid, dear boy. Splendid. All down to you, I must say. And this handsome chap is...?' Oscar beamed at Ben.

'Ben. My son.'

'Well, I might have guessed. He's a chip off the old block, that's for sure. Hello Ben.'

There was no reply from Ben but instead he managed a small smile and a shy look.

'Our table is ready,' Hetti moved forward and took Oscar's arm, leading him away.

It was odd. I couldn't make it out. They just seemed the most unlikely couple. I shrugged and turned my attention back to Ben.

'Hungry?'

'Mm.' A nod of the head.

'Ah, looks like our food is coming now.'

Later, we shared a dessert of sticky toffee pudding with caramel sauce and ice cream. Oh, alright, so I know I said I wanted Ben to grow up on healthy food, but you've got to have a bit of a treat now and then, haven't you?

I asked for the bill and the manager approached our table.

'The gentleman who was here earlier, with the young lady with the beautiful red hair? He paid your bill, sir.'

That was decent of the old boy. Totally unnecessary though.

61

Hetti

October arrived and my phone pinged one day with a text from Jack, the plumber.

Got a washing machine for you, if you're still interested?

I most certainly was interested, being as I never got to Argos last month, but had ended up in hospital instead.

Oscar had gone back to live in his own house and I'd driven into Norwich to use his washer/drier once or twice. We took the opportunity to have lunch together while the clothes were laundered and at least I could check up on him at the same time.

Toby seemed as elusive as ever. They'd met for lunch in Norwich that day and Toby had driven Oscar back to Wisteria Cottage, but their contact seemed to become more and more infrequent. I really didn't like that guy. What was his game?

Jack was at the door at nine the following morning, telling me that he didn't have long to get it installed, as he wheeled in the reconditioned machine. 'Got an urgent job to get to up at Attleborough, so I need to get this one installed pronto.' I thanked him for taking the time to deliver a much-needed washing machine to Wisteria Cottage.

'I'll take the old one out to the van first — presumably you'd like me to dispose of it for you, yeah?' Jack raised his eyebrows in expectation of my reply. I nodded my agreement.

He installed the 'new' machine, stopping to read texts that seemed to be flying into his mobile at a rate of ten per minute. He was shoving the washer into the space under the draining board when I recalled Jack's remark on our first meeting; something about Nathan. Curious, I asked him about it as I handed over the cash for the washer.

'Nathan? Oh yeah. Had a bit of —' Jack's phone's ring tone played out some rock music I'd never heard in my life and he apologised as he took the call.

'Yeah, yeah. Will do. On it mate, on it.' He ended the call and looked at me.

'Gotta dash, Hetti. Sorry. What was that you were saying?'

'Oh, never mind. Not important,' I'd hardly finished the sentence, and he was gone.

62

Nathan

Halloween came and went, followed swiftly by Guy Fawkes' Night and now Christmas approached. Our first Christmas together, my little man, Ben and me. I think I was more excited than he was at the prospect. I wondered if he still believed in Santa, if indeed he ever had. Mandy wasn't exactly the maternal type, that was for sure. She never got in touch, not even to reply to my weekly texts letting her know that Ben was doing fine. Nothing. I thought it was very odd, but to be honest, that was the way I liked it.

I'd mated the ram with the ewes successfully and looked forward to the lambs arriving in the spring. A quick calculation told me that the due date was early April. Great stuff. When I told Ben, he became very excited at the prospect of seeing baby lambs gambolling in the fields in the spring.

It was the last week of term before Christmas and I went to the school to see Ben perform in the nativity play. He was chosen to be one of the "cattle are lowing" and it meant that he had to wear a cow's head with horns, which we made of Papier-Mache and painted brown one Saturday afternoon. The cow's head was like a motorcycle helmet, so that Ben's face was totally visible. The rest of him was 'human' — the costume was a very simplistic version of a cow — it comprised the cow's head, his school trousers and a brown jumper. I never thought I'd derive so much pleasure out of spending an afternoon making a cow's head for my son to wear in the Christmas play!

As I sat with parents and grandparents watching the performance, I felt a huge lump the size of a rock in my throat, as the children sang *Away in a Manger* and I could see Ben joining in. He had come a long way and grown in confidence in the months since I'd brought him to live with me in Norfolk. He was, as yet, still not as outgoing as I'd like, but, so far, I was happy with progress. He wasn't so shy with the other kids and seemed to have one or two special friends. His busy-body teacher had chilled out a bit too and there had been no further altercations between us.

On the Saturday before Christmas we went to the Wymondham Charity Christmas Craft Fayre, where all the stuff was made by the proud vendors. A white, fluffy knitted lamb caught Ben's eye and I bought it for him – a nod to the expected lambs next spring. We also bought seasonal food: homemade chutneys, mince pies, hams and cakes. We had hot spicy apple drinks with sausage rolls, which we ate in the street as we meandered along. Christmas carols were being sung by a number of choristers from a local classical choir gathered outside the Cross Keys pub and we stopped a while to listen to their dulcet tones, that invoked the Christmas spirit. I gave Ben a fiver to drop into the bucket that was being shaken at the crowd. Proceeds in aid of local charities.

We came to a stall on Market Cross where homemade candles, soaps and Christmas cards were on sale, along with an assortment of Christmas decorations.

A Christmas Tree! Why hadn't I thought of it before? Well, of course I'd need to buy a tree for Santa to leave presents underneath for Ben. How could I overlook that? I was really getting into it now. We bought a few decorations that Ben had chosen and I asked the rosy-faced woman where I might find a decent tree.

'Thass a real tree, you mean, right? Not one of them horrible plastic ones?' The woman gazed at me from underneath her woolly red hat.

'Yeah. A real one, that's right. Do you know the best place to get one around here?'

'Well now, you're in luck, my man. Just walk down towards the Abbey and you'll find a boy selling proper trees. Good prices too. And that money is going to charity, so thass a good cause.'

I thanked her and we wandered down Market Street and turned into Church Street where, outside the arts centre stood a young man surrounded by trees of different sizes. One or two people examined the specimens.

'Which one would you like, Ben?' I put my arm around his shoulders. 'You choose.' He looked up at me. 'You can have whichever you want.'

Ben looked at the trees on display and pointed to a small one, with thin, sparse branches. It looked rather sad and lonely, propped up against the wall.

'Are you sure? Look,' I said, pointing out some bigger, fuller trees, 'what about one of these?'

'Can we really have a big one, Daddy?' He still rarely spoke and when he did his voice was tiny and quiet.

'Yes, of course we can. We can have whatever we want. What about this one?' I touched the top of a tall, full tree that stood out in its majesty.

Ben's eyes were like saucers.

'Really? That great big one, Daddy?'

'Well, would you like it?'

A very enthusiastic nod of the head. 'Mmm!' More nodding.

The vendor tied string around the tree and took the twenty quid note I shoved into his hand.

'Shall we go home and put the tree up, then?'

Another keen and eager nod, accompanied by a beaming smile.

As we turned to face the charity shop on the corner of the street, I caught sight of a huge silver, glittering star in the window. Perfect for the top of our Christmas tree.

The kindly, elderly volunteer's eyes shone as she handed the star to Ben and took the one-pound coin from me. Bargain!

It was awkward trying to manoeuvre the tall tree through the doorway, as we left the shop, and I ended up backing out.

Hetti

December, 2018

Christmas. How time flies. Was it only a year ago that I'd spent the holiday with my Aunt Pat in north Norfolk while Daniel had been spending Christmas god-knows-where? I'd been so disappointed, thinking he didn't love me after all, but then after Christmas Daniel asked me to move in with him and I soon put any nagging doubts out of my mind.

So much had happened in one year but still no sign of Daniel. I hadn't set eyes on him since that day in Gentleman's Walk, strolling by the coffee shop and I was beginning to wonder if it was actually him that I'd seen. Of course, I'd updated the police, but without any evidence or further leads, they were as useful as a chocolate teapot. So, things were just about as dismal as ever, where my stolen money was concerned. There was one good thing, though; my periods had normalised and the nausea had ceased.

Daniel's face was now plastered all over Facebook, both mine and Oscar's and was getting shared left, right and centre. I'd often thought that Facebook — social media in general, actually — was an amazing invention that had, unfortunately, huge potential for abuse. I mean, some of the comments that people write on there are just beyond the pale. They don't call them keyboard warriors for nothing. Would they be so rude and obnoxious if they met the person face-to-face? Probably not. Social Media certainly had its downsides. However, if the police couldn't find Daniel, then I hoped with all my heart that Facebook would. The only reason I'd not posted about Daniel before was because I was so ashamed of allowing myself to be fooled by him and felt excruciatingly embarrassed about letting everyone that I knew find out about it. But shame wasn't going to find him and I wanted my money back. I posted several pictures of him, taken from different angles, and wrote: *Last seen in Gentleman's Walk, Norwich, summer 2018. Any sightings, please PM me. Thanks!*

Tosca was back, but only part time. Nathan's little boy had apparently taken a great liking to the dog and missed him a lot, so Nathan and I agreed to share responsibility for the hound. Well, it was only for another six months; Olivia would be back in the summer.

Wymondham folk apparently love the annual Christmas Fayre and so I decided to go and see what was on offer. I'd left Tosca tied with a long lead to the gazebo and took the land rover into town to take a wander around. As I'd tied up Tosca, he'd started whimpering a bit and gave a little bark, but when I'd looked around, I could see nothing.

'What's up, boy? What are you trying to tell me?'

Then I'd heard a rustle in the vegetation the other side of the garden fence and walked over to investigate.

'Hello? Anyone there?' I called out.

Nothing.

Oh well. Probably a rabbit or something. I wrapped an old duvet around the dog. I wouldn't be long, but I couldn't let him get cold, but neither could I leave him indoors and risk coming home to a scene of devastation.

'Now you behave, Tosca. I won't be long but I don't want to find you up to mischief when I get back.'

Tosca, in his usual manner, had jumped up and licked my face.

'Okay. Good boy.' He really was much better behaved these days. Being with Nathan was good for him. He'd trained him well.

I tucked him up in the duvet again and set off for town. As I drove along, I thought about Tosca's bark, his alarm call, letting me know that there was something not quite right going on near the cottage. Could it have been anything to do with the times that I'd been in the garden and felt that I was being watched? Weird. Oscar would probably call my uneasiness 'stuff and nonsense', but I felt instinctively that there was something sinister going on. I'd never actually seen anyone or anything, but had the sense, with absolute certainty, that there was something odd. I tried to shrug off the feeling as I approached the town.

With very little money to spare, I knew that I could get a nice, reasonably priced handmade Christmas present for Oscar and something for dear old Aunty Pat as well. I'd asked her to come and spend Christmas with us in Wymondham, but she was totally non-committal, saying only that she'd think about it.

Okay, time to get into the Christmas spirit and find some affordable presents.

Nathan

Same day

'Ouch!' The scream was followed by a mild expletive. 'Watch where you're going!' I turned to see Hetti on the pavement outside the charity shop, hopping on one foot, a grimace spread across her face.

'Sorry! Didn't see you there.' God, she looked hot. Black skinny jeans on legs so long they seemed to go on forever, a snowy white, fluffy fleece jacket and enormous bright pink scarf wrapped several times around her neck and tied at the front. She wore flat heeled boots with her jeans tucked in and I noticed, probably for the first time, that we were exactly the same height. Her wild, red hair tumbled down, cascading over her shoulders and down her back, giving her that look of an Amazonian goddess. A felt a definite stirring in the nether regions and felt my face grow hot and red.

'Oh hi! It's you! And you too, Ben! Hello darling. How are you?' She bent down to look Ben in the face. What I'd give to have her calling me 'darling'! I was almost jealous of Ben! She looked so relaxed and — dare I say it? — almost pleased to see me.

'Yeah, we're good, thanks. Just doing some Christmas shopping, as you can see. How's your foot? I hope I didn't crush it!'

'I'll live.'

'And Oscar? How's he doing?' Hated to bring up the subject of the old boy, the constant reminder that Hetti wasn't free for me to pursue, but I hadn't forgotten his generous gesture of paying for our Sunday lunch that day.

'Oh, he's doing great! He's back home now, but he's going to come back to Wisteria Cottage for Christmas. Well, actually, he wants us to go out for Christmas lunch, so we'll probably do that, rather than cook.' I loved the way she was so animated when she spoke and her eyebrows went up and down in motion along with her other facial expressions.

But hang on a minute. Did she say Oscar had gone home?

'Er, Oscar's gone home?'

'Yeah. He lives in Norwich.'

'And you live in Wymondham?'

She stood there with a perplexed expression on her face. Like I'd asked her the most totally bizarre question.

'Er, yeah. Why?'

People were trying to get by as we blocked the pavement and we moved along, the three of us together, and the Christmas tree, which seemed to be taking on a personality of its own.

Hetti

Same day

I'd been standing on the corner of Damgate and Church Street, trying to decide whether to buy one of those lovely

Christmas trees I'd seen for sale outside the arts centre, or to first take a look at the stalls of handmade crafts up at Market Cross, when suddenly, a pain shot through my foot and it was excruciating. Someone had backed out of the RSPCA charity shop and stepped right on my foot. I let out a swear word. Well, I know I shouldn't have sworn in the street, but I think in the circumstances I could be forgiven for my bad manners. I was hopping up and down when I looked up and realised it was Nathan and his son standing there. I couldn't help being pleased to see them. Nathan was handsome in a Ross Poldark sort of a way, with his long, black curls tied into a pony tail at the nape of his neck. His little boy was a dead ringer for his dad, too. A miniature version of Nathan. I started to feel something that, well, actually it was nothing like anything I'd ever felt before. But I reminded myself that Nathan was a married man with a child and I was to keep away. Anyway, after Daniel, I wasn't in a hurry to get involved with any guy any time soon. There was still no sign of Daniel and I didn't for a moment believe that I'd ever get my money back.

We were blocking the pavement so the three of us moved away and up the street towards Market Cross. I could smell the pine needles of their Christmas tree and resolved to go back to buy one for myself after finishing my Christmas shopping.

'What have you got there, Ben?' I said, as we strolled up the street. Ben held up his Christmas star for me to take a closer look. 'Wow, that's a beautiful star. Is it for your Christmas tree?'

He nodded his little head.

'Will you put it on your tree yourself? You'll need steps to reach the top of that big tree, or perhaps Daddy will have to lift you up.'

Ben looked down at his feet but Nathan gave me a wide smile that made my hormones wake up big time. I swiped away the thought from my mind and reminded myself yet again that Nathan was not available.

'He doesn't speak much. He's a bit shy, aren't you Ben?' Nathan smiled reassuringly at his son.

The boy looked away.

We reached Market Cross where all the Christmas stalls displayed homemade crafts. Nathan offered to take us all to the *Mad Hatters* for coffee and cake, but aware of and uncomfortable with my changing feelings for this man, I made my excuses and left Nathan and Ben to it.

I bought a bright purple woolly handknitted scarf for Oscar (his favourite colour, don't you know!) and a scented candle for Aunty Pat. I stopped to listen to some carol singers outside a pub and found myself joining in. The conductor, a very smiley lady in her sixties looked over at me and when the song came to an end she came over to where I was standing.

'Hello. I'm Tess, the musical director of the choir. Do you enjoy singing? You have a lovely voice.'

I was quite taken aback and wasn't sure what to say through my blushes.

'Er, yeah. I do. Sorry, didn't mean to intrude.'

She waved away my comment, reached into her coat pocket and handed me a flyer, saying, 'There you are. Our contact details. Come and join us after Christmas, if you'd like. You'd be very welcome. We're a friendly bunch and we could do with some young blood. We rehearse Tuesdays, seven-thirty in the evenings. It's all on there.' She smiled at me warmly and moved back to start the next carol.

I returned to the arts centre in Church Street and bought a small tree. In the *Star Throwers* charity shop opposite I bought a few second-hand Christmas decorations then made my way back to the car.

On the way to Wisteria Cottage, I felt all warm and fuzzy, driving along in the Veramobile, as I'd come to refer to the land rover. I'd done my Christmas shopping on a shoestring, bumped into Nathan and Ben and got invited to join the local choir. It felt heart-warming. Oscar had been telling me for months that I must learn to trust again and not let Daniel totally destroy my faith in humankind.

Easier said than done. But I must try. I knew I must try.

Tosca jumped up and down and whimpered as I untied him and allowed him back indoors. He was used to sleeping either indoors or in a shed at Nathan's place, but there wasn't really space in here, so I had to have him in the house at night, now that it was winter. Dog hairs ruled supreme, covered my clothes, the carpets and furniture and clogged the vacuum cleaner.

I lit the fire and Tosca settled down on the hearth rug. As I drew the curtains that evening, I saw that it had started to snow.

Nathan

Same day

We skipped the coffee and cake because I realised the tree wouldn't fit inside the tea shop, and anyway, my invitation was just an excuse to spend some time with Hetti. Once home, I found a bucket and filled it with soil to install the pine tree. I'd bought a tree with roots to help avoid the dried pine needles falling to the floor and getting trodden around the house or stuck into our stockinged feet. I lit a log fire and made hot chocolate with marshmallows, much to Ben's delight. As we sat at the hearth, eating mince pies from the Christmas market and drinking the hot chocolate, we started sorting through the decorations. I'd found a set of Christmas lights and now set about testing them. I plugged in the lights and screwed each bulb up tight until all of the lights illuminated in unison. Ben looked on, quietly excited.

First, we wrapped sparkly Christmas wrapping paper around the bucket, then wound the lights around the pine branches. We took it in turns to hang the baubles and tinsel then I lifted Ben onto my shoulders so that he could tie the star to the top of the tree. It was a bit skewwhiff, but hey, this was Ben's effort and I wouldn't dream of adjusting it. Instead, I applauded it.

'That's brilliant, Ben!' I said, clapping my hands. 'Well done you!' My beautiful boy treated me to a bright smile.

I'd bought a bright red Christmas stocking and pulled it out of the drawer in the kitchen.

'Here we are, Ben. Time to hang your stocking for Santa to fill.'

Did I detect a little look of wonder on my little boy's face?

'Go on, hang it from the mantelpiece. Or do you prefer to leave it under the tree?'

Ben took the stocking from me and held it for a moment. He moved towards the tree and carefully placed it on one of the branches. I was surprised that it stayed there, but the tree was fairly sturdy and did the job.

'When Santa fills it, he'll have to leave it under the tree.'

'Why Daddy?'

'Well, because with all those presents he's bound to bring you, because you're such a god boy, it will be too heavy to hang back on the tree.'

A big smile.

I went to pull the curtains and saw the forecast snow gently falling in the yard.

That evening, once we'd had supper and my son was tucked up in bed, I poured a glass of wine and opened my emails. There was a message from Mum and Dad, looking forward to coming to spend Christmas with me and Ben. It would be the first time they had met my son. I felt guilty at not introducing him to his grandparents yet. They did know about him, of course they did, right from the beginning, but I'd been taking a cautious approach to settling Ben in his new life and didn't want too much too soon. My parents — in particular Mum — were itching to meet him and spoil him rotten. I'd shown Ben pictures of his grandparents, so he knew of their existence, but he'd just given a tentative nod of the head by way of acknowledgement.

Matt called. 'Wanna come out for a pint, mate? I'm in Wymondham.'

'You're forgetting I've got a small son, Matt. Can't just drop everything to go out on the piss.'

'Can't you get a babysitter?'

'You're kidding! I can't get a babysitter at a moment's notice. I'm a dad, Matt. I have responsibilities. But perhaps we could get a pint together one lunch time next week, while Ben's at school. Only one, though.'

'Okay, I get it. You're not in the habit of being drunk in charge of a kid.' Matt laughed heartily.

'And it will have to be early in the week. He breaks up for Christmas on Tuesday.' We made arrangements to meet at the Green Dragon.

I replied to Mum's email and closed the laptop.

Sitting by the fire, I thought back to the afternoon at the Christmas Fayre and Hetti. She was a bit friendlier these days and I just wished she wasn't in a relationship with that Oscar. Nice enough guy, but bloody hell, he was the last person I'd expect a girl like Hetti to be hitched to. But perhaps they weren't married. She'd said he lived in Norwich. Maybe they were just in a relationship.

I washed up the wine glass and wandered upstairs. As always, I looked in on Ben to see him hugging the fluffy white lamb I'd bought him that day, snoozing contentedly. Toffee was curled up on the end of the bed, where she spent most nights, despite my protestations. My heart warmed.

My first Christmas with my son. I couldn't wait.

63

Hetti

Few days later

Christmas was getting closer and I was becoming very aware that my money was running out. I went online and searched the Wymondham Facebook page. Sometimes they advertised local jobs on there so I decided to take a look.

There were only a couple of job adverts. A hairdressing salon was looking for a qualified stylist, which was no good for me, but someone else wanted a cleaner three times a week. I gave them a ring.

'I want someone reliable,' the woman said, in a voice that sounded vaguely familiar but which I could not place, 'and do you have a car, because I might want you to get me some shopping sometimes.'

'I believe that I am a reliable person,' I said, in my best telephone voice. 'And yes, I do have the use of a vehicle.' I was reluctant to call the Veramobile an actual car. That description would be pushing it a bit.

'Alright. Good. Would you like to come and see me?'

Sparrow Woman answered the door. I thought I was seeing things, but it was definitely the same woman who had brought Tosca to Wisteria Cottage that day, demanding that I take him off her hands. Same pinched little face, a plethora of wrinkles, short, frizzy hair flecked with grey. Little bird-like eyes that stared then squinted at you suspiciously. She reminded me of the Geraldine McEwan version of Agatha Christie's *Miss Marple*. She even dressed in a similar fashion with her nineteen-fifties style calf-length pale green, woollen dress with a bow that tied at her throat and beige, crocheted cardigan.

'Hello Hetti,' now she smiled and her face transformed to a softness that was definitely absent when I'd first met her all those months ago.

'Oh. Are you Miss Higgins?'

'Yes, dear, I am. Do come in.' She stepped aside and let me enter the hallway of her tiny house. Glancing around as I walked in, I could see immediately why it would have been impossible for her to take care of a dog like Tosca in this limited space.

'This is a nice place, Miss Higgins. Would you like to show me what you'd want me to do?'

'Yes, come through,' and she led the way to the lounge, a small room that had French doors leading out to a tiny back garden. 'I'll need to you dust and polish and vac this room, every time you come and once every two weeks, clean the insides of the windows. I have a chap who comes to do the outside once a month. I also need you to clean out the fire place and set the fire ready for me to light it in the evenings.'

I made a mental note.

'How's that Dalmatian? She said, as she touched the mantelpiece and wiped imaginary dust from the tips of her fingers. 'He really is a bit of a handful, isn't he?'

'Er, yes, he is. Well, actually, he's quite a bit better behaved these days. I had to leave him for a while with Nathan at the smallholding just down the lane and he's been really good with him. Really trained him well. Tosca actually does what he's told, nine times out of ten these days.'

'Well, that's good news. Young Nathan is good with animals. He was meant to be a vet, you know, until...' She cut herself short and looked away.

'Until?'

'Oh, I never gossip about people, dear,' she said, turning back to me, 'it's not my nature.'

So, she didn't "gossip" but would drop a hint that she knew something about Nathan, while refusing to say what it was. Not for the first time, I was left wondering what had happened to Nathan. Jack, the plumber, had also mentioned something; some tragedy?

'Come through to the kitchen.'

I followed her out of the room into the hall and to the left was the smallest kitchen I'd ever seen. One person and a cat would have been a crowd.

'In here I need you to clean everything — surfaces, sink, floor, cupboards — everything, every time you come. Then once a month, I need you to clean the refrigerator. And defrost the freezer, too.'

'How often? The freezer?'

'Oh, probably once every six months or so. I'll let you know.'

'Okay.' I took out my phone and started making notes.

'There's a downstairs cloakroom,' she moved across the hallway and opened a door. There was just enough space in the room for the toilet and a minute washbasin. The vacuum cleaner was propped up in one corner. 'This needs thoroughly cleaning every time you come.'

I made a note.

'Come upstairs, dear,' she said, and took hold of the bannister, making her way up, very slowly, one painful step at a time.

'There's the family bathroom,' she indicated with an index finger to her left, 'but I don't use it much, so a quick going over once a week will be fine. Likewise, with the second bedroom.' I made more notes.

She walked across the landing, saying, 'of course, you'll have to vacuum all the carpets up here every time you come.'

'Right,' I made a note.

Miss Higgins opened the door of her bedroom and entered, 'My bedroom needs to be dusted and polished and vacuumed every time you come, and the bed linen changed once every two weeks.'

She opened the door to a tiny ensuite shower room.

'I'll need you to clean my ensuite thoroughly,' she emphasised the word, *thoroughly*, 'every time you come.'

'Okay, fine,' I murmured, making a note on my phone.

'And naturally, you'll need to clean the insides of all the windows up here every two weeks, just as you will downstairs.'

'Fine. Is there anything else?'

'Yes, you'll need to sort the bins and be sure to use the correct recycling bin for each item and I don't like to see the rubbish bin too full — it indicates that there is not enough recycling going on.'

'Absolutely.' I made a note.

We walked downstairs. At the front door, I turned to Miss Higgins. 'So, er, have you got others to see, or —?'

'No. You'll do. Fifteen pounds an hour. Two hours each time you come and you'll be here three times a week. Mondays, Wednesdays and Fridays.'

I didn't know if I was pleased that I'd have a bit of an income or terrified at the prospect of facing Miss Higgins every time I turned up to clean her house.

'Thank you. What time would you like me to arrive?'

'Monday morning, nine o'clock sharp.' That would be the first Monday after Christmas, then. 'Don't be late, dear. I don't like unreliable people.'

'Of course.' I turned to walk outside. As I stepped onto the garden path, I looked back at Miss Higgins. 'Oh, er, you said something about possibly needing some shopping done?'

'Yes, very occasionally. And if I need you to go into Norwich for anything, I'll pay you extra. See you Monday. And don't bring that dog.'

As if I would.

64

Hetti

Christmas

Late afternoon on Christmas Eve, Oscar arrived by taxi and we trimmed the Christmas tree together before dinner. The festive tree glittered in the corner of the room, dripping with the tinsel and baubles and Christmas lights that I'd bought in the charity shop last week. Two Christmas presents, one for me and one for Oscar, colourfully wrapped with lots of glitter, lay under the tree. I remembered the Christmas Fayre last week, when Nathan's son, Ben, had shown me his Christmas tree star. What a gorgeous little boy, but painfully shy. I thought about their Christmas, how they would spend it and it occurred to me that although I'd seen Ben two or three times, I'd never seen the boy's mother. I wondered what she was like. Was she pretty? What colour was her hair? Was she petite? The boy looked so much like his dad that it was hard to imagine what his mother might look like. I shrugged. Nathan's wife. Why was I thinking about her? I didn't even know her. Was I jealous? Maybe. Just a little. I shrugged and tried to dismiss the thought from my mind, only for it to return, popping into my head, annoyingly.

Nathan had been over to Wisteria Cottage that afternoon to take Tosca back with him. I'd told him that Oscar, and possibly Aunty Pat would be coming and he'd pointed out that adding a fully-grown Dalmatian to the mix could cause a little chaos. It was certainly peaceful and quiet without the Dalmatian in the house.

After dinner Oscar and I sat by the fire with a glass of mulled wine and apple tart and whipped cream — Oscar's favourite dessert — that I'd made especially for him as a treat.

'I shouldn't be encouraging you to eat sugary puddings, Oscar. Far too many calories! And whipped cream is definitely a no-no, normally. But hey! It's Christmas, isn't it?'

'Yes, indeed,' he said, 'Christmas is a time for treats. And I am lucky to be here at all, so I intend to enjoy myself!'

'Absolutely! You'll just have to work a bit harder in the gym after Christmas to make up for it. We need to take care of that poor heart of yours!'

Oscar raised his glass and chinked it against mine. 'To healing hearts and apple tarts!' He took a small sip of his drink. 'And a very Happy Christmas to you, Dear One!'

'Healing hearts, Oscar? I do hope your heart will completely heal.' I raised my glass to him again after taking a sip.

'And may your dear little heart soon be healed, my love.' Putting his glass down to free his arm he hugged me to him. I was so happy and grateful that he was here with me for Christmas. It could have been so different.

My phone rang and it was Aunty Pat, calling to say that she'd decided not to come to spend Christmas Day with us after all. She didn't want to travel in the ice and snow, even though I'd offered to go and pick her up and that anyway she had someone with whom she could have Christmas dinner.

I ended the call and looked out of the window. It was still snowing. This was my first ever white Christmas.

Oscar chuckled as he mischievously speculated that Aunty Pat had probably found herself a gentleman friend. I laughed too, thinking that it was unlikely, but really did hope that she would have company and wouldn't be spending Christmas Day alone.

I rummaged through Olivia Hargreaves-Brown's CD collection and found an opera titled 'Tosca'. The beautiful soprano voice of Angela Gheorghiu singing an aria filled the room and I felt my emotions raw and close to the surface. We listened for a while in silence to the opera singer's vocal gymnastics.

Oscar took my hand. 'One of my favourites, this one. Do you know the story, Hetti?'

'I don't think I do, no. What's she singing about?' The soprano's voice tugged at my heartstrings.

'Oh well, it's the usual story — you know — eternal triangle between a woman — that's Tosca — and two gentlemen — well, to be more precise, one's her lover and the other's a bent copper!' Oscar laughed at himself. 'The story is set in Rome in the early nineteenth century, I believe. Napoleonic times, anyway.' He got up and picked up the CD cover and came back to sit on the sofa next to me.

He read the blurb on the back of the cover. 'Yes, that's about right. Sad ending, of course. Old Puccini loved a good old tragic finale.'

I was lying back on the sofa, my head resting on Oscar's shoulder. The soprano playing Tosca was wreaking havoc on my senses, when suddenly I sat bolt upright.

'Hang on a minute!' I grabbed the CD cover out of Oscar's hands and looked at the back blurb. 'Tosca is the woman!'

'Well, yes.'

'But Tosca?'

'Yes? What about her?'

'I mean the dog.'

'The dog?' Had he had too much mulled wine? My godfather was being rather dim.

'Yes! The bloody dog. The Dalmatian. He's a boy!'

'Yes, he's a boy. And?'

I jumped up off the sofa in exasperation and faced Oscar.

'He's a boy and she's given him an Italian girl's name!'

'Yes, Dear One. That's right. So, what?'

'Why did she give him a girl's name when she knew he was a boy?'

'Hetti darling, I have no idea. Come. Sit down and enjoy the opera and this delicious mulled wine. Any chance of another piece of apple tart?'

I got up and walked through to the kitchen, muttering to myself, 'He's a boy with a girl's name, for goodness' sake. No wonder the bloody dog's neurotic!'

Nathan

Christmas morning and Mum and Dad were due to arrive soon. Ben had opened his presents that Santa had left in his stocking under the tree, we'd eaten breakfast, checked the sheep and taken the dogs for a walk. The snow had stopped falling overnight and the morning sun shone down, making the white ground, trees, hedges and rooftops twinkle like millions of stars.

I hoped that the excitement of Christmas and the occasion of his first meeting with his grandparents wouldn't overwhelm Ben too much. There was definitely something not good about his past that I didn't know about. I had my suspicions that there had been some — shall we say — unkind behaviour that he'd experienced. I wondered about Mandy's parents. They'd rarely been mentioned, although, as far as I knew, they were still around.

I heard the car pull into the yard and went to open the door to my parents. As I did so, Ben disappeared upstairs, his toy car from Santa in one hand and the knitted lamb in the other.

'Where are you going, Ben? Grannie and Grandpops are here.' Toffee gave a little bark as she tore down the stairs and headed for the front door, jumping up as if to try and open it. Tosca sprang to life from his prostrate position in front of the fire and joined in with the barking. I grabbed his collar and shut him in the kitchen, commanding him to "stay!"

I opened the door and Toff ran out to the car. Mum and Dad were unloading presents and luggage. When they saw me standing there, they dropped what they were doing and ran over to me with open arms.

'Nathan, my darling boy!' Mum hugged me so tight I thought I'd burst and Dad offered me a firm hand to shake. They looked well. Now in their late fifties, Mum and Dad had both got the youth genes. Mum still had lustrous, thick hair and Dad was tall, with a rod-like straight back.

'Welcome, Mum, Dad. Merry Christmas!' Cold air made white clouds of my breath as I spoke. They hugged me again. I had a lump in my throat. My parents had always been so accepting, whatever stupid thing I'd got up to as a youth. Having Ben with me had made me appreciate all the more how fantastically lucky I was to have them. I'd always been secure in their love.

'Happy Christmas, darling!' Mum's nose and cheeks were growing red with cold. 'Where's Ben?' She looked behind me towards the house.

'Er, Mum, we'll have to take it slowly,' I said, almost whispering. 'He nipped upstairs PDQ when he heard your car pull in. He's still got some issues. Need to take it gently.'

'Of course, love.' My parents looked at each other and nodded in unison as my mother spoke. 'We understand, don't we Geoffrey?'

'Yes, we do.' Dad slapped me on the back, then said, 'come on lad, help me get these things into the house.'

With Toffee at her heel, my mother went into the house and, being Mum, headed straight to the kitchen to put the kettle on. As Tosca ran out into the yard. I heard Mum's cries and ran into the house, throwing my load onto the sofa as I went to her aid.

'Oh, god, no! Mum! Are you okay?'

'Perfectly fine, love. Silly me. Just help me up.' I took her arm and once she was upright, I led her to the sofa and sat her down.

'Take it easy, now. I'll check you over in a minute, when we've got everything out of the car.'

'That's okay, love. I'm just fine. Go and help Dad.'

'Whatever have you done, Sheila?' My father was at the front door.

'Oh, the dog. It was my fault. I shouldn't have gone into the kitchen.'

'Are you hurt?' Dad looked at my mother, then at me.

'I'm fine, Geoffrey, really, don't fuss.'

'Is that all your stuff, now, Dad? Can I shut the door?'

'Yes, that's it. But what about the Dalmatian? He went tearing down the road.'

'Don't worry about him. He'll have gone home. Remember, I told you? I have him some of the time but he belongs to someone else.'

Mother was rubbing her hip.

'Let me take a look at that, Mum,' I said. Bloody hell, Ben's first Christmas with me and my parents and we have this drama.

I took Mother upstairs and helped her to lay on my bed. She was, thankfully, wearing a full skirt that was easy to lift up and I could see that nothing major had occurred. I pressed gently over the area. Mum winced a bit.

'I think you're okay, Mum. But you'll have a lovely bruise there tomorrow, and maybe feel a bit stiff, too.'

'Oh, don't worry, I've got some Arnica in my handbag. I'll put some on and I'll be right as rai —' She was no longer looking at me, but staring at the doorway. 'Oh, and who's this lovely boy?' She pulled down her skirt.

I twisted my head around so quickly that I risked getting whiplash. Ben stood at the door, hugging his woolly lamb.

I held my breath.

Slowly does it.

'Would you like to come in and meet your Grannie, Ben?' I held my hand out to him.

He took one faltering step, then stopped.

'I'm afraid Tosca knocked Grannie over and I was just checking her injuries. Nothing broken.' Mum lay there smiling through eyes that glistened with tears. Toff appeared from nowhere and jumped on the bed. I got up and moved over to my son.

Hunkering down to his level, I looked him straight in the eyes.

'I know it all feels a bit overwhelming, little man,' I said, in a low, soft voice, 'but these are my Mummy and Daddy and they love you as much as they love me and as much as I love you. And it's Christmas Day, so we are going to have lots of fun together.' I put my arms around him and hugged him firmly but gently to me. I kissed him on the forehead. 'Shall we try and say hello to Grannie? Would you like that?'

He looked beyond me to his grandmother. She smiled encouragingly at him and held out a hand, beckoning him to her bedside.

Ben looked at me.

'It's okay, Ben. I promise. Grannie loves you loads and wants to be your friend.'

From under lowered eyelids, he looked first at me and then at my mother, who by now had lowered her hand, swung her legs round and was sitting on the edge of the bed.

My son stepped slowly towards his grandmother. The dog had fallen asleep on the end of the bed, oblivious to the emotional turmoil playing out around him.

Ben took another step and my mother reached out and touched the side of his face.

'What a beautiful boy you are, darling.' She rubbed a thumb over his cheek and with her other arm, folded his small frame into her.

He let her do it, unresisting. Downstairs, I could hear Dad unpacking things in the kitchen. The sound of rustling paper giving the game away that there were lots of Christmas gifts to be opened later. On the bed, the dog stretched out in her sleep and sighed.

Mother stroked Ben's soft, black hair with her fingers. She held him at a slight distance and took his face in her hands once more.

'Happy Christmas, Ben darling. I am so very happy to meet my lovely grandson, at last.'

'Do you like my woolly lamb? My Daddy bought it for me.'

Hetti

On Christmas Day, Oscar made scrambled eggs with real cream, chives and smoked salmon for breakfast. We had Buck's Fizz mixed with lots of orange juice and just a little Prosecco. After breakfast, we exchanged presents from under the tree. Oscar was delighted with his purple scarf, handmade, warm and very cosy. I received a big hug of thanks. The colour was perfect on him. His smile stretched from ear to ear and reached up to his twinkling eyes.

Oscar handed me my present, which came with more warm hugs and kisses on both cheeks. We laughed when I unwrapped the parcel to find a purple woollen hat, with matching scarf and gloves. Shining sequins sparkled on the hat, on the ends of the scarf and around the cuffs of the gloves. When I tried on the gloves, I felt something cylindrical-shaped inside one of them. Curious, I pulled it out to find five-hundred pounds, in fifty-pound notes, rolled up and secured with an elastic band.

'Oscar!' I squeaked. 'Oh, Oscar, you shouldn't have!'

'You deserve it, darling girl. Treat yourself.'

Wearing our new, Christmas woollies, wrapped up warm against the frost and snow we took a gentle walk down the lane.

'Good to walk off the excesses of last night's pudding and this morning's cholesterol-laced breakfast!' Oscar gave a hearty laugh as he clapped and rubbed his hands together.

The frosty, snow-covered fields and hedgerows glistened in the winter sun, looking like a scene from a Christmas card.

People with their dogs and toddlers in strollers, nodding and smiling, wished us good morning and a Happy Christmas.

It was late morning and we made our way back to Wisteria Cottage. Oscar had booked our table at *The Queen's Head* for two o'clock. Plenty of time, but we didn't want to stay out in the cold for too long.

As we arrived at the garden gate, I reached into my coat pocket for the front door key. Snow sprayed around the front garden as a very exuberant Dalmatian tore across the lawn towards us.

'Stay!' I commanded, holding up my hand like a traffic policeman. For once Tosca did as he was told, but only for a second, before he ran towards me, whimpering and licking for all he was worth.

'What's he doing here? Isn't Nathan supposed to be having him today?' Oscar patted the dog, rubbing his ears and shoulders. I looked around the garden and over towards the holiday cottage that was my nearest neighbour. There was a thin line of smoke rising weakly from the chimney. The second-home-owners must have come for Christmas.

'Well, yes, he is, but Tosca has obviously escaped. It's what he does. When he's there, he wants to get back to me and when he's here he scarpers off to Nathan's. I need to take him back, otherwise, what will we do with him when we go out to dinner?'

It was far too cold for him to be tied up outside and I wasn't going to give him the opportunity to wreck the house while I was gone. The shed was no good for him either, because it was full of stuff that he could easily ruin and anyway, it was too cold.

'Come along, then, Dear One. Let's take him to Nathan on our way to lunch.'

'Okay. Let's go.' I took hold of the dog to lead him to the land rover.

Oscar turned to walk towards the side of the house then stopped in his tracks, moved forward and looked down at the snow-covered lawn. He bent his knees to get closer.

'Footprints in the snow.'

'Yes, Oscar. The dog's.'

'No darling. Not *paw*prints. *Foot*prints. Look!' He pointed to a line of indents in the snow that led from the back-garden fence to the window of Wisteria Cottage. The vegetation was so overgrown that, despite the lack of leaves, there was no clear sight of the holiday cottage, apart from the chimney top.

I thought of the number of times that I'd been in the garden and had a feeling that I was being watched, but dismissed the idea as silly fantasy. Now I shuddered again, but it wasn't to do with the chill in the air.

I looked at my watch. We needed to leave immediately.

Nathan

It went better than I ever dreamed it could. Ben was still very quiet, but relaxed and happy in the company of his grandparents. I don't think I'd ever been so proud, not to mention relieved.

Ben opened Christmas presents from Grannie and Grandpops and thanked them politely. He sat on Grandpop's knee and told him, in a very quiet voice, that he had been a "cattle are lowing" in the school nativity play and thought it was better than being a shepherd or Joseph or something like that, because he got to wear a cow's head that he helped Daddy to make.

It was getting close to the time we needed to leave for Christmas lunch in Wymondham.

'Come on Ben, time to get tidied up for going out. Come and wash your hands and face and clean your teeth and then you can put on your new clothes.'

My mother had gone absolutely overboard with new clothes for the boy. She dismissed my admonishment, telling me in no uncertain terms, 'He's my first grandson and as his grandmother I am entitled to spoil him. And it is the first time I've ever been allowed to buy him anything, so there!'

She was right, of course. Mother always is.

I was just helping Ben into his new coat when I heard the familiar engine sound of a certain land rover, as it pulled into the yard. My heart did a little flip, my testosterone levels shot up and my libido immediately went on red-alert.

I left Ben with his Grandpop and opened the door to see Hetti parking the car. The Dalmatian came barrelling towards me.

'Sit! Stay!' He stopped just short of me, no more than a half a metre away.

'Good dog.'

'Hi! You certainly know how to handle dogs, Nathan. Merry Christmas!' Hetti strode across the yard, looking stunning in her signature white skinny jeans, that white fluffy fleece jacket and those red curls of hers bouncing around. She was wearing a bright purple hat with shiny bits on it, matching scarf and gloves. She seemed to be totally unaware of her own sex appeal. Despite the snow and ice and freezing temperatures, I could feel myself getting hot.

Oscar followed behind her, saying, 'A jolly Merry Christmas to you Nathan!' Seeing him had the effect of chucking ice-cold water over my libido. Damn! Why did Hetti have to be so gorgeous and yet so unavailable?

'Merry Christmas, Hetti and Oscar,' I said, nodding to him. I looked back at Hetti. 'It's a white one, too.'

'Yes! My first white Christmas!' She raised her arms, spreading her hands as if to take in the whole scene, did a little pirouette and giggled like a small girl.

'Me too,' I said, smiling. 'Never seen a white Christmas before in my life, not even in Norfolk.'

'Wow. Oh, er, sorry about Tosca. I had to bring him back, because we're going out for lunch and I can't leave him.'

'That's okay. I can put him in his shed, he's fine in there with his blankets and there's a heater too.'

'Like a five-star hotel!'

'Yeah. Well, a five-star dog shed.' They both seemed to think this was hilariously funny for some reason and their laughter rippled around the yard, but the truth was, Tosca had it good in his dog shed. There was heating, lighting, blankets food, drink and dog toys. All the creature comforts a self-respecting Dalmatian could wish for.

Tosca, still sitting where I'd commanded him to stay, watched me very closely. I knew he was waiting for me to let him get up and move his cold backside off the snow.

'Hello. Happy Christmas.' It was Mum at my side, smiling broadly at Hetti.

Oscar stepped forward, took her hand and kissed it. 'And a jolly, happy Christmas to you too, dear lady.' What a charmer. "Dear Lady"? Was this his usual chat up line?

I made the introductions, invited everyone to go inside where it was warm, then took Tosca to his shed. I heard Mum say, 'Actually, we were just getting ready to go out for lunch ourselves.'

Back in the house, Ben was sitting on Dad's knee, having his shoe laces tied, as if not capable of doing it himself, which he most certainly was. He seemed to be lapping up the attention from doting grandparents. It was heart-warming. He looked great in his new trousers, white shirt and bright red, woolly jumper.

Dad's face lit up when he caught sight of Hetti.

She walked over and ruffled Ben's hair. 'Hi Ben. Are you having a lovely Christmas? Looks like you've got lots of presents.' Ben nodded, still clutching his woolly lamb.

Hetti seemed to be looking around the place as if looking for someone or had mislaid something. She saw me watching her, and quickly said, 'Well, it's lovely to meet you, but Oscar and I need to go. We've a table booked at the *Queen's Head*.'

'Really? That's where we're going,' Mum said, a big smile on her face.

'What time is your reservation?' Oscar said.

'Two.' Mum and I said in unison.

'Well, I'm blessed! We have a two o'clock booking too, don't we Hetti? Why don't we all go together?' Oscar would have made a good Santa, I thought, with his white hair, red nose, jolly expression and ample belly. All he needed was the beard and the red suit.

'Yes! What a lovely idea,' said Mum. Dad agreed.

I was torn. While the prospect of spending time with Hetti was very appealing, it was torture to see her with Oscar, knowing they were an item and that so long as he was around, I stood no chance with her.

Ben slid off his Grandpop's knee and took hold of Hetti's hand, ready to leave with her. Seemed that the decision had been made. I nipped upstairs to get my coat and scarf. They were all leaving the house as I came down, Mum and Hetti head-to-head in conspiratorial conversation and Dad carrying Ben across the snow to the Audi. Oscar was already in the land rover.

On the drive home, Ben fell asleep and Mum and Dad chatted about the Christmas meal and how lovely it had been that the day had turned into an impromptu party to include Hetti and Oscar. The pub staff had been very accommodating and happily pushed our tables together to make a table for six.

Ben had sat at the head of the table, like a little lord of the manor.

'I do like Hetti, darling,' Mum said.

'Yes, me too. Lovely girl,' Dad concurred.

'Don't go getting any ideas you two. Hetti is spoken for,' I said, hoping to halt the line of conversation.

'Oh, that's a shame,' said Mum. 'So, where is her boyfriend then? Why didn't he have dinner with her today?'

'He did, Mum. It's Oscar.'

Dad's laughter resonated around the car.

'What's so funny?'

'Nathan, are you completely naïve or just plain blind?' Dad laughed even louder.

'Will you please stop laughing and tell me what's so funny?'

'Haven't you noticed, son?'

'Noticed what?'

'Oscar.'

'What about him?'

'Well, he's as camp as a row of tents!' More hearty laughter.

Dusk had fallen and ahead in my headlights I could just make out the greyish coat of a muntjac deer. I slowed down to let it scuttle across the road. Mum wanted to show Ben the deer, but he was still snoozing, his head dropped forward.

'Well, I know he's a bit limp-wristed, Dad, but they're a couple. It's a fact. I've seen them, holding hands as they walk together and kissing too. And she was distraught when he had that cardiac arrest.' We had discussed Oscar's health over dinner at the Queen's Head, so they knew the story and again Oscar had praised my quick actions in performing CPR, making my parents very proud. 'And if you must know, Hetti told me herself that he is her world.'

Mum reached forward from the back seat of the car and touched my shoulder. I glanced at my rear-view mirror. Ben was still asleep.

'Nathan, darling, Oscar is Hetti's godfather.'

'Godfather?'

WTF?

'How do you know that?' Each word came out in an octave higher than the previous one.

'They told me. It was when you took Ben to the toilet in the pub. I asked how they'd met and Hetti told me that she'd known Oscar all her life and that he was her godfather. It's true, Nathan. Really, it is.'

Have you ever felt like a total dickhead and yet utterly elated at the same time?

No?

I have.

65

Hetti

2019

Late February. Snowdrops peeked through the ground and the sun tried to shine for at least a few minutes a day. Spring was just around the corner. The winter would be gone in no time and we could look forward to some long, warm summer's days.

I'd joined he choir and every Tuesday we met at a local hall to rehearse *Faure's Requiem*, for our Easter concert, which we were to perform in the Abbey. Tess, the musical director, had been right when she'd approached me at the carol singing at Wymondham Christmas Fayre. They really were a friendly group of choristers and I felt uplifted every week as I went home after rehearsal. It was good for me to get out and meet new people who didn't know about Daniel.

I'd been working for Miss Higgins for a couple of months and although she was a stickler when it came to standards of cleanliness, she was happy with my efforts. Actually, she was really quite nice, once you started to get to know her.

I was cleaning her oven one day when my phone pinged in my pocket. Removing my rubber gloves, I looked at the screen of my iPhone.

I didn't recognise the number. I wondered if it was Daniel, getting in touch to threaten me in some way. Oscar and I had plastered Daniel's photo all over Facebook, along with our mobile numbers and a request that people share until it went viral and to contact one of us direct if they had any information. I did worry that if, or rather when he found out he'd come looking for me to do me harm. With a rapidly beating heart, I opened the message.

Hi Hetti, I've seen your man. He's left Norwich for his own safety. I might know where he is. Call me if you want more info. A friend.

With a rapidly beating heart, I shoved the phone back in my pocket and returned to the task of scrubbing away at Miss Higgins' oven with all my might.

A friend. They'd signed the message: 'A friend' — but if this was a friend, well, why didn't they identify themselves so that I'd know who they were?

I finished the cleaning, picked up my wages from Miss Higgins and left. Once outside, I called Oscar.

'But darling girl, you must go to the police immediately.'

'What if it's a hoax, or a trick for Daniel to find me?'

'That is exactly why you must take this to the police Hetti, my love. They will be able to trace that number, get onto that person and find Daniel.'

I called into Wymondham police headquarters on my way home. A police officer made a note of all the information I gave her and said someone would be in touch.

Two days later, Tosca barked excitedly as we heard a car on the drive. I answered the door to two police officers, an older man and the same young woman that I'd spoken to at the station the day that I received the anonymous message.

'Have you got news?' My heart beat like a drum with the anticipation of what they had come to tell me. 'Have you found Daniel?'

'Can we come inside for a moment please, love?' PC Sheryl Conway's demeanour made it perfectly clear to me that there was something very serious afoot.

I stood aside to let them in and Tosca, who had been barking enthusiastically, came bounding towards the two officers.

'Tosca! Sit!' He actually did as he was told, much to my surprise. Why was it that whenever Nathan gave an order, the dog obeyed? With me, it was still hit and miss.

'Would you like to sit down, Hetti?' PC Sheryl asked, softly. A terrible sense of foreboding came over me. I knew for sure that what she was about to tell me was not going to be happy news. Had Daniel been found? Was he dead? Or alive and spending my money, living the high life in some exotic location?

I sat on the sofa.

'Are you alone, Hetti?' The older man looked around the room. What was he looking for? Some secret lover to come bouncing out of a cupboard and run out of the house naked?

'Yes. Why?'

PC Sheryl spoke gently. 'I'm afraid we have some bad news for you, Hetti.'

66

Nathan

Spring, 2019

Very soon, the ewes would be ready to lamb. They were still out grazing in the field and I kept an eye on them every day. March was drawing to a close and the lambs would be born early April. Excited at the prospect of baby lambs being born, Ben rode his bike along the lane at the weekends whenever I took him with me to the field. He was slowly, but surely growing in confidence and was speaking more too. He wasn't the most verbose of kids, and when he did speak, his voice was very quiet, but I was relieved that he seemed to be leaving behind the selective mutism gig.

I'd read widely on what the different experts said about selective mutism in children, hoping to find an insight into my son's reluctance to speak. But it seems that the causes of selective mutism are unknown. Not much help there then. Doctors did agree though, that children with the condition tended to suffer from a lot of anxiety, although, with others it seems that there was no logical reason at all for their refusal to speak.

I'd turned myself inside out, trying to think what could have happened to my son to cause his selective mutism, but in the end, I knew that I had to just let it go. Nothing, no researching, analysing or digging into his past would change things. All I could do was to give him all the love and security that he needed and hope that whatever memories he held would fade and never return.

I drove him to school one Monday morning in late March and watched him as he walked into the playground. He happily joined in the chat with the quieter members of his class. Ben was still unready to engage with the more rumbustious of kids. But that was okay. Slowly does it; you can't rush these things.

I watched as Miss Abbot stood supervising the children entering the school building. She looked over to me and I raised a hand in greeting. She nodded and smiled. Things were good. I was relieved that there had been no further disagreements with Ben's teacher, after the time that she'd suggested he must be missing his mother. I'd still, in all these months, had no word from Mandy, despite my regular update texts, which always went unanswered. But hey, perhaps I preferred it that way. Ben didn't seem to be suffering from the lack of a mother's love in his life. Says a lot about Mandy's mothering skills.

Walking back to the car, I heard the clip-clop of stiletto heels as one of the yummy mummies rushed along the pavement to catch up with me. I glanced briefly sideways at her. She was petite, with a blonde bob and an ample set of boobs that she took pride in showing off to full advantage.

'Morning, Tracey.' I carried on, looking straight ahead, striding purposefully towards my car.

'Nathan! Good morning! How are you?'

'Fine, thanks,' I said, without looking at her.

'I've made chicken cacciatore — way too much as usual — would you like some? I could —'

I carried on walking. 'Very kind, but no thanks, Tracey. I have plenty of food in the house.'

'Oh, it's no trouble, Nathan. I could pop round with it this afternoon, if you like.'

I stopped and faced her.

'Tracey, like I said, it's very kind of you, but it is also quite unnecessary. I have plenty of food in the house and I know how to cook a half-decent meal for my son and myself. So, please, don't go to any trouble on my account.' I nodded at her, turned away and in three steps was at my car.

I drove off without a backward glance.

I had animals to see to.

It felt good to be alive as I cruised along the lane to check on the ewes. The sky was covered in white, fluffy clouds with a little bit of blue sky doing its best to poke its way through. Now the weak sun shone through the windscreen and I reached into the side of the driver's door to find my shades.

I thought back to Tracey. Once upon a time I'd have had no hesitation in accepting her offer of afternoon sex. There's something very enjoyable about having a woman as sexually enthusiastic as Tracey to satisfy the male libido and no strings attached. Well, at one time, a lot of years ago, I would have jumped at the chance. But that was before... I kicked the memory into touch. That was before I met Erin. And anyway, these days I was more interested in Hetti than any of the mothers of Ben's classmates. I needed to man-up and ask her out, now that I knew she was single and not tied up with Oscar. It was easier said than done though, after all these years as a celibate and anyway, I had Ben to think about. I wasn't going to leave him with a babysitter while I went out on a date.

I pulled in by the side of the field and got out of the car. There was something in the air that unsettled me now, but I couldn't think what. I cast my eyes around the field. Most of the sheep — I knew them by sight and could identify each and every one of them — were huddled in the corner, close to the ditch. I counted them, feeling that something was amiss. There was one ewe not accounted for. I walked along the ditch that ran parallel to the field, looking for a stranded stray ewe. Hetti sprang to mind; the first time I'd met her she'd rescued an injured sheep that had fallen into the ditch.

The thought of Hetti always had the same effect on me. I wanted her. God, how I wanted her. I was over the moon to discover that she and Oscar were not a couple. What a total idiot I'd been, thinking that those two were in a relationship. As if! I felt a familiar stirring in the very spot that any thought of Hetti Lewis always hit.

I reached the bridge over the ditch and bent down to look into it. Something caught my eye.

Moving closer, my Wellington boots sank into the soft undergrowth as I stepped down the embankment and into the water to get a closer look.

Oh god, no.

67

Hetti

A unty Pat was dead.
    'Is there someone you can call, Hetti?' PC Sheryl's voice
was soft and gentle. I was sitting on the sofa. Stunned. 'Hetti?'
    'Pardon?' I was having trouble taking it in and missed
what she'd asked.
    'Can you call someone, love? You don't want to be on your
own after news like this.'
    Oscar. I would call Oscar. Later.
    'What happened? How did my aunt…?' I looked from her to
the window. Tosca, sitting at my feet, put a paw on my lap,
his head cocked to one side as if asking me what was wrong.
    'Well, apparently she had been feeling unwell since
Christmas, but carried on as normal.'
    'I invited her for Christmas. She didn't want to come.' Oh,
poor Aunt Pat. She must have been feeling too ill to travel
and made the excuse that she didn't want to drive in the
snow. I looked back at PC Sheryl. 'So, why didn't she get
better? What was wrong with her?'
    'We don't know. There'll have to be a post-mortem
examination. She was found by her cleaning lady yesterday
morning, lying at the bottom of the stairs. I'm so sorry, love.'
    'At the bottom of the stairs? Had she fallen down? Down
the stairs?' The thought of dear old Aunty Pat lying there for
god knows how long, alone, probably in pain and frightened
was too much to bear and I started to cry.
    'Try not to upset yourself, Hetti. Shall I make you a cup
of tea?'
    The good old British answer to all crises. Make the tea.
    'No thanks. I'll be alright. I'm going to phone my godfather.'

The funeral was supposed to be a quiet affair but just about
everyone in the north Norfolk village attended. The little
church was packed and some people made do by standing
outside, despite the cold. I'd never seen so many flowers as
there were lying around the graveside and the smell was

exquisite. A carpet of colour, bright and vibrant, spread around the mound of soil that covered my aunt's coffin.

Mr Lambert, the solicitor taking care of Aunty Pat's affairs attended the service. Leaving the church, he discreetly handed me an envelope. He shook my hand, then Oscar's, raised his hat and said goodbye.

We had arranged to have a lunch afterwards in the village pub. It was a small party: Oscar and me, and four close friends of Pat's. During the afternoon, people popped into the pub to offer condolences and pay their respects. Before today, I'd had no idea now popular my Aunt Pat had been. Oscar and I stayed all afternoon, being greeted by people who had known and loved my dear old Aunt. It was touching to see so many people who had remembered her taking me into her home as an orphaned child, and bringing me up as her own. Their faces still recognisable, if a little worn with the years.

'Was my aunt alone on Christmas Day,' I asked one woman who told me that she and Pat had been best friends since they were at primary school. I vaguely remembered her face, but couldn't recall her name.

'Well, that was the thing. We thought she was coming to you, dear, that's what she said. But then, she didn't go. It wasn't until after New Year that I realised she'd been at home on her own all that time. I think she was too proud to let anyone know she hadn't been feeling well. She was very independent.'

It was a mini stroke; the post-mortem examination had found. That would have made her unfit to travel to Wymondham. A couple of months later she had a massive stroke, fell down the stairs, banged her head and died instantly.

Once Oscar and I were on the train home, I took the envelope out of my bag.

'It's an invitation to hear the will being read,' I said, handing the paper to my godfather.

Three days later, as I sat in Mr Lambert's office in Cromer, I found out that Aunty Pat had left me the house where she had raised me from the age of seven. Sums of money had been bequeathed to the village church roof fund, to cancer research, the British Heart Foundation, to the local children's charity and the British Refugee Council.

She also left me all the rest of the money that she had in the bank. After the payment of outstanding bills, fees and expenses, I was left with close to a quarter of a million pounds.

The news staggered me. Aunty Pat had always been so frugal, despite giving me a good childhood and providing everything a girl could possibly need.

I silently thanked Aunty Pat, wherever she might be resting and vowed not to let the likes of Daniel Jones get his thieving hands on even a penny of it.

68

Nathan

The ewe's throat had been slashed. Her dead lamb lay, covered in bloody effluvia, beside its mother. It had been cut out of the belly of the pregnant ewe.

I tried to move the two dead animals out from under the bridge and their blood flowed freely into the ditch water.

Running back to the car, I jumped in, grabbed my mobile and called the police.

The Wymondham plods were there in no time. The area was cordoned off and guys in hooded overalls picked over the scene and took stuff away in sealed plastic bags.

By the time I'd finished with interviews and statements at the police headquarters it was time to pick up Ben from school.

Seeing my son coming out of the school gate was the best thing that had happened since I'd dropped him off that morning.

'Shall we go for a cake in town before we go home?' I'd had one hell of a day and fancied a bit of relaxation, a cup of tea and something to make up for having missed lunch.

Ben nodded vigorously. He was developing quite an appetite for *Mad Hatters* homemade cake and I made a mental note to keep a check on his sugar levels.

He climbed into his car seat, I buckled him in, planted a kiss on his cheek, then jumped into the driver's seat and off we went.

'Daddy?'

'Yes, son?'

'Can we go swimming again soon? It's indoors so it won't be cold, will it?' I was taken aback by his fluency of speech.

'Sure, we can do that.' I was glad he seemed keen. 'Perhaps at the weekend. Let's see how things go.' I saw him through the rear-view mirror, nodding his acceptance. A little smile played across his face.

It was only a couple of minutes to the town centre. We had less than an hour before the tea shop closed for the day, so

I parked in the central car park and we walked briskly up the hill. Ben held my hand for a while before letting go and skipping ahead.

A flock of pigeons took flight over Market Cross. That's when I saw her. That unmistakable, glorious hair. That slender body. Those tight little buttocks at the top of long, skinny legs. She was wearing a short, red skirt, thick, black tights and flat-heeled ankle boots. It was still not warm enough to go without a coat and she had on the white fluffy jacket that I'd seen her in before and the purple sparkly scarf. The matching hat and gloves were gone.

69

Hetti

I'd been out of touch with all my girlfriends since Daniel had done a runner last summer. In fact, the last time I'd seen them was the night before I'd discovered Daniel's betrayal; I'd stayed the night at Louise's place after our girls' night out and gone from there straight to the appointment at the bank. It was now late March and I'd ignored all of their attempts to contact me. So, it had been months and months since I'd spent any time with Jessie and Louise and Izzie. I'd been so ashamed and embarrassed about what Daniel had done that I couldn't face anyone. Not one of them had ever been happy about my choice of boyfriend. If ever we bumped into them, which was rare, he'd be distant with them and moody and always made up some excuse as to why we had to hurry along. Individually, each of them had voiced their opinion. They concurred, variously that, 'He's a loser, Hetti.' 'He's so moody.' 'He's right up himself.' 'What do you see in him?' 'You can do better than that.' And, yes, now there was that little bit of self-pride, which made me want to avoid hearing them say, 'I told you so' to my face.

Oscar, as always, was right. He told me now, in no uncertain terms, that ghosting my friends was out of order, rude, totally unacceptable and that it would serve me right if they all told me where to get off. But added that I should contact them anyway. I picked up the phone, took a deep breath and called them one at a time.

'Splendid, darling!' Oscar was delighted to hear later that day that not Jessie, nor Louise, nor Izzie had rejected my call. Every one of them was happy to hear from me. Very contrite, I'd explained the reason for my silence. But they already knew, because they'd seen it on Facebook and had shared the hell out of my post every day since they'd seen it. Much to my surprise, and totally in contrast to what I felt I deserved, they were sympathetic and supportive and revelled in thoughts of what they'd like to do to Daniel Jones (all of which involved deadly and painful instruments like red hot pokers and various unmentionable regions of his body) if ever they came face-to-face with him again. In no time at all we were arranging to meet up for a girls' evening out in Norwich.

The following afternoon, I went into *Hemlock's* Jewellers in Wymondham and bought three different sets of necklaces with matching earrings. I'd seen them displayed in the window the week before and went back to get them as presents for my three besties. The grey-haired assistant gift wrapped each boxed set with a lovely, sparkly ribbon giving the perfect finishing touch.

With a spring in my step, I walked with my purchases in my bag up Market Street, towards the station to take the train to Norwich. A familiar figure sat on a bench on Market Cross, talking into his mobile phone. His waist length hair fell in a pony tail around his shoulders. With his free hand, he was gesticulating as if the caller could see him. He looked anguished and very upset. His body language spoke volumes. As I got closer, I saw, just as I had thought, that it was the waiter from the Thai restaurant. The call ended and now he sat with his head in his hands, looking tormented.

'Hello there. It's Chaiyuth, isn't it?'

He looked up at me. 'Hello, madam.' He smiled through his sadness.

'Are you okay?' He was wringing his hands now.

'I'm okay, *krup* madam.'

'My name is Hetti. Please, you don't have to call me "madam". And anyway, I don't think you are okay. You look a bit sad to me,' I said, sitting down next to him. 'Would you like to talk about it?'

'It's my girlfriend. She English student at university. I take final exams this year and then I go back to Thailand. But she want me stay here in England with her.'

'And what do you want to do, Chaiyuth?'

'I have to go back Thailand and get job. Be lawyer. Or lecturer in university. I cannot stay in England.'

'But, if you didn't have to do that, would you want to stay in England, with your girlfriend?'

'No.' He looked at me and shook his head when he said it, pretty emphatically.

'Well, there is nothing else to it, then, is there? When you have finished your exams, you will go back to Thailand.'

'Girlfriend very angry with me. She doesn't understand.'

'What doesn't she understand, Chaiyuth?'

'I cannot have visa to stay in England. My student visa will end when I have finished my exams. So, I cannot stay, even if I wanted to.'

'Why doesn't she understand that?'

'She does understand that.'

Now I was confused. He'd just told me the girlfriend didn't understand; now, apparently, she does.

'I don't think I understand, now, Chaiyuth. Are you saying that she does understand, or that she doesn't?'

'She understands about the visa. That I must go back to Thailand. But she want me to stay. For me to stay in England, she says she will marry me. Her family have much money. Very rich, by Thai standards. My family not rich. Medium poor. I have to work. Help my family.' He looked at me with sad, dark brown, almond shaped eyes. 'I don't want marry with her. I want to go home to my country and work. I am a proud Thai man, *Khun* Hetti. I don't want to be married and certainly not for money or visa. That is what she doesn't understand.'

Well, that was pretty clear, I'd say.

'I think you should do what you want, Chaiyuth. Your girlfriend sounds pretty selfish to me. You're a lovely guy and you deserve better than that.' Here I was, passing on the wisdom of my own mistakes, like some old sage.

'You think this of me?' He was smiling but his eyes filled with tears. I took his hand and held it in both of mine.

'Yes, I do,' I said, looking straight into his eyes. 'And I am sure there are lots of lovely Thai girls in your home country. You could choose anyone.'

Suddenly, the sadness and tension in his expression was gone and Chaiyuth smiled with the whole of his face. I touched his face with my thumbs and wiped the tears from his cheeks. We laughed together now. He put his hands together in prayer position. The *wai*, as the Thai people call it.

I got up to leave and he stood up too. We hugged and his hair tickled my face. I'd never seen such long hair on a guy before. It reached his waist.

'What will you do with all this hair when you're a hotshot lawyer in

Thailand?'

Chaiyuth laughed. 'I will have to cut it short and be a smart gentleman!'

We both laughed at this and I started walking towards the station to take my train.

Over my shoulder, I waved and said, 'Hope to see you again before you leave England, my friend.'

'Yes, yes! Please come back to the restaurant, *Khun* Hetti.'

I turned to see Nathan walking on the other side of the road, Ben skipping a metre or two ahead of him. I lifted my arm and waved.

'Hey Nathan!'

He completely blanked me.

Nathan

Damn it! She did have a bloke after all. They were standing there canoodling in the middle of Market Cross. In broad daylight too. My heart sank to my boots. Just as the day was looking up, my mood came crashing down again.

'Come on, Daddy. We're here. Let's get cake!'

Ben took my hand and led me into the tea shop. I pulled myself together and ruffled Ben's hair. 'Yup! Cake here we come!'

It was already dark and I sat on the sofa with a cup of tea. Ben had been worn out and was in the Land of Nod as soon as his head touched the pillow, his white, fluffy lamb tucked into the crook of his arm.

Evenings were still cold and I'd lit the fire.

What a day. Started off well enough but went downhill very quickly. Finding the slaughtered sheep was disturbing to say the least. Then, seeing Hetti with another guy, I was so jealous and pissed off that I didn't speak or even return her wave. Not proud of that. Behaved like a sulky brat. Get a grip Nate. But I must have misread all the signs, because I really thought that we were starting to be a little more friendly with each other, especially after the Christmas lunch and having to see each other because of sharing Dalmatian duties.

A knock at the door interrupted my thoughts and as I went to open it, I saw the lights of a police car through the window.

'Hi.'

'Mr Brookes?'

'Yeah. What's it about? The sheep?'

'I'm afraid it is. There's been another killing.'

'Another one?' Didn't see that coming. I thought they were coming to tell me they'd made an arrest.

'A dog walker reported that he found a dead sheep. It's one of yours and it's obvious that it's been killed the same way that the other one was.'

'Shit. Who could be doing this?'

'Got any enemies, sir?'

'What?' Frantic thoughts were tearing around in my brain.

'Sorry. We have to ask. This looks very much like revenge attacks.'

'I don't know of anyone, anyone at all who would want to do such a thing.'

'No one with a grudge, then?'

'No. Well, not as far as I know. I don't make it a habit of going around making enemies. Keep myself to myself, usually. I've got my son living with me. He's only six. I have quite a lot on my plate, what with looking after him and running the smallholding. I don't have that much to do with locals, but I haven't fallen out with anybody.'

'Okay, Mr Brookes. We advise you to keep everything as secure as you can. Make sure the sheep are out of the field at night and think about installing CCTV in your yard. You need to be vigilant. Don't take any chances.'

I got hold of Jed Bailey and gave him the news. He organised a couple of guys to come over and help me get the sheep into the safety of the bigger barn in the yard, where I left them during the colder nights of winter. Jed's daughter came to sit with Ben, who was still fast asleep, so that I could go out. It was dark and that impeded our work.

I counted the animals in the shed. There was one missing. I counted again, thinking I'd made a mistake, but it turned out I was right first time.

The babysitter had left, so I couldn't leave the house to go back and search the field.

That night my sleep was disturbed by dreams of dead sheep and dead lambs.

And my dead baby daughter.

The following morning, immediately after dropping off Ben at school, I drove down to the field. With a sinking feeling at my very core, I searched for the missing sheep. I knew the worst before I even found her. The ewe's throat was ripped open and, just like the other two, her lamb lay lifeless beside her.

The police arrived within fifteen minutes and once again my field became a crime scene, cordoned off and guys wearing anti-contamination gear as they searched for forensic evidence.

What sick bastard was doing this?

Hetti

Well, that was weird. I was sure he'd seen me. He was looking straight at me when I waved. I thought we'd become friends. I mean, we were sharing looking after the dog and he'd willingly bought the special food that Dalmatians need and had been really good at training him. Tosca was much better behaved these days. And Nathan Brookes had saved my godfather's life, for heaven's sakes! For that I would owe him a debt of gratitude for the rest of my life.

Then Oscar and I had had Christmas lunch with Nathan and Ben and the grandparents. His dad was lovely and I got on really well with his mum, too. As we were leaving Nathan's house for Christmas lunch, I'd asked her, discreetly, where Ben's mum was. I'd actually expected to see her that day and was surprised that there was no woman, other than Sheila Brookes, in the house. As we'd walked across the yard, she'd told me in hushed tones, a bowed head inclined towards me, that the woman was, 'no longer on the scene, dear. And jolly good riddance, too.'

I'd received the information with a mixture of intrigue and pleasure.

'Not that she was ever very much on the scene,' Sheila Brookes had continued, 'bit of a trollop, between you and me.'

'Oh,' I'd said, 'that was rather sad,' but something inside me knew, perfectly well, that I didn't find it sad at all, even though I knew I should have.

'No, my dear. Ben is better off here with his daddy.' And she gave me a little conspiratorial wink. 'He doesn't need a mother like that.'

Nathan was growing on me. Yes, I admit it; he was. But I was still smarting from Daniel's utter betrayal and was in no hurry, I firmly told myself, to get involved with a man again, any time soon.

And now, I thought, as I hopped on the train to meet my friends, Jessie, Louise and Izzy for long overdue evening out in Norwich, it was just as well that I didn't get involved with Nathan Brookes, if he's the sort of guy who will just cut you dead in the street.

70

Nathan

'Nat'an Brookes?'

Even after all these years, I couldn't forget the sound of that unmistakable Irish reflection in her voice. I turned around slowly and there she stood at the entrance to the yard. My mouth felt as dry as sawdust and my heart pounded in my chest, like heavy rain thrumming down on a taut tent. The blood chilled in my veins.

'You are Nat'an Brookes, aren't you?'

She moved closer. A cold wind whipped around the yard, despite the mild, sunny spring afternoon.

I seemed to have lost the power of speech. I nodded.

'Sure, y'are. Nat'an Brookes. To be sure, I'd know you anywhere.' That familiar Irish lilt, returning from long ago.

I froze. All these years...

Erin.

It was Erin, but not Erin. Well, not my Erin. My Erin was the same build, height, the same beautiful, tawny hair, the facial features indistinguishable — but the eyes... Those eyes of Erin's — my Erin's — were unique. They would twinkle and shine like exquisite emerald stars on a dark night.

The eyes that looked at me now were cold, dark and filled with hate. It was as though a pernicious alien being had somehow managed to inhabit the body of the woman I'd loved for so long.

'Speak up, Nat'an Brookes. Anyone would think you'd seen a ghost!'

And I thought I had.

I really thought I had.

'I see you went ahead and had another child, then? After the babby girl died? A boy, right? I've seen him. Seen you taking him to school. Taking him out on his bike. Taking him to see the sheep.'

The grip of fear and foreboding shot through my whole body. She'd seen Ben? Watched us from afar? Stalked us?

'How...? How did...?' I couldn't get the words out.

'How what? *What?* How did I find you after all these years? Well, let me tell you, Nat'an Brookes,' that Irish accent laced through with a good deal of menace and threat, 'not too difficult once I asked around the village.'

She'd mentioned the sheep. My blood ran cold.

'I've been watching you from afar. Watching and waiting.'

I found my voice. 'What do you want?'

Whatever it was, I was scared witless. I'd never seen a pair of eyes as wild and unnerving as those that held me in this woman's glare.

She laughed. It wasn't a laugh of mirth. No. This laugh was vile, like some villainous character in a horror movie. A bitter, malicious laugh that seemed to echo around the yard.

An image of Ben sprang into my mind. 'Please, I don't want any trouble —'

I took a step towards her.

'Trouble? Of course, you don't, Nat'an Brookes. Sure, you're a coward, aren't you? A spineless invertebrate.' She spat out each syllable like poison spewing from the mouth of a snake. 'But we can make this easy for you.'

I stopped dead on the spot. Unable to move. I had to force my mouth to start. 'What do you mean? Make what easy?'

She reached for her jacket pocket and produced a flick knife. The blade shot out and shone in the sunlight. My jaw dropped and I could feel my guts plummeting to the ground.

'Hey, look. Hang on a minute—' She interrupted me with that menacing laugh of hers that reverberated around the yard.

'You know that cuddly little ewe of yours out there in the field? The one that your boy is so fond of? Well, I thought to myself, why should it have an offspring and live to rear it when you,' she moved closer and held the knife in front of my face, waved it about as she spoke, 'when you impregnated my twin sister,' she hissed the words like a venomous cobra, 'and then stood and watched both Erin and the babby die, eh?'

She spat in my face. I tried to wipe saliva away with my shirt sleeve. I don't know why I didn't do what any normal person would have done and get the hell out of it, but it was like my feet had taken root. I started to tremble. The first trigger sign of my PTSD.

'And then I thought,' she continued in a sing-song voice, her tone rising and falling, 'why should any of the other ewes enjoy their lives and their little lambs? So, I slit the throat of another and another. It was very satisfying.'

'Wh — what?' My knees shook. My heart pumped so fast I could almost feel the blood coursing through my veins. My hands were sweaty and clammy. The image of my baby girl, laying in my hand, shot to the forefront of my mind.

'Oh, yes. Very satisfying.'

I was horrified, revolted, incredulous and absolutely terrified in equal measures. I just could not believe what I was hearing. This crazy woman had actually come all the way from Ireland, after all these years, to accuse me of killing Erin, the one and only love of my life and our baby daughter, then threaten to kill Ben and me. I could hardly find my voice.

'Wh - what?'

'Stop feckin' saying "what", you wet bastard!' She was shouting now. 'You killed Erin and her babby.'

She made the sign of the cross in front of her chest. 'May the Lord bless them and keep them in his love.' I kid you not, she actually crossed herself and sent up a prayer while holding a knife to my neck and threatening to kill me. You couldn't make this crap up.

'Now I'm going to repay the compliment. Reciprocity, right? An eye for an eye. That's what the Holy Bible says. An eye for an eye and a tooth for a tooth. Hah!' Was she actually quoting the fucking bible at me in the same breath as threatening to murder my son and me? My baby girl's little face came back to me. The trembling got worse. I started to sweat. My skin felt clammy.

'I'll see to your son first,' she said, and then, when you've watched him suffer and die before your very eyes, like you did Erin and her bastard wain, I'll deal with you.' Her words were measured; her voice frighteningly composed.

'No, please, leave my son alone. Don't hurt him. You'll regret it if you hurt one hair of my son's head.'

Áine Byrne took a step closer and touched the jugular vein in my neck with the very tip of the knife's blade. I took a sharp intake of breath.

'And then I'll see to your woman, the redhead.'

Hetti

Spring 2019

April heralded a hint of spring and choir was all of a frenzy, trying to get the performance perfected for the upcoming concert in the Abbey. Evenings were lighter and there was a little more warmth in the air.

I'd heard nothing more from the author of the anonymous text, so presumably the police were on the case. They'd taken my phone to check the log and I got it back twenty-four hours later. Oscar had lent me an old phone with a pay-as-you-go SIM to use in case of emergencies. Funnily enough, it was quite nice to be away from social media for a few hours. Who says millennials are glued to their phones?

The spring-like weather prompted me to take the Dalmatian from Nathan's, where he'd been camped out for a couple of days, and go for a walk along the Tiffey river. Before I left, I posted a message on Facebook, reminding friends about the concert in the Abbey that night.

Things had been a little cool between Nathan and me since the day he'd blanked me in the street. What the hell had that been about? I mean, we'd been friendly enough since Christmas, so why the sudden change? Talk about capricious!

I'd taken to jogging along the riverbank, while Tosca trotted alongside me on the lead. Today would be the perfect day for it. He was slightly better behaved these days. After the exercise, I'd go for a drink. Somewhere dog-friendly. Not the *Mad Hatters*. The memory of the scalding incident was still never far away from my mind. We walked down Church Street, where I'd bought the Christmas tree — that day seemed like an age ago now — and sat outside at the *Green Dragon*. I ordered a lemonade and lime cordial and the barman brought a bowl of water for the dog.

'Looks like you could both do with a long, cool drink,' he said. 'Been for a jog?' He was tall, slender and wore his blond hair cropped short.

'Yes.' I handed him the money for the drinks. 'We went along the Tiffey riverside. One of my favourite places.'

'Are you from around here? Not seen you before. I'm sure I'd remember a striking-looking girl like you.'

I felt myself blush. Not used to being chatted up and this was definitely a chat-up line, if ever I heard one.

'No, not really. Grew up in north Norfolk, but originally from Sussex.' I patted Tosca on the back. 'I'm dog sitting this one while his owner is away travelling.'

'Nice one –'

'Simon, will you stop chatting up the women and clear these glasses in here?' The middle-aged woman stood with her arms folded across her chest, meaning business. 'You're here to work, in case you'd forgotten!'

'Sorry — gotta go.' He winked and was gone.

I smiled to myself and took a long drink.

Back at Wisteria Cottage, I tied Tosca to his gazebo and went into the kitchen to make a lasagne for dinner. The choir's concert was that evening and I needed to eat dinner early. Oscar was at home in Norwich, but he promised that he'd be at the Abbey to hear me sing with the choir. I'd got used to seeing more of him and missed him when he was away from the cottage. I'd bought a folding put-you-up bed in one of Wymondham's many charity shops, so that when Oscar stayed overnight, I could be more comfortable than I had been sleeping on cushions on the floor.

Losing my beloved aunt was still raw; I found myself remembering things that we had done together when I was growing up. She really had been a good guardian to me and I missed her terribly now, even though we hadn't seen much of each other in the last couple of years, we'd kept in regular touch by phone. Recalling the funeral and the huge turnout of villagers reminded me of what a force for good Miss Pat Lewis had been.

I was still reeling from the shock of the huge sum of money that she'd left me in her will. The house was less surprising. I knew there was no one else that she could leave it to. And I had no idea what I would do about the house, but Oscar had advised me to take my time and not rush into anything. I had to admit, though, that it was good to have a few quid in the bank so that I didn't have to worry about money these days. I'd kept my job though, cleaning for Miss Higgins, even found myself looking forward to my visits three times a week.

Daniel's betrayal still loomed large in my mind and I was determined not to let things go until he'd been found and brought to justice. The police had been very quiet about the case. Whenever I enquired, I was told firmly that investigations were ongoing.

As I started gathering the ingredients for that evening's meal, I heard Tosca whimpering and barking. Sometimes he did that when the postman arrived, and in which case I would ignore him, but for some unfathomable reason, this time I felt compelled to go and check things out.

The dog was straining on the leash, trying to make for the garden fence that separated the Wisteria Cottage from the holiday let cottage nearby. I could hear that familiar rustling of undergrowth and vegetation from where such noises had come on earlier occasions.

'Hello? Is anybody there?' I walked towards the fence.

No reply, but footsteps hurrying away.

I'd forgotten about the footprints in the snow episode, but now it came back to me. Who the hell was this person? Why did they keep spying on me? I shivered. It couldn't be Daniel, could it?

Back in the kitchen, I prepared the ingredients and layered the lasagne dish, alternating the filling with the pasta sheets, then sprinkled the cheese on top and put it on top of the cooker ready to bake in the oven later.

I tidied up the kitchen, finished the salad, covered it and left it in the fridge. I nipped upstairs and laid out my clothes for the concert. Downstairs, I set the timer on my phone for five minutes before the cooking time would be up and popped the lasagne in the oven. Locking up the cottage, I untied Tosca and walked him back to Nathan's place. I had just enough time to drop the dog off and get back before dinner was ready.

Nathan

Jesus Christ. This mad woman was actually Erin's twin? Unbelievable. They had surely not shared space in the same womb? Erin and she were the total antithesis of each other. The pure gold and the pure evil. The light and the dark. I don't mind telling you, I was absolutely bricking it. Had I been the religious type I'd have been on my knees praying. But I wasn't; so, I didn't. And anyway, it would have been a bit tricky trying to sink to the ground while this lunatic held a knife to my neck. So, I just stood there with trembling legs, transfixed, scared for my life, but, more so, that of my son. Thankfully, he was safe at school. For now.

I tried to regulate my breathing, a technique I was taught after the PTSD diagnosis, following the loss of Erin and the baby. Slowly, breathing in; slowly, breathing out. And repeat. And repeat. Terror turned to sheer anger.

'You know what?' I began, as I started to feel the bile rise to my throat. I spoke with a clenched jaw; my words slow and deliberate. 'I didn't kill Erin. And I sure as fuck didn't kill our sweet baby daughter, either.' As I uttered the word "daughter" I felt my voice crack and tears gathering behind my eyes. The memory of her tiny, lifeless body lying in the palm of my hand had haunted me for all these years. Who the hell was this psychotic bitch to intrude on my grief? For five years I'd been reliving the nightmare of that day in the hospital, emotionally destroyed over the loss of my beautiful Erin and our sweet little girl. I should never have left her alone in the ward, while I went to feed my bloody face. The nurses had told me — insisted — that I go and get some breakfast. Promised she'd be fine with them. That they would take care of her. When I'd got back to the ward, her bed was empty and stripped bare. My poor Erin had died alone. With no one there to hold her hand or kiss her goodbye. And I'd never recovered from the guilt of having left her just so that I could take sustenance into my own body while the life in Erin's was slipping away. I could never forgive myself.

But it wasn't me who killed Erin. Erin died because she gave her kidney to save the life of this bloody psycho standing in front of me now and that was the cause of her death. That and a screwed up dogmatic religion that denied a woman the human right of contraception and that proscribed sex before marriage. Sex before marriage was not a joyful expression of love; oh no. To their twisted reasoning, it was a mortal sin, punishable by hell and eternal damnation. Erin had been indoctrinated with that crap, so no wonder she dare not let her parents find out that she even had a boyfriend, let alone

had been taking the pill. Erin had died of complications —
eclampsia — after a pregnancy and a birth that occurred
too soon after the live donor transplant. A procedure I knew
nothing about until it was too late. My lovely, warm Erin and
our baby should still be here with me, alive, vital, warm. Not
dead, buried, cold, in the ground. It was this evil cow who
should be dead. How the fuck dare she?

All the years of torturous memories, of grief and guilt over
losing Erin and our baby rose up to the surface now and
overwhelmed me to the point where my overriding emotion
was savage rage. My fist, clenched hard and tight, thrust
right into the sick bitch's solar plexus, like a marshmallow
being smashed with a sledge hammer. Caught by surprise,
she gasped and fell backwards. This was the first time in my
life that I'd ever hit a woman. And I swear it would be the last.
Dad had always taught me that there was never any excuse
for a man to hit a woman; but this was one twisted, nasty
and dangerous individual. And she needed to be stopped.

Reaching for the knife that had fallen to the ground Áine
started to get up, cursing me like a bloody fishwife. She had
a mouth like a sewer, this 'good Catholic girl'.

In the blink of an eye, a black and white fuzzy image
whizzed past me, heading straight for Áine. Tosca knocked
her back to the ground and she rolled onto her back, in an
attempt to get up. He was having none of it; steadfast, he
sat on her chest, his front paws on her shoulders, strong
and proud. I thought he was going to bite her. I really did.
And I'd have been tempted not to stop him. But Tosca? Bite
a human? As if. So, what did he do? He held her down and
licked the face off the psycho.

I took the opportunity to grab Áine's wrist and relieve her
of the knife that she now held, before she decided to stab
the dog with it.

'Will you get this crazy feckin' mongrel off me?'

Who the hell was she calling a mongrel? And a crazy one
at that! Talk about the pot and the kettle. And it seems that
Tosca also took great exception to being referred to as a
mongrel, because the licking stopped and he held her in a
steely stare, eyeball to eyeball. An ominous rumbling sound
started in the pit of his stomach and travelled up to his
throat, culminating into a full-blown growl. His lips peeled

back, exposing healthy, pink gums and a set of large, very sharp and potentially lethal teeth. Áine's face set in a twisted grimace of sheer terror.

'Get this feckin' animal off me, you eejit bogtrotter!' Lovely turn of phrase this woman had. Well, alright, I know that was a bit hypocritical of me. I can eff and blind for England. Erin used to tell me off for 'cursing like an Irish tinker', as she put it. She rarely swore herself, so to hear the 'clone' of Erin screaming profanities was kind of surreal.

Another growl. The dog meant business.

'Good dog, Tosca. Stay! Good boy!' I was relieved but my heart remained firmly in my mouth. I wanted to call the law, but my phone was in the house.

'Hey, Nathan. Got a bit of trouble, have you?' Hetti's voice sent music to my soul. She didn't wait for a reply, instead she was tapping the screen of her iPhone with her index finger, no messing about.

'Yeah, police.' She gave her name and our whereabouts. 'We have an emergency out here. Some woman has been slaughtering sheep and threatening a man with a knife. Please send armed police and handcuffs. What? No armed police? Oh. Okay, so it's not America; no need for the sarcasm. Well, send lots of police with tasers, then. And be quick about it. Use blue flashing lights and sirens.'

She threw the dog's lead at me. 'Here, use this to tie her wrists together, or better still, her ankles.'

Jesus Christ on a bike. She was wonderful.

And Tosca was a total hero.

Hetti

The last thing I expected to see when I arrived at Nathan's place was a madwoman holding a knife to his neck. And this lunatic really meant business. I'd heard the conversation and had to act quickly. The only thing I could think of was to order Tosca to attack the woman. Nathan's life, possibly mine too and probably that of the dog, come to think of it, depended on someone disarming this nutcase of a woman. But I know my limitations. There's no way I was going to be able to do it. Trust me, I'd win Wimp-of-the-Year Award any day.

So, I whispered in Tosca's ear, very firmly and clearly, 'Go Tosca! Go get her! Now!'

For once in his life, the erstwhile totally disobedient Dalmatian did as he was told.

The police cars screeched to a halt in the yard like a scene from a police drama, sirens and blue lights everywhere. They took the crackpot away in handcuffs. I was pleased that they'd remembered to bring those.

'You saved my life there,' said Nathan, as we both patted the dog and told him what a good boy he was. 'I don't know what to say, Hetti.'

'Well, you could start by telling me why you so rudely blanked me in the street some weeks ago, Nathan.'

'Sorry about that, Hetti. The truth is,' he stopped petting the dog and stood upright. 'I saw you with your boyfriend and, frankly,' he went back to stroking the dog, 'I was jealous.'

'Boyfriend?' I stood upright. 'What boyfriend? I haven't got a boyfriend.'

'The dude with all the hair going on.' He straightened up so that we were on a level with each other.

'What the bloody hell are you talking about, Nathan?'

'That guy. Long hair. Pony tail right down his back. You were wrapped around each other in the street. Just before you turned and waved to me.'

I laughed out loud. Then took a moment.

'He's a waiter in the Thai restaurant.'

'So? What do I care what your boyfriend does for a living?' He stroked the dog again. Tosca had never had so much fuss made of him.

'So, if you must know, he's not my boyfriend. He was having a bit of girlfriend trouble. He was upset. I talked to him and he felt better.'

'Really?'

'Yeah, really. And what, exactly, were you jealous about?'

He stopped petting the dog and face-palmed himself, slapping his hand to his forehead. A small smile started to creep across his face. He took my face in his hands. I looked into his eyes. We were exactly the same height. His mouth moved closer to mine.

And my bloody phone timer went off.

'My lasagne!! I have to go!'

Nathan let go of my face and dropped his hands to his sides. He had a "WTF?" expression on his face.

'Your lasagne?'

I started running out of the yard. 'It's in the oven. It'll be burnt. I have to —'

'Get in the Audi. I'll drive you.' He took my hand, we ran to his car and jumped in. Tosca was sent into his five-star shed, Toffee was nowhere to be seen and we arrived at Wisteria Cottage just in time. The lasagne was cooked to perfection.

Hetti

Two hours later

Ben, Nathan and I sat at the kitchen table in Wisteria Cottage, feasting on rescued lasagne and salad. Nathan had gone to pick up Ben from school and, at my suggestion, brought him back for dinner. Ben was quiet, but relaxed. He seemed to be taking it all in his stride. Nathan finished his meal, leaned back on his chair and patted his taut abdominals.

'Mmm. That was delicious. Quite a cook, aren't you?'

'Glad you enjoyed it. Is yours good, Ben?'

I was treated to a little nod and a 'yummy'.

'I have to get ready for the concert now.'

'Concert?'

I explained that I'd joined the choir and that we were performing in the Abbey that evening.

'Can boys come to your concert, Hetti?' I was surprised, not exactly at Ben's question, but that he had spoken unprompted. I'd only ever heard him speak when he was spoken to and even then, he was very quiet.

'Yes, I'm sure they can. Would you like to come? With Daddy?'

Nathan looked at me, obviously pleased at the invitation.

'Tell you what,' he said, smiling, 'why don't we all go together? You go and get ready, while I wash the dishes, and then I can drive us to the Abbey.'

Upstairs, I quickly showered and changed into my long, black skirt and black, long-sleeved top – the classical choir's ladies' uniform. I piled my unruly tresses up high on my head and fixed them with sparkly clips. I put on a diamante necklace and matching pair of diamante drop-earrings — remembering that Tess, our renowned musical director, had told us that she'd like to see a bit of bling on us to offset the black, as she takes us through the dulcet notes of Fauré's Requiem. I put on a pair of black ankle boots and walked slowly down to the sitting room, holding the skirt with one hand and the wobbly bannister with the other, hoping to avoid tripping on the stairs and breaking my neck.

A long, low, appreciative whistle emitted from Nathan's lips.

The Abbey was packed to full capacity. I'd forgotten that I'd mentioned the concert to Miss Higgins and we bumped into her at the door. How nice that she came. I took my place in the choir and could see Oscar, Nathan, Ben and Miss Higgins sitting together. Much to my surprise, Toby was there too. Perhaps he wasn't so bad after all. Oscar gave me a little wave.

Wine and juice were served in paper cups during the interval and people mingled and chatted about what they'd enjoyed most about the performance so far. At the end of the concert, the audience gave a standing ovation and demanded an encore. This was most unusual, apparently. Unprecedented. Tess was somewhat nonplussed, but looked really chuffed. She smiled at the audience, gathered herself and chose a suitable movement for us to sing again.

As people left, the chink of cash dropping into charity buckets made a gratifying sound.

Ben sat up on Nathan's shoulders as we all walked together down the path of the Abbey graveyard towards the car. Oscar gave me big hugs and told me how splendid it had all been and how proud he was of me. I whispered in his ear, 'Uncle Oscar, what's with Toby?'

'All good, Dear One. He's decided to mend his ways and commit to me.'

'I just don't want you to get hurt, Oscar.'

'Don't worry my love. I think he's here to stay.'

'What's that?' Toby butted in.

'My god daughter is worried that you'll break my heart, dear boy. But I've told her that you're ready to settle down now.'

'That's right. No need for you to be concerned, Hetti. I'm a changed man. I've realised where I'm better off.'

'I should jolly well hope so, too!' I said. And I meant it.

'I simply cannot live without Oscar's delicious home-made apple tarts.' Toby said, winking at me in the lamplight.

He'd just better mean it.

'How's the crazy Dalmatian?' Toby had a mischievous expression on his face.

'He's better behaved, but still very boisterous.'

'Just be glad it's just the one and not one hundred and one Dalmatians, Cruella!'

Oscar gave him a dig in the ribs. 'Enough of that, Toby!'

As we left the grounds of the Abbey and stepped onto the pavement, I realised that I'd left behind my music folder.

'Carry on to the car,' I said, running back to the Abbey. 'I'll catch you up.'

In the Abbey, some of the choristers and Tess were still standing around chatting.

'Did you enjoy it, Hetti?' Tess smiled at me warmly.

'Yes, I did, Tess.'

'Good! Then you'll come back for the summer concert?'

'You bet!'

Nathan

I turned and looked back but there was no sign of Hetti. I'd offered Miss Higgins a lift home. We'd all moved along slowly because she used a walking stick but even so, we'd already reached the carpark. Where had Hetti got to? Oscar and his boyfriend had already left and were on their way back to Norwich. They'd had a little lovers' tiff; something about Toby wanting to get home but Oscar wanting to buy us all a drink. In the end I said that I needed to get Ben home to bed, even though it was Saturday tomorrow and no school. That seemed to settle the matter.

But I was feeling a bit anxious about Hetti. She should have caught us up by now. Miss Higgins said that perhaps Hetti had just got chatting with someone, but suggested it might be a good idea to walk back to meet her. Wymondham wasn't the same these days, she said. Not like the old days, when you could leave your door unlocked at night and the family silver would still be there in the morning.

We walked slowly back along Market Street towards Church Street.

Hetti

Feeling very accepted, happy and welcome in my new home town, I left the Abbey and started to walk down Church Street to catch up with the others. I reached the *Green Dragon* pub and stood with my back to it, waiting for a car to pass so that I could cross the road. I felt the sudden shock and the pain as a hand grabbed my hair and my arm was twisted up my back. My music folder fell to the ground.

'Keep quiet. Don't make a sound, or you're dead.' I could feel his hot breath on my ear, his voice muffled.

I struggled and he pulled tighter on my hair, shoving my arm further up my back. 'Let go of me!' I yelled, while I kept on struggling.

'Still! Keep still,' he said through his teeth.

Like hell I would. I managed to twist around to face him. He was wearing a Batman's Joker mask and a hoodie pulled over his head. I recoiled and gasped in horror.

He pushed me backwards into a bush that formed part of the garden of the *Green Dragon* pub.

Bloody hell. What a day. First Nathan and now me. What was it with these crazy people? You couldn't make it up!

My heart was playing the drums on my ribcage.

He was strong, but shorter than me. At that moment, I was — ridiculous, I know — hoping that Tosca would turn up. Of course, he wasn't likely to, being as he was languishing in his five-star shed. I had to think of something and I had to be quick. I hooked my right leg around the back of the guy's knee and with supreme effort, flipped forward. To my great and not unpleasant surprise, he let go of my hair, loosening his grip on my arm, as he went head first over me and fell to the ground with a satisfying thud.

A carefully aimed kick rendered him writhing in agony, his chances of fatherhood probably diminished. There was something rather comical about Batman's Joker rolling around on the ground, screaming and holding his genitals.

'Nice one, babe!' I looked up to see Simon, the flirty barman from the Green Dragon making for the assailant. He was on his mobile, calling the police. He ended the call, put his phone in his jeans pocket and turned to me. 'I'm impressed. Wouldn't want to get on the wrong side of you! Where did you learn that trick?'

'Self-defence class as a kid, one summer holidays. And that was the only defence move I can actually remember.' I could still hear my heart thumping in my ears.

The assailant recovered sufficiently to try and get up. Holding up my long skirt, I gave him another kick, this time in the leg. He rolled over and I kicked him in the bum as he made to get up. He collapsed back on the ground, moaning and groaning. I was glad that I wasn't wearing silly shoes. My days of sporting ballet flats were, after the Sheep-rescue-from-the-ditch incident, long gone.

Simon leaned over Joker Man, pulled down his hood and tried to rip the mask off his face. 'The police are on their way. Don't even think about getting up, or you'll get another kicking.'

Nathan

Reaching Church Street, we could hear a commotion going on by the Green Dragon. People were starting to gather, forming little groups. Not wanting my son to witness any unpleasantness, I left him sitting on a low wall on the corner of the street, in the care of Miss Higgins. A few people had gathered around. It was dark, but I could see Hetti and a dude from the pub standing over someone on the ground. The barman was doing something with the head of the guy on the ground.

Thinking that someone had been hurt, I sprinted to the scene, arriving in time to hear a loud screech.

It was Hetti.

Hetti

Joker mask was off and he scrambled to his feet, sufficiently recovered to take off down the street. I ran after him, carrying the mask and bumped straight into Nathan.

'*That's Daniel!* He's got my money. Stop him!' I yelled, without realising that Nathan had no idea who Daniel was. It didn't matter. He jumped to it.

We both ran the short distance up the street, keeping Daniel within sight. If he turned the corner, we could lose him. I was gasping for air, my lungs on fire.

'Catch him!' I yelled at anyone who could hear me. 'He stole a hundred-grand from me! Stop him!'

I could see Miss Higgins and Ben sitting on the low wall on the corner. Daniel was nearly at the corner of the street. Suddenly, he was on the ground and Miss Higgins — Sparrow Woman, remember? — was standing over him, giving him a good hiding with her walking stick. Daniel's hands were in defence position and he was whimpering and pleading with her to stop.

Pathetic!

Now, it seemed that half the population of this sleepy little market town was out in force, gathered around Daniel Jones, thief extraordinaire, who was about to spend a lot of time looking at brick walls and iron bars on windows, if I had anything to do with it.

Nathan

I grabbed the bastard by the scruff of the neck and dragged him to his feet. People were recording on their mobile phones. The police were on their way, someone said. A woman said she recognised Daniel, but couldn't place him, then someone else said the same and a man holding a bag of takeaway food said he thought he recognised him too. They were all pointing at him and nodding. I kept a tight grip on him.

'Thass him off that Facebook, ain't it?' A woman with a small dog said.

I wished to god I knew what was going on. This was all totally bizarre.

'Ben?' Where was Ben? I cast my eyes around the immediate area. Three yummy mummies from Ben's school, all dolled up on a girls' night out, stood across the road. One of them held Ben close to her, shielding him from the altercation, her hands wrapped around his head.

She raised a hand, as if to say that Ben was okay and turned so that his back faced the incident and he couldn't see what was going on. Tracey was one of the girls on a night out. She smiled at me, faux coy, stuck her chest out and wiggled her fingers at me in a wave. Inappropriate, Tracey. Really, inappropriate. This is not the time, nor the place. Not that any time or any place would be.

Miss Higgins watched the show from her vantage point sitting on the wall. No doubt she needed to sit down and catch her breath after the exertion of giving Joker Boy a good belting. She got up and whispered to me, 'Your boy's fine. Good job we caught the thief!'

'Thanks. He'll have a few bruises on him tomorrow. That walking stick of yours is lethal!'

'When I heard Hetti say that this was the man what'd stolen a hundred-thousand pounds from her, I remembered her telling me about him. Well, I had to do something. So, I tripped him up with my stick and then walloped him with it. Nasty young bugger.' And she looked like such a sweet little old dear, too!

I looked at Hetti. Her hair was all over the place and she was pushing it back off her face, straightening her clothes and rubbing her arm. The mask had dropped to the ground.

'Did he hurt you?'

'He yanked my hair and shoved my arm up my back. It's okay. He got it worse than me. Hopefully the kick I gave him has scuppered his chances of ever becoming a father. I'm not usually violent, but he stole a hundred-grand from me.'

'Yeah, so I gather. Well, he's been caught now. Has anyone called the law?'

'Yes, the barman from the pub.'

As Hetti spoke, Daniel tried to wriggle free and run off. I grabbed his hood and yanked him back, turned him around and held him by the scruff of the neck.

'You fucking tosser! You're not going anywhere but a police cell this evening.'

He spat in my face.

Outstanding.

And that was the second time in one day that I'd been spat on. I'd need antibiotics at this rate.

The police arrived just in time to see me headbutt the bastard.

Hetti

The police were about to arrest Nathan for assault, but several of the Wymondham folk who'd come to watch the action stepped forward with their mobile phones and showed footage of the whole incident, so the police thought better of it.

'You'll all need to make statements later.'

Several people complained that it was getting late and they needed to get home.

'My dinner's getting cold,' moaned a man with his takeaway.

'My husband'll be worried where I've got to,' said a woman with a little dog.

'Okay. Give your details to PC Cotman, here and we'll be in touch,' one of the officers said.

They took Daniel away in handcuffs, but not before I slapped him

right across the face and called him a lot of unrepeatable names.

'Miss Lewis,' said one police officer, 'you cannot slap him. It's assault.'

'Oh yes, I can,' I said. 'He swindled me out of a hundred-thousand pounds. And that's theft and fraud and all kinds of other criminal offences. He's a dirty crook.'

'It's not true. I haven't got your money, Hetti!' Blood dripped from his nose.

'You'd better have it, Daniel Jones. All hundred-grand of it. And my holiday money too!' I picked up the Joker mask and thrust it at him. 'Here; I think this belongs to you.'

Of course, it was a bit awkward for him to hold the mask, what with him being handcuffed, so one of the police officers took it from me. Vital evidence, obviously.

Nathan took Miss Higgins home, dropped me off at Wisteria Cottage and took Ben straight home. We were all too tired to talk in the car.

I was never so glad to see my bed as I was that night. What an emotional rollercoaster of a day. The extraordinary events started to unfurl in my mind. As I curled up under the duvet the memory of Nathan's almost-kiss in his yard that afternoon — which seemed like a lifetime ago now — lulled me into a rosy, cosy sense of wellbeing.

And I knew that I wanted more, much more of Nathan Brookes.

71

Hetti

After breakfast the following day, feeling cautiously hopeful that the hundred-thousand pounds would soon be back in my account, I made my way to the bank. I asked to see the manager and kept my fingers crossed that the money would still be there. Daniel could well have spent the lot, for all I knew.

'Daniel Jones is in police custody and I want my money back.' I hadn't even sat down in the bank manager's office, as I said it.

'I'm afraid it's not quite that simple, Hetti,' said the same man who had told me all those months ago that a Promise is Like a Butterfly, or words to that effect.

'Why not? Where's my money? Has he spent it?'

'It's safe. All of it,' he said.

What a relief! So, when Daniel said last night that he didn't have my money, he was telling the truth for once in his pathetic life. He didn't have my money. But the fact remained that he had stolen it.

'Good. So, when can I have it, then?'

'I'm afraid you cannot have access to it while the police are in the process of putting together a case against Mr Jones.' He went on to tell me that he'd been updated by the police that morning.

Turns out, as he explained to me now, the bank had frozen the account the same day I'd reported the matter, so Daniel couldn't get his grubby little hands on the money. Not one penny of it. That was a highly gratifying thought. But I still had issues with the bank.

'Why didn't you tell me in the first place that you'd frozen the account?' I glared at the bank manager. 'All these months I've been desperate to recover my money, living from hand to mouth — do you realise I've been bloody well dog sitting a demented Dalmatian because I couldn't afford anywhere to live? And all the time you knew my money was safe. How could you do that to a person?' I was one heartbeat away from bashing my fist on the desk.

The bank manager informed me, very calmly — bordering on patronisingly actually, if I'm honest — that they had been carrying out the internal investigation and at the same time, the police were doing their bit too, but that it would have been illegal for them to tell me that they'd frozen Daniel's account.

'Even though it would have meant that I'd had had peace of mind, knowing that he couldn't get hold of a penny?'

'I'm afraid so, my dear.'

'Don't patronise me.'

I left the bank, still feeling elated, but also rather exasperated.

Next stop: the police.

I knew straight away that this was no insignificant case when the constable took me to see the chief superintendent in charge of the investigation.

And so, the story started to unfold. Daniel Jones had been involved in a drugs-running game. You really couldn't make it up. Daniel? Oh, for goodness' sake!

The police knew about it but didn't have enough evidence to charge anyone.

'You see, Miss Lewis,' said the police chief superintendent, 'we wanted to get the drugs baron. Daniel Jones was merely a mule.'

It was all going over my head. What on earth was he talking about? Barons and mules?

'I don't understand,' I said, scratching my head. 'What's a "mule", exactly?'

'Well, my dear,' he said, like I was intellectually a bit slow. 'What does a mule — as in the animal — normally do? What is it used for?' I felt about five.

'Er, carries stuff?'

'Yes, that's right.' His spoke his words slowly, drawing out each syllable.

'So?'

'So, my dear,' he touched the tips of the fingers of one hand with the fingertips of the other, making a shape like a church spire, in a self-important sort of way, 'Daniel Jones was drugs running for the big boss in the organisation. And we are talking Class A drugs here. But we were trying to catch the ring leader, not just his lackeys. It was very fortuitous that you reported the fraud. It took many months, but your quick actions in giving the information to the fraud people at the bank and reporting the matter to the police have led us to gather enough evidence to prosecute not only the mules, like Daniel, but also the drugs baron.'

I sat there speechless. Just couldn't process what the middle-aged man sitting across the desk from me in high ranking policer's uniform was telling me. Daniel? Engaged in all this? Serious, organised crime? Drugs? Class A drugs? He never touched drugs, as far as I knew. Didn't smoke at all and hardly ever had an alcoholic drink.

'This is going to be hard for you to hear, Miss Lewis, but Jones was stringing you along right from the moment you first confided in him about your trust fund.'

'How do you know that?' I couldn't bear it. Daniel had never loved me at all. What an absolute fool I'd been. And what a lesson to learn. I vowed there and then that I would never again allow myself to be swept off my feet in a whirlwind romance. I should have known that Daniel was moving things too fast. I thought it was because he loved me. What an idiot I'd been. From now on, I'd take things slowly. At my own pace. Never trust again.

'Did he tell you that?'

'Never mind that now, my dear,' said the chief superintendent, getting up from his chair; my cue to leave. 'I cannot give you any more information at the moment, but all will be revealed in the fullness of time.'

'Well can you tell me, if he was getting drugs money, why he needed to steal a hundred-grand from me?

'He owed the baron for drugs. He was supposed to sell the drugs and hand over the money and keep his cut. But he spent the money. They were putting pressure on him.'

'So, he stole my trust fund money to pay off his drugs debt?' What an appalling thought.

'I'm afraid so. Weren't you even a little bit suspicious when he started spending vast amounts of money? That brand-new car, for example?'

'No. I thought he was doing well in his job. That's what he said, anyway. And don't turn this around to make it look like I was the one to blame. He's the criminal, not me!' Typical. Blame the victim.

'What happens now?'

'He'll be charged. The whole gang will be charged. They'll appear in the magistrates' court where they'll be referred to Crown Court. This is a very serious crime. They're all looking at hefty sentences.'

'They?'

'Yes, we have all of them in custody. Once we got Daniel Jones, he sang like a canary and a dawn raid here and there this morning swept up the rest of the mules as well as the baron.'

It sounded like a 1980s TV police drama.

Daniel? A drugs baron's mule? Not the baron, then? He wasn't very ambitious, was he? Just an insignificant little nobody. Hah!

The chief superintendent opened the door to let me leave and a beefy guy walked in. Looked like he'd been overdoing it in the gym.

'Ah. Miss Lewis, this is Detective Sergeant Greenwood from the fraud squad. He's been dealing with the other side of the crime – your hundred-thousand pounds.'

Greenwood shook my hand.

'When can I get my money back? The bank say that they froze Daniel's account and that means the money is safe. When can I get it back?'

'The case against Jones is watertight. He's fessed up. We can give you a crime reference number to take to the bank and they should refund your money to you within a matter of days.'

Music to my ears.

72

Nathan

'You must have grown wings on your car, Mum! I didn't expect you for another hour, at least.' I picked up her overnight bag, linked her arm and led her into the house.

Ben was still sleeping soundly when I woke up and called my parents. I gave them very few details over the phone about the Áine incident yesterday, but knowing that something serious had occurred was enough to make Mum jump straight into her car and arrive at the smallholding in record time.

'Where's my lovely grandson?' Doting grandmother cast her eyes around the room.

'Still sleeping! It was a very late night.'

I made coffee and warmed the croissants that Mum had brought with her. We sat at the kitchen table and over breakfast I gave her an outline of the events of yesterday.

Mum started clearing up and Ben came into the kitchen, yawning. She put down the dishes and held out her arms. Ben ran straight into them and she hugged him tight.

"My! Look at this big boy!' She held his face in her hands. Toff suddenly started barking excitedly and there followed a light tap on the front door.

Hetti. The very sight of her sent my hormone levels through the roof.

'Good morning!' I couldn't hide my delight at seeing her.

'I've come for Tosca. I thought it only fair.'

'It's a lovely surprise to see you, Hetti,' said Mum, who had appeared at the front door, holding Ben's hand. 'Come in and have coffee and something to eat.'

'Hello Sheila. Thanks. That would be lovely, so long as I'm not intruding.' She ruffled Ben's hair. 'Hi Ben. Just woken up?' He nodded.

'Not at all, Hetti,' said Mum, 'you're very welcome!' We went through to the kitchen and Mum made more breakfast while I put the coffee pot on.

Toffee jumped up on Hetti's knee, as she sat at the kitchen table.

'Get down, Toff!' I said, 'you know you're not allowed up there.' The dog immediately obeyed.

'I wish I had your powers of command,' said Hetti, totally unaware of the power that she held over me. 'Tosca hardly ever does as I tell him. Although, I must admit, with your training, he's a lot better than he was.'

'Tosca obeyed your command at a most crucial moment yesterday afternoon, if I remember correctly.'

'Okay, we won't go there, Nathan,' cut in Mum. She knew the whole story. Now she was keen for Ben not to hear any of it.

'We went to hear Hetti singing in a concert at the Abbey last night, Mum. And very good she was too!' I said, trying to change the subject. It wasn't the best idea I'd ever had. Talk of last night set Ben off.

'Grannie, there was a baddy and he was going to hurt Hetti and Daddy rescued her!' Ben's little face was a mixture of astonishment and pride. 'And the policemen came and took the bad man away.'

'Yes, I heard about that darling. And we won't talk about baddies any more today, will we?' Mum held me in her stare.

'That's right.' I nodded.

'Ben, would you like to come out with Grannie today? We could go to the park, or to the swimming pool or whatever you'd like and then we could have some nice lunch. What do you say?' Mum was up to something.

'Yes please!' Ben jumped up and down. It was good to see him so lively and confident.

'If it's okay with Daddy, of course.' She raised an eyebrow at me. 'Why don't you and Hetti take the dogs out for a nice, long walk? I'm sure you have lots to talk about.' So that was it. Mum's scheme was becoming clear.

We took both the dogs and let them off the lead once we reached the field. The sheep were safely ensconced in an enclosure close to the house and the crime scene — the field where the sheep had been slaughtered — had been cleaned up by police forensics. New lambs were due to be born to the surviving ewes any day now.

'So, Hetti, what was all that about Daniel Jones stealing your money? What's been going on?' I was wary about bringing it up, but we both knew that we had a lot to talk about. And it was the reason Mum had suggested she took Ben out for a while, so that Hetti and I would have a chance to discuss things.

'I was a complete fool, Nathan,' she said, looking down at her feet as we walked along. My hands were in my pockets. I left them there to stop myself from doing what I was desperate to do, but knew I shouldn't: take her in my arms and kiss her for a long time.

'I thought we were in love. That I could trust Daniel. He was so totally into me to start with. Very attentive. When he asked me to move in with him, I took it as a sign of his commitment to the relationship. And when he suggested we buy a house together I saw that as confirmation of his commitment. How wrong can you be?' She sighed. 'I was so stupid.'

The memory of a day, a long time ago, came to mind. 'You know,' I began, 'I met an old woman at a bus stop once. It was the day that I found out that Ben had been born and that... well about...' I shook my head to try and rid myself of the memory.

'What?'

'Nothing. Something that happened. Well, anyway, I ended up telling this wise, wrinkly old woman all about it. She said something to me that I've never forgotten.'

Hetti looked at me. 'What was that, Nathan?'

'She said, "Everybody makes mistakes. Forgive yourself and move on". Easier said than done, but I've never forgotten it. Maybe that's what you should be doing. Forgive yourself and move on, Hetti.'

She shrugged her shoulders. 'Sound advice, but yeah, easier said than done.'

Toffee ran up to me with Tosca hot on her heels. I picked up a stick and threw it. The dogs tore off into the distance.

'Will you get your money back? I mean, he stole a hundred-grand from you. That's a hell of a lot of money.'

'Yeah. It's a lot of money and it was my trust fund. Left for me by my parents. They died in a crash when I was about seven.'

I stopped in my tracks and looked at her. She'd never mentioned this before. 'Jeez, Hetti. I'm so sorry. I had no idea,' I said, and in a heartbeat my hands were out of my pockets and I went to wrap my arms around her.

'Please, don't.' She took a step back.

'Sorry. It's just... I'm sorry.' I put my hands back in my pockets and she looked down again. We walked on.

'My parents are to me now just a wonderful memory of two people who absolutely adored me. And I was lucky because they left me in the loving care of the two best people a little girl could wish for: Oscar and my dear late Aunt Pat.'

'Your Aunt Pat?'

'She died a couple of months ago.'

'I'm sorry.' Another trauma that Hetti had gone through, that I'd known nothing about.

'So am I,' she said, her voice quieter now.

She wandered off into thoughts of her own, that I was not privy to, as we carried on strolling along side by side.

The dogs returned, Tosca carrying the stick between his teeth. I threw it again and they ran after it.

After some minutes, I said, 'Must have been tough, though. I mean, I can't even imagine life without my parents. They've been with me through thick and thin. No matter what stupid choices I've made.'

'I can tell they're good people, Nathan,' she said, glancing at me. 'I enjoyed meeting them on Christmas Day. And your mum is great with Ben.'

'Thanks. Do you remember very much about your mum and dad?'

'I do remember bits. Like little flashes from a dream. And I miss them, even though I was very young when they died. But my darling maiden aunt, Pat, and dear old Oscar gave me all the love and care a little girl could need or want. I lived with Aunt Pat, but Oscar would visit a lot and take me out. And he always took me on holiday; every summer.'

'That's very touching, Hetti.' We stopped and I tried to hold her hand. This time, she didn't resist. But she didn't respond either.

In the meantime, my testosterone levels were wreaking havoc on my libido.

We walked on in silence. It was strange to be at the field and no sheep. I shook my head in an effort to rid my mind of the image of the three of them that had been slaughtered by Áine, their unborn lambs lying lifeless beside their mothers. If she'd got her way, I'd have a slit throat too. I shuddered and started focusing on my breathing to avert another PTSD trigger.

As if reading my thoughts, Hetti stopped and looked me in the face. 'And you, Nathan? What's with the crazy Irish bitch?'

My laughter reverberated around the whole of the South West Norfolk countryside.

'What's so funny?'

'Sorry, Hetti.' Could I really tell her how her turn of phrase totally turned me on? Best not.

'Well?' Hetti stood still in front of me, a quizzical look in her beautiful eyes.

'The crazy Irish woman is the twin sister — identical twin sister — of a woman I loved very much and one I will never forget.'

As we walked on, I told Hetti the whole gut-wrenching story. All of it. About my tiny baby girl lying dead in the palm of my hand; about Erin dying alone, without me there to hold her hand, or to say goodbye. The guilt that I felt would never leave me. And about me falling apart so badly that I didn't take my final exams. Instead, I'd left university, after nearly four years of very hard work, without a degree. How I was diagnosed with post-traumatic stress disorder, which can still be triggered from time to time.

'How old were you when this happened, Nathan?'

'The baby and Erin died on my twenty-second birthday.'

'Oh my god.'

I started to cry softly and covered my face with one hand. I used to think that it was weak for a man to cry, but had learnt that it's better to let emotions out rather than feed the PTSD.

She reached out and held me in her arms.

After a while – time was hard to measure — I got a grip of myself and we walked home in silence, holding hands.

Mum's car was not in the yard, so presumably she was still out with Ben, spoiling him rotten. A police car pulled up.

'What's up?' I said as an officer got out of the car and walked over towards us. Another officer followed him.

'Nathan Brookes?'

'Yeah, that's me.'

'The woman who attacked you yesterday? Áine Byrne?'

'What about her?' I hadn't seen either of these guys before. Not when Áine was taken away by police yesterday afternoon and not when Daniel Jones was arrested last night either.

'She's saying that it was you who attacked her.'

'What? That's ridiculous!'

'We need you to come down to the station with us, Mr Brookes.'

Hetti

Unbelievable. That lunatic woman was actually accusing Nathan after what she did to him, not to mention what she did to his sheep and threatened to do to Ben.

Nathan put Tosca in his five-star shed and Toffee in the house, leaving water and food for them both.

'I'm coming with you, I said, as the officers escorted him to the car. 'I was there and I saw everything,' I said and walked with them to the police car.

It was a short ride to the police headquarters in Wymondham. On the way, the police were not very talkative. I asked questions but they were very vague and evasive.

Nathan was taken to one room and a woman police officer led me to another.

Two officers questioned me and took a detailed statement. It had only happened yesterday afternoon and although a lot had occurred since then, I remembered everything.

'She's completely bonkers, you know,' I said, after giving a blow-by-blow account of what I'd seen. 'Nathan went through a nightmare when his little girl was stillborn and then his girlfriend — the mother of the baby — she died shortly afterwards. He's still heartbroken about it, you know. Yesterday that madwoman was accusing him of murder and she was going on about the bible and an eye for an eye. I heard her. She was going to slit his throat, like she did the sheep. It triggered his PTSD.'

'That's very helpful, Miss Lewis.'

'What happens now?'

'Miss Byrne is being assessed by doctors as we speak. She's in a secure unit on the psychiatric ward.'

'Thank goodness for that!'

The door opened and a male officer walked in. He was one of the ones who'd driven us to the station.

'We have taken Mr Brookes' statement. They're free to go.'

Outside, Nathan took his mobile phone out of his pocket and called a taxi to take us home. Just as the car arrived, a police officer came out.

'Can you come back inside, please, Mr Brookes?'

Now what?

Nathan asked the taxi driver if he could wait; the answer was a grumpy 'No!' and he drove off.

Inside, we were taken to a room and left alone for over half an hour.

'What do you think it is they want?' I said. Nathan took my hand and I let him. I was still wary of trusting a man again, but I found Nathan's touch very reassuring. I thought about the almost-kiss yesterday. I still wanted more.

'God knows.'

The door opened and in walked a different officer altogether.

'Just checking a few things. And we've had a call from the hospital about Miss Byrne. What the doctor says confirms what you've told us today. The woman is very ill. She's bipolar. Went missing a few months ago from a psychiatric hospital in Ireland and her family and the police have been looking for her. She's been in an increasingly manic state, probably due to not taking her medication. And things are more serious because she's a transplant patient and she's not been taking her anti-rejection medication either.'

Nathan visibly tensed up. 'To think, Erin died because she gave a kidney to that woman and she's abused it.'

'It's a lot for you to process, Mr Brookes, but Áine Byrne is a very sick woman. We need to remember that.' I instinctively took Nathan's hand.

'I'm amazed that she's not been found before,' I said. 'How did she hide for all these months?'

'We believe she's been squatting in a holiday home in Wymondham. Officers are out there now checking the house.'

Memories of strange rustling sounds and the sight of footprints in the snow flooded my mind.

Outside, Nathan called again for a taxi.

'I need to go straight home, Nathan,' I said.

'Sure. You okay?' Nathan gave the driver directions to Wisteria Cottage.

'They said Áine had been squatting in a holiday home, right?'

'And?'

'Well, it's probably not connected and you'll probably think I'm being paranoid, but I've been having some strange things happening — to do with the holiday home next to me.

The taxi driver pulled up outside Wisteria Cottage and Nathan paid him.

I checked over the cottage and we went out into the garden. Through the bushes I could see and hear movement.

'I'm going over there to check things out, Nathan.'

'Not without me, you're not.'

It was late afternoon and almost dusk as we reached the holiday home a few minutes later. Police were combing the area. Blue and white tape cordoned off the property. I tried to move forward.

'Nothing for you to see here, Miss. Move on, please,' said the officer at the cordon.

Another officer that I recognised from Nathan's place yesterday came over.

'You're Miss Lewis, right?'

'Yes, I am and I was wondering what you're looking for. Because I've had a feeling for months now that someone was watching me from the garden of this property. And at Christmas, I found footprints in the snow, leading from the adjoining fence to the door of Wisteria Cottage, where I live.'

'Did you report this?'

'No, I didn't. I imagined I'd be laughed at. But now I think the person squatting here in recent months was Áine Byrne. Am I right?'

'You are, yes. Now, please, leave and let us get on with the job. You have nothing to worry about any longer. Miss Byrne is being taken care of.'

'Thanks. That's all I wanted to know.'

I started to turn to walk away when something else occurred to me.

'Just a thought. That anonymous text that I got — the one saying they'd seen Daniel?'

'What about it, Miss Lewis?'

'Well, you might just want to check Áine Byrne's phone. Only, the text says the person had seen "your man". That's all.'

The police officer gave me a blank look. 'And?'

'Well, that's an Irish expression, isn't it? "Your man". The Irish say it when referring to a man that someone knows, don't they? Why would the anonymous texter say "your man" instead of referring to Daniel by name? I mean, I named Daniel Jones on my Facebook post. An English person wouldn't say "your man", they'd use his name, wouldn't they?'

'That's very astute of you Miss Lewis. We will be looking into that for sure.'

We turned and started to walk back to Wisteria Cottage. Nathan suddenly stopped in his tracks.

'That anonymous text message.'

'What about it, Nathan?'

'You're right. It must have been Áine. She threatened to kill you too. Referred to you as, "Your woman. The redhead". I remember now. She was probably trying to lure you into a trap with that anonymous text message.'

'Just as well she didn't manage it! She had plenty of chances. God knows how the bipolar mind works.' I tried to laugh it off, but inside I was horrified at the very thought.

Nathan's phone rang.

'Hi Mum. Ben okay?'

He took my hand and squeezed it. We walked hand-in-hand towards Wisteria Cottage, as he talked on the phone.

'Good, good. He's not wearing you out, is he?'

He smiled at me.

'Not at all implying that you're too old to look after your beloved grandson, not a bit of it Mother!' He was laughing now, his eyes shining as he looked at me.

"Okay, Mum, so what is this plan of yours?'

73

Nathan

One week later

I'd been up most of the night, in the barn with the ewes in lamb. I hadn't returned them to the field, since Áine had been on the rampage. For one thing, they were so close to birthing, for another, I still felt pretty unnerved about the slaughters that Áine had carried out. I knew she was now securely locked away, but even so, I wanted them safe in the barn. Lambs were safely delivered at short intervals throughout the night. Ewes merely bleated weakly, with a low tone, while pushing new life into the world and for most of them it took less than ten minutes. I'd busied myself, making sure the new mums had plenty of warm water to drink and anything else that they needed to make life a little more comfortable. Some needed electrolytes administered by syringe, but most looked like pros, as if they gave birth every week and it was no big deal.

With no more than two hours' sleep, I woke up at nine. Mum had taken Ben to school and wasn't back yet. Knowing her, she was probably in Norwich, shopping. Dad was going to come and stay in a day or two, so Ben would get plenty of attention. I hadn't told Ben about the baby lambs before he went to school. Visitors to the barn had to be restricted for a while. The new mums needed time to accept their young and learn how to be mothers.

I heard a dog barking frenziedly as I stepped out of the shower. It could only be Tosca. Wrapping a towel around my waist, I looked out of the upstairs window to see Hetti and Tosca returning from their walk. Tosca was pulling Hetti towards the barn and she was — comically, as always — trying to drag him back to his five-star shed.

I banged on the window, opened it and called out to Hetti. Over the dog's barking, she obviously hadn't heard me and carried on trying to persuade him to go into the shed. I banged on the window once more and yelled again.

'Hetti! Don't let him near the barn.'

She looked up at me.

'Easier said than done. He's concerned about something in there.'

'Yes, it's the lambs!'

Still damp from the shower, I threw on some clothes, ran down the stairs and out to the yard.

Grabbing the lead, I shut Tosca in the shed and sprinted over to the barn. Three more ewes had given birth and the lambs were happily suckling colostrum from their mothers. I made sure they had plenty of warm straw and checked the mouths of each of the lambs. A warm mouth indicated that mother's milk had passed through it, so sticking a finger inside the mouth was a sure way of knowing that they'd been fed. If not, the mother needed to be encouraged to feed their baby. Happily, they were all fine, as it was evident that very lamb was successfully feeding.

Plaintive bleating filled the air. It wasn't any of the new mums; they were all happy. Looking around, I spotted the ewe that Hetti had rescued from the ditch all those months ago. It had separated itself from the rest of the flock and was lying in the corner of the barn.

'Oh, what beautiful creatures!' Hetti stood at the barn door.

'Stay there, Hetti. The animals shouldn't have too many people around them at this time,' I held my hand up as I called out to her and moved over towards the troubled ewe.

It didn't take long to see that the unhappy ewe was having trouble pushing the lamb out. She started fidgeting, fretting, bleating, moving in circles, trying to make a bed. Poor creature. I wondered how long she'd been struggling. I pushed more warm, comforting straw around her.

'It's okay, girl. You're doing fine. Let's just take a little look at what's going on in there.' I rubbed the back of the ewe in an effort to reassure her, turned her around, laid her on her belly across a bale of straw and examined her rear end. Putting two fingers of each hand inside her, I felt the lamb's head but not the front feet. The head of the lamb was slightly turned into the wrong position. The ewe was becoming even more distressed.

I tried to feel around inside her for the lamb's two front feet so that I could turn the infant around and pull it out by the limbs. It wasn't going to be easy. The ewe was fretting and wouldn't keep still long enough for me to help the birth.

I looked up to see Hetti still standing at the door of the barn.

'Hetti, I need some help. Could you get over here without going anywhere near the new mums and lambs? I think they've all bonded, so they should be okay, but you never know. Best not to take any chances.'

Hetti didn't move.

'How can I get to you without disturbing them, Nathan?'

I pointed to the side of the barn, where there were no sheep. 'Walk around the very edge of the —' The ewe suddenly started fidgeting again, kicking her legs. I held her steady. 'Walk around the very edge of the barn by the wall. I need you to hold onto her while I get the lamb out.'

'Okay. I'm coming.' Tentatively, she entered the barn and, pressing herself against the wall, slowly moved towards me.

'Right. She's very skittish and distressed and not cooperating. I need you to keep her still while I get the baby out.' I glanced around at the other ewes and lambs. All fine there.

'Right. What shall I do?'

'I'm going to turn her around and I want you to straddle her.'

Hetti made a face.

'Won't I hurt her? I'm a bit heavy to be sitting on a sheep.'

'I wouldn't ask you to do it if I thought it'd hurt her, don't worry.'

She looked down at the animal. 'Oh! It's Bah-Bah! I recognise the markings on her face.'

I honestly thought Hetti had lost it.

'Bah-Bah?'

Hetti coloured up a bit.

'Er, yeah. She's the one I got out of the ditch, isn't she? When I spoke to her that day, I called her "Bah-Bah"'.

A wide grin spread across my face. Hetti's face was beetroot red.

'Well, I had to call her something!'

I gave a little laugh. 'Whatever,' I said, still grinning. 'Climb onto her back.'

Hetti made to get onto the animal as if it was a horse.

'No, not like that. I need you to sit on its back and face towards its rear. Like this.' I demonstrated.

'Okay, like this?' She climbed onto Bah-Bah (really? She actually called it that?), facing backwards.

'Great. Now, whatever she does, stay there and hold her steady. She's not very happy, so it's likely she'll object strongly to what we are doing.'

'Okay, let's do this.' I loved her enthusiasm.

I kneeled down on the straw and examined the ewe's rear end. This time, with Hetti holding the animal still, I managed to catch hold of the head and twist it a little, which meant that the front feet were now visible.

'Okay, hold her still, Hetti. The lamb's about to be born.' I pulled, the ewe pushed, Hetti held her still and between us we brought new life into the world.

'Aah! How gorgeous!' Hetti's delight was written all over her face.

'Stay there, Hetti. Hold her still. There's another one coming.'

The ewe moved, gave a low-toned bleat and another lamb slid out.

'Stay there, Hetti. I need to examine her.'

All was well.

In the house I put the kettle on to make coffee. I cleared my throat and took a deep breath. 'Hetti,' I began, 'there's something I've been wanting to ask you.'

74

The Finale

Hetti

'Hetti, darling!' Oscar sounded in fine fettle as he took my call. 'What news have you for your old Uncle Oscar? We so enjoyed the concert, Dear One. I said to Toby —'

I interrupted Oscar, shut him up, launched in and told him everything. About the mad woman; that Daniel had been caught; that I was to get all of my money back, that'd I'd helped to deliver two baby lambs — Oscar gasped in all the appropriate places — and that Nathan had invited me out to dinner.

'Splendid, darling! Simply splendid!' This, it seemed, was the most exciting news of all: not that I was to get my money back but that I had a date with Nathan. 'Where is he taking you?'

'The Thai place that you took me to that time. It was lovely, wasn't it?'

'Excellent choice, darling. Now, tell me, what are you going to wear? And be sure to put your glorious tresses up, you know you look absolutely *gorgeous* darling, with your hair piled up.' He elongated the 'gor' bit of the word.

'I don't know what to wear. I don't want to overdo it, otherwise he might think I'm trying too hard.'

'Hetti,' he drew out the 'He' syllable of my name in the way he sometimes did when I was a child, to let me know he was warning me about something naughty I might have been about to do.

'What?'

'Don't play games with him darling. Just be yourself. Forget Daniel. This is Nathan and a jolly good chap he is too. You both have hearts to heal, but you and Nathan must learn to trust again. So,' he continued, in a lighter tone, 'do tell, when did he ask you out?'

'Actually, it was his mum's plan. We'd just got back from the police station when she called and said that she wanted him to take me out to dinner and she would have Ben for as long as was needed. And that he was to go out and enjoy himself for once.'

'Well, the scheming little minx!' Hearty laughter from Oscar's end of the phone line. 'I do approve! I liked Sheila immediately I met her at Christmas.'

'Yes, but then the lambs started being born, so he didn't ask me out until that morning, after I'd helped play the midwife.'

'How perfectly splendid! Now Dear One, go and get into something really nice, put those gorgeous curls of yours up with those sparkly little things you wore in your hair for the concert — you looked so delicious — and go and have a wonderful time. This is a new chapter in your life, my love.'

'I love you, Oscar.'

'And I love you too, Dear One. Now I must dash — I've got an apple tart in the oven — can't let it burn. Off you go! Go! Get ready!'

I laid the shimmery, cowl neck midnight blue dress that I'd decided on wearing, on the bed and shoved the other clothes back into the wardrobe. It was an easy choice; I only had two dresses. The rest of my clothes were skinny jeans and tops. I had exactly fifteen minutes to get showered and dressed.

Nathan turned up at the precise minute that he'd said he'd arrive. He looked me up and down, appraisingly.

'You look edible.'

Kissing me lightly on the cheek, he added, 'and you smell divine.'

'Shall we go?' I said, with the merest hint of a smile.

'*Sa wat dee, krup, Khun* Hetti!' Chaiyuth greeted us with a huge smile, a bow of the head and his hands poised in the '*wai*'.

'Hello, Chaiyuth! It's great to see you again. This is Nathan.' Another *wai*.

'Let me take you to your table.'

We ordered a pile of food, not really knowing what it was, but were guided by Chaiyuth's expertise. I decided against wine, because Nathan was driving and said he wouldn't drink before getting behind the wheel. So, we agreed on sparkling water. We ate and drank and talked about the sheep and the lambs and laughed. He told me that he'd let Ben keep as a pet one of the lambs that I'd helped deliver earlier in the week and that the boy had named it "Hetti" after me.

'Well, that's a first! I've never had a pet lamb named after me before!'

It was as though we'd always known each other. At one point, as Nathan was telling me a funny story about his time at school, I laughed so loud that the whole room went quiet. People turned around and looked at me momentarily, before going back to their meals and conversation.

Looking around the restaurant, amused rather than embarrassed, Nathan's face lit up with a broad smile as he turned his attention back to me.

We finished our meal and sat drinking coffee after the waiter had cleared the table.

'So, what are your plans, Hetti, when Olivia gets back from her travels?'

'I'm going to university. In Norwich.'

'Brilliant!' His face lit up even more. 'But, I mean, where will you live?'

'On campus.' Did I detect a fleeting flash of disappointment in his eyes?

'I see. And what are you going to study?' Maybe I'd imagined it.

'Well, I was going to do English and Drama. But I think I've had enough drama in my life in the past few months, so perhaps I'll just do English.' We both laughed at this.

'Whatever you decide to study, you will love uni, Hetti.' A wistful expression crossed his dark features. 'It's a great university that you've chosen.'

'Thanks, I'm sure I will. It's got a really good reputation.'

I thought about what Nathan had told me, about how he'd been so devastated after losing Erin and the baby girl that he'd dropped out of university without taking his finals. He'd also told me that his parents had supported him totally but that he'd never stopped feeling guilty about wasting all the money his dad had paid for his degree studies, which had come to nothing.

Thinking about this for a moment, I asked him, 'What about you, Nathan? Have you ever thought of going back to complete your studies? You wanted to become a vet, right?'

He nodded.

'Well, it seems you've had lots of experience with animals, running the smallholding. And you were really impressive, delivering the lambs. Why not go back to university and finish?'

Nathan Brookes took my hand in his. 'I might just do that. You've inspired me.'

I don't know why, but I pulled my hand away. Nathan didn't react, but lowered his eyes momentarily, then asked for the bill.

We drove home in silence. I was deep in thought. About the past nine months in general and, in particular, the more recent events involving Daniel and the crazy Irish woman. About Daniel's betrayal that still stung and the hurt went deep. And I thought about Nathan; the loss of his baby girl and Erin must be unbearable.

Oscar's words came back to me: *You both have hearts to heal.*

Nathan pulled up outside Wisteria Cottage.

'Thanks for a great evening, Hetti. Sleep well.'

You both have hearts to heal. You both have hearts to heal. Oscar's words bounced around in my brain like a mantra. You both have hearts to heal.

With my hand on the car door handle, ready to get out of the car, my encounter with the cancer patient at the hospital, who had been crying with joy that her treatment had been successful, came to mind. Her words, loud and clear: *Live every day like it's your last, because it might be.*

I paused and looked at Nathan, my hand still on the door handle.

'Erm, I was wondering, Nathan — I — erm —'

'Yes?' He looked at me, his expression not easy to read. I took a deep breath.

I held my breath. 'I quite fancy a glass of wine. Would you like to come in and join me?' I breathed out.

The full moon lit up the inside of the car enough for me to see the twinkle in Nathan's eyes and a smile spread across the face of the man I knew I'd fallen in love with. I also knew for sure that I wanted to spend the rest of my life with Nathan Brookes.

'I don't drink and drive.'

'I know you don't. And I don't expect you to,' I said, looking at him sideways.

'So, if I were to have a glass of wine, then I'd just have to stay the night, wouldn't I?'

'Yes, indeed you would.'

'Right.'

'So, are you up for it, Nathan Brookes?'

He reached out and held my face in his hands. His lips met mine, first lingering softly, then more urgently, drowning me in a tsunami-sized release of emotional and sexual tension.

'Oh yes, Hetti Lewis,' he murmured, through his kisses. 'I am so up for it.'

*****

Printed in Great Britain
by Amazon

32768218R00160